I0693126

The Alchemist

First Edition

Published by The Nazca Plains Corporation
Las Vegas, Nevada
2009

ISBN: 978-1-935509-40-0

Published by

The Nazca Plains Corporation ®
4640 Paradise Rd, Suite 141
Las Vegas NV 89109-8000

PUBLISHER'S NOTE
The Alchemist is a work of fiction created wholly by *Sky Unending*'s imagination. All characters are fictional and any resemblance to any persons living or deceased is purely by accident. No portion of this book reflects any real person or events.

Male Cover Photo, Martin Garnham
Art Director, Blake Stephens

Dedication

This book is dedicated to my dearest mother.
And to Barry. My heart goes out to you.

The Alchemist

First Edition

Sky Unending

Contents

Prologue

"It shall not be condoned."

A simple assertion stated icily by the petite lass seated on the throne of the veiled empire of Vand, would put an end to the forbidden affair. Her pet chimera screeched an ear-piercing scream. The fanciful creature knew what his mistress' tone implied.

"Black shall pay for his treachery and White will suffer for his chicanery," she asserted, her cobalt eyes saturating to a milky white. Black was a name she rarely used. She would call White by no other name.

The pet chimera screeched even louder, flitting about frantically, knowing that death of a Perpetual was approaching. He glided along to the seven vision stone that the mistress was glaring at and peered into the sight unfolding in front of him

The guardian of the empress of Vand, Arangyunus, better known as Black, was embracing the empress' greatest enemy, and had his lips firmly pressed against White's lips. His 15 feet long silver grey wings were folded against his back while the shining pearl white wings of the guardian of the city of Immaculata, White, were wrapped around both their bodies encasing them as one.

The petite girl grimaced once more as she watched the vision before her. She looked to be a child about 4 with golden tresses that reached all the way to her feet. With soft pink lips and blue eyes that were steadily turning white with rage, she looked incapable of the many horrors attributed to her, but her chimera, Pi, knew better.

"Mistress Woe, what do you intend to do?" Pi enquired telepathically. Speech was not a gift bestowed upon this half foot long chimera.

One word was stated by the empress Woe. "Obliterate."

"Black? But he is your own essence!"

The little girl did not reply. Instead she closed her eyes and when she reopened them, they were black.

In the vision ahead of the two watchers, suddenly the darker lover flinched, breaking his kiss with the keeper of the light.

"What's wrong?" White questioned, with a sudden fear in his eyes.

"Nothing I just felt as if…" he gazed upon the worried eyes of his lover. The Keeper of the light was more beautiful than anything that could ever be created. Ignoring the sensation a moment ago, he pressed his mouth against this magnificent angel who closed his eyes and accepted his lover.

Another throbbing pain shot across Black's torso compelling him to break the kiss again.

"What's wrong Black? What's Happening?" White quickly unfurled his shining pearl wings letting Black out of his hold.

"She's found out!" he yelled as he reeled under seemingly imaginary blows with both of his hands tightly pressing his chest at the centre. His heartbeat got louder as a throbbing pain became unbearable.

His lover immediately shut his eyes and tried to figure out where the pain was being channeled through. His thoughts raced along the insides of Black's but it was hopeless as the bond between the Mistress of Vand and Arangyunus, better known as Black, was pre-natal. He reopened his eyes and quickly ran to the side and held his new found lover in his arms; the one who was soon to be obliterated.

"No, No, No!" he cried. "How can she do this?" but his sounds were drowned out by the thumping of Black's heart, which was booming so loud that it felt like it was going to explode. It was soon going to. And the thumping was getting louder.

"Witenhoem!" cried the dying lover, using the name his mistress had forbidden him to use. And then in an explosion of grey fumes and ash, the Keeper of the dark, the Guardian of the mistress of Vand, the sworn enemy yet lover of the keeper of Light ceased to exist. All that remained of him was dust and ashes, covering the body of the one who held him as he was extinguished. And for the first time in centuries the pearl shining wings of the Angel, the Keeper of light, were blemished by grey soot and ash, the remains of his new found love that was to be no more.

"NO!" cried White, letting out an all pervasive shriek. And burst into sobs cradling his countenance between his palms. A strange site; one of the most powerful Perpetuals reduced to this.

Back on the throne of Vand, the little girl watched unstirred as tears of blood trailed down from the corners of her black eyes.

·····

A Boner Book

Episode One

"Here, want one?" Aiden offered Tinka. He was surely going to exact for the 'missed calls' incident. Or so, thought Aiden to himself, as he extended his hand with the cream biscuits towards Tinka. He knew these were her favorite and she would not resist them.

"Ooh Melbies!" she squealed in delight as she promptly took two of them and stuffed them into her mouth, chomping ravenously. Aiden carefully watched her face, holding his breath. A few moments later Tinka slowed down her munching and got a funny look over her face. And then she clasped both of her hands over her mouth and screeched. "Yuk, what's wrong with them??"

"Wrong? Nothing wrong. Except… maybe for the fact that I scraped off all the cream from the biscuits and put toothpaste inside them!" Aiden had the smirk of the century on his face.

"You Basta…" The rest of the sentence was left incomplete as Tinka lunged forward to try and smack Aiden on the head who easily dodged her. Moments later she could be seen gargling over the sink in the ladies room of the coffee shop. Cursing under her breath as white foam spewed out from her mouth. She was going to have to come up with some really evil plan to get one back on Aiden this time. Boy, would he be in trouble now.

"That was totally evil!" she declared as she came back and sat next to Aiden in the café.

" I mean, you are so going to get it from me now." She stated to a seemingly unaffected Aiden busy guffawing away.

"Stop guffawing like an ape! It wasn't that funny."

"Yes it was!"

"No, it was not!"

"You should have seen your expression with your mouth plastered with all that minty goo! Damn, I should have got my camera!"

"Aiden Writer, you are in deep shit now!"

"Yeah Right! That's the exact same thing I said to you when you could not stop giving Chas all those missed calls from my phone, if you can recall any of your past evil deeds," replied Aiden haughtily, referring to the previous week when Aiden made the mistake of telling Tinka he had a crush on their class branch Co-ordinator. Tinka went all out after that, using Aiden's cell phone whenever she could get a hold of it, to just give a single ring every time on Chas' number. A few embarrassing return calls later, vengeance was first priority on Aiden's mind.

"Well that was cute, and kinda funny."

"So was this!" replied Aiden with an air of triumph. Then he cheekily extended the packet containing the maligned biscuits towards the enraged female. "Want some more?"

Tinka replied by slinging her bag and smacking him over the head.

"Oww!" cried Aiden. "That hurt!"

"Well it should."

Aiden and Tinka had first become friends in the 8th grade when a friend of Aiden's had commented that Tinka possessed 'very large boobs'. That was still in the 8th grade when Aiden's new found homosexuality made it hard for him to hear guys labeling girls as sluts and bitches. His friend had challenged him to go and say it to her if he had the guts. That very night Aiden called Tinka up and told her what his friend thought of her assets. "What?" she had reacted. "Is that all he likes about me?" Chumminess came easily to them after that and they became as thick as thieves; always together, and always referred to as a couple. Few of their close friends knew the truth though.

"Well gotta head back and finish my presentation." Tinka nodded her head. "Miss Marple's gonna kill us with those submissions and presentations you know."

"Yeah, excuses. Nowadays you never have time for me," Aiden stated with a mock frown on his face.

"Yeah dolt!" I spend more time with you than any of the guys I date! I mean, we are practically married!"

"Ewww."

"Well eww from my side too, but it's true."

"Double eww."

"Eww all you want, I am gonna be heading back, and you, my 'husband' Aiden, are gonna be dropping me back to my room."

"As your Excellency desires!"

"Her Excellency desires that you pick her and Aditi up at 11:00. We are going to 'Earthquake' tonight!"

"Cool! Aditi's coming to Earthquake too?"

"Yes, you better believe it. The gorgeous Indian Chick is coming along. She's finally mixing with the other girls now. So if you wanna bring along some guys who wanna discreetly drool over her, feel free."

"Umm, we'll see."

"I am sure Chas would love to come!" Tinka knew she was asking for it.

"Yeah, I bet he would," replied Aiden appearing to be nonchalant but knowing that Tinka would surely see the seething person inside him.

"Or maybe Dominic would!" This time Tinka hit a sore spot. She was already getting back at him for the Melbies prank. Aiden flashed her an angry glare. Dominic was the guy that Aiden had been in love with for a long time, though he would never admit it to anyone. Tinka wondered how he managed to keep it all bottled inside. She had never seen someone so madly besotted with anyone before. And even more fierce about keeping it all to oneself. One thing she had learnt was that Aiden Writer had endurance.

"I'll just get Jason along." He muttered finally. Jason Bradley was one of Aiden's roommates.

"Okey Dokey!"

Dropping her off at her dorm, Aiden sped towards his. Maybe if he hurried he could finish all of his assignment work and squeeze in a little bit of tennis playing time with Steve and Jason, if any of them would agree to come along with him that was. Steve Johnson was his second roommate.

. . . . .

"Hey guys!" Aiden boomed as he swung open the door of his room.

A very lukewarm hey came back from Steve who seemed busy reading a Mathew Reilly novel and a very enthusiastic 'wazzzzuuuup' came from Jason who stretched out his hand to high five him.

"Anyone for Tennis?" he enquired.

"Yeah sure." Steve said pertly as he slammed down his book. As bookish as he seemed, Steve was never one to pass up on a game of tennis.

"You guys go ahead." Jason chimed in. "I'll play a little baski and join you later. Jason was the most athletic of the trio and at the same time the most affable, friendly and naive. His innocence caused him to be the butt of jokes at most times but everyone loved the five foot five inch dude and Aiden always considered himself lucky to have such a great roommate. Aiden was academically the most brilliant of the three, and that too by a long margin. With the highest CGPA in his class, he always had his friends pestering him as to how he achieved great grades, when he studied so little. "Sheer genius" he would tell them.

"Well I'll just be playing for a half hour or so, but you can join Steve later if he is still at the courts," replied Aiden while carefully taking out his tennis togs from a neatly folded bundle in his cupboard. Steve just picked up something from the heap lying on the bed and slipped it on.

"Ok then see you later."

"And yeah, don't forget, tonight we are going to 'Earthquake' with Tinka and that new Indian babe Aditi." Aiden knew Steve would not be interested and never bothered informing him.

"You gotta be kidding me! Aditi Agrawal. Fucking-A!"

"Yup, Aditi Agrawal"

"Shit, how the hell do you properly pronounce her name? Gotta ask someone that!"

Steve and Aiden left a beaming Jason in the room who was now happily rummaging amongst his side of the room searching for his basketball. How the hell could someone not find a basketball? Aiden would never understand, His friends would badger him to no end about being such a stickler and a neatness freak, but that's the way that he liked things.

. . . . .

40 minutes of tennis later, Aiden was exhausted and grumbling. His serve was as bad, if not as worse than when he had started playing tennis a year back, his backhand sucked and his reaction time also seemed screwed up. Steve mercilessly routed him for a 6-1 victory.

"Sheesh! I suck! I really do," Aiden grumbled to himself, slamming his racket on the bench as he slumped down and guzzled on a bottle of water.

"Yup, you sure do!" added Steve.

Aiden glanced at Steve. Steve sure was a mystery to him. The guy was lazy as hell most of the time, just lying around, sleeping 10-12 hours a day, watching movies or playing on the comp, but he could sure be active when he wanted to. Aiden was enervated to the core after a furious tennis session but Steve appeared to be hardly breaking a sweat. Steve was unarguably the best-looking amongst the 3 roommates and also the most moody. But he was also the only other person other than Tinka who knew about Aiden's sexuality in the university he was studying in.

"So. You're going to the Earthquake with Tinka and Jason?"

"And Aditi."

"Yeah, her too."

"Yup."

Aiden knew Steve had something on his mind but knew he would just have to be patient if he wanted to hear it.

"So nowadays, you're not sleeping around with any guy?"

Aiden was taken aback. This was pretty straight-forward for Steve. Steve had accepted Aiden's sexuality when he had come out to him, but was never very comfortable with the details regarding it. On the other hand there was Tinka who always demanded things right down to the most graphic and sordid detail from Aiden.

"Nope! No one."

Steve then took a deep breath. "Why don't you do something about Dominic and ask…"

"Hey, howzzit going?"

Jason interrupted the two as he strutted onto the courts with a basketball in his hands. The petite guy clad with an arm and head band was smiling as his usual self. Jason looked at an annoyed Steve and a red faced Aiden.

"People, are we playing?" Jason was never good at picking up hints and had no clue that he had interrupted something, much to the relief of Aiden.

"Yeah, sure… err…" stuttered Aiden. "I'll just go and… um… you continue with Steve." Aiden looked about frantically and caught sight of Steve with a blank expression on his face. 'Always difficult to read' he thought.

"So 11 PM at night right?"

"Yup, be ready!" stated Aiden as he scurried about collecting his items in a rush to get away from there. He left the court hastily as Steve's eyes followed him till he exited and Jason continued rambling to Steve telling him about how he had obtained details about Aditi and how he had found out that she really loved cats.

. . . . .

"It's been eons since an Alchemist has appeared on the material plane," the dulcet voice of the Empress of Vand stated.

She cast her blue eyes upon the bowing masculine figure before her.

Black.

That was the name he was famously known as. The guardian of the empress of Vand, the dark silver 'seraph', the keeper of the Dark, all were names and titles bestowed upon him. Arangyunus was his real name, but very few Perpetuals knew that. His Silver grey wings stretched across more than 30 feet from one tip to the other and a dark crystalline glint sparkled across his sinewy torso. The tips of the wings had black streaks highlighting the edges. The scene looked peculiar, for an entity of such seeming power to be bowing in respect in front of an ostensibly four year old child.

The Empress shook her head and her long golden tresses swayed. "The alchemist has to be won over."

Her pet chimera, Pi flitted noisily. "Black will take on the required form and descend upon the material plane?" This message was telepathic and was directed only towards the Empress of Vand.

"Yes Black will do the required." And she gazed upon the eyes of her guardian as he lifted his silver eyes to meet hers. Brilliant sparkles of white and blue light scintillated across his form as the wings slowly disappeared and the Perpetual's body slowly changed color to a pale flesh tone. At the end of the transformation, present in front of the Empress and her pet was a naked man, bowing waiting for his mistress to give the next command.

"Go, Arangyunus. Perpetrate the necessary."

And with that order from his mistress, Black stood up, a powerful male of the human species. His form slowly shimmered and disappeared. A few seconds later he appeared on the material plane. This would be the most difficult errand his mistress would ever send him on. Only, he did not realize it yet.

"Mistress, are you certain that Black should be employed for this task." Pi, the telepathic chimera had doubts. "The Alchemist is an event occurring in a millennium. Should you not descend upon the material plane yourself and handle this yourself?"

"The Alchemist possesses powers beyond the Perpetuals. And that power has never been correctly harnessed. Force will under no circumstances lend us his powers, because they are his to use."

"So overwhelming with lust will bend him towards our side?"

"Perchance. Or maybe it will require more than that."

.....

The door of the bar swung open as the 4 of them walked in. Aditi being led by an over courteous Jason followed by a pair of haggling 21 year olds; Aiden and Tinka.

"What do you mean 'the debate club is not good enough'? The debate club of our uni is fab and I Aiden, am definitely the best speaker."

"You would not be the best speaker if there were no other speaker's left darling. I think Mr. Rodrigues would oust you in a debate." Mr. Rodrigues was the head janitor in the university campus. He was dumb.

"What? You saying that he can raise arguments better than me?" Aiden was flaring as he took the seat opposite Jason and Aditi.

"You would not recognize a cogent argument if it hit you on the head and ran all over you." Tinka knew exactly how to push Aiden's sore spots to get a rise out of him. She gracefully sat on the seat beside Aiden.

"And what about your..."

"Guys Please." Jason interrupted Aiden with a pained expression on his face. Aiden immediately felt guilty when he thought about how badly Jason wanted to meet this Aditi girl. He turned and saw Tinka was in too with a guilty expression on her face. Then he saw Jason pleading him with his eyes. Jason really had the hots for this Tinka girl and he wanted things to start of on the right foot today.

"Well Aditi, the two of us are always at opposite warheads releasing all kinds of ammunition on each other. It's not actually as bad as it looks." Tinka smiled as she said that. Aiden also had a big grin over his face, realizing once again that other people might not find their 'friendly' banter to be as friendly as they considered it to be.

"Yeah, tell me about it, motormouth marathon" Jason whistled under his breath. Then before Aiden could figure out what he had said he quickly turned towards Aditi, "Hey Aditi, you like cats? My grandma lives close to the campus and her cat just gave birth to 5 kittens last week!"

Aiden clunked his head against the table in his mind as Tinka nudged his foot under the table. This had to be the cheesiest way to start a conversation with someone.

"Um, yeah…" Aditi replied looking at Jason with a weird look on her face.

"Great, you can come over with me sometime to my grandma's place and we can… err cuddle and pet." Tinka, Aiden and Aditi all glared at Jason.

"Pet the kittens… the, the little fur balls… all soft and cuddly." Jason' face was as red as a beet root. He could obviously not believe the words that were leaving his own mouth.

"Uh huh…. maybe sometime." Aditi had a 'what-a-bozo' look on her face.

Just then a black girl with golden curls and an apron appeared and introduced herself as the waitress. "What will you guys have?"

Tinka glared at Jason, who looked sheepishly at Aiden who was busy looking at Aditi wondering whether the 'why do I have to be unwittingly paired up with this bozo' look on her face was indeed what he was deciphering it to be. Jason really wanted to not screw up tings with this girl and he and Tinka would have to take matters into their hands for now. Tinka apparently had the same thoughts on her mind for as soon as the drinks were ordered she asked Jason.

"So, how's basketball coming along these days?"

Jason face lit up at the mention of the game. "Yeah that's' right" Aiden thought, keep the conversation to sports and Jason would not have any trouble.

Over the next 15 minutes Jason' sports abilities were discussed in detail. His being in the uni's Basketball team or 'Baski' as he referred to it, even though he was the shortest player on the team. His being on the uni's tennis team, a feat Aiden had spent grueling hours of practice to achieve, and Jason seemed to play tennis effortlessly. His being on the swim team and even an ace track athlete. Aditi seemed to be taken in by his athletic achievements and looked at Jason with a new admiration. Jason just seemed to bask in the glow of his abilities and was back to his effervescent affable self – the one that did not blunder like a drunk on 36 shots of vodka when he was with girls.

As Jason and Aditi got engrossed in their own conversation, Aiden motioned over to Tinka to let the two be. They excused themselves and headed over to the bar.

"Well that starts of something between Jason and Aditi." Stated Tinka as she flopped down onto one of the bar stools and motioned the bartender to come over. The guy sitting on the adjacent seat glanced at her and then fixed his gaze on her breasts. Aiden noticed and scowled a bit. He slowly settled onto the stool next to Tinka still frowning at the guy, which seemed to have no effect on him.

"Well you've got an admirer." Aiden said pointing with his chin to the lecher on Tinka's right. "Or rather should I say your body parts have another admirer?"

The guy coughed and looked away as Tinka whirled around to see what Aiden was talking about then shook her head and looked at the ceiling in a helpless gesture.

"I was saying, that Aditi looks like she's into our buddy." They booth looked at Jason and Aditi animatedly laughing over what appeared to be a very jovial conversation. "She could probably pick him and toss him out if he causes any trouble." She said laughing to herself. Aiden joined in the laughter. It was true; Jason was not exactly shorter than her, but pretty short indeed and Aditi apparently had stilettos on for she stood more than a couple of inches over him if they were both standing.

"So Aiden, when are you going to get hooked?" she said with a solemn expression on her face.

"Don't know." Aiden took a deep breath and continued, "When the mood is right I guess?"

"Mooood? What the hell do you mean by that? How about now?"

"And you're supplying prince charming I suppose?"

"Yeah, he's behind me!"

"What?" Aiden glanced behind her. " 'Mister-I-can't-keep-my-eyes-of-women's-large-boobies'?"

"No not him you moron!" Tinka said haughtily. "The guy behind the lecher, the one in the black shirt."

Aiden leaned forward to look behind her. The guy who he had first scorned at now scowled back at him. This time, Aiden ignored his look and looked at the guy next to him. Blond hair, nice face and good looking. He had a prominent dimple on his cheek.

"And what makes you think he may be interested in me?"

"Well…" Tinka stated with an air of omniscience, "I noticed him giving you the eye before, when we were with Jason and Aditi…." She paused to gulp at her drink. "And besides he never once glanced at my breasts when I settled down here" she stated as if it was the most non-hetero thing to do on the planet.

"Yeah right! And that gives me the authority to go and make a pass at him…."

"Of course it does!" Tinka stated triumphantly cutting Aiden off.

Aiden swallowed before his next words. "Mrs. big Doosies boosies do not get stared at and she expects the guy to be a crooked one eh… someone here sure is conceited!"

"Oh stop with your smart ass replies for once. Why don't you just give it a chance?"

"He's probably straight you nut! You just want me to get a black eye. I have never met a single gay guy in this place even once! The probability that he caters to my kind is absolutely minimal!"

"Stop thinking with your logical head for once. Why the hell won't you go and make a pass at him! It's not like he'll think you are from outer space or something. Even if he is straight, I am sure he has heard of gay guys to figure out where you're coming from."

Tinka took a deep breath before she added the last bit. She still had more to say, "Stop saving yourself for that Dominic Paige."

2 more minutes of exasperated arguing later Aiden got up, straightened his shirt and advanced slowly towards the subject of their argument muttering and cursing Tinka under his breath. But he knew better than to argue with her when she was in those headstrong moods. "Just do as she says." He murmured to himself and cautiously approached the blond guy.

"Hi, can I buy you a drink?" Aiden looked questioningly towards the blond dude sitting alone on a barstool, returning his inquiring look with a puzzled one.

Aiden extended his hand. "My name's Aiden." The guy shook the offered hand hesitatingly, his puzzled countenance morphing into a slight scowl.

"So what's your name?" Aiden was wondering if he would have to do all the talking.

"Josh." He said and then shut his mouth. Aiden noticed how beautiful his lips were. The guy had a dimple only on his left cheek, the one Aiden had seen before and none on the other. It made him look real cute to Aiden. The music in the club was booming really loud and Aiden found it difficult to listen to what Josh was saying, if he was saying anything that is.

"Listen, are you waiting for someone or can I take this seat here?"

"Whatever, take it." he replied nonchalantly, not seeming too pleased that this over-friendly guy was piling onto him.

Aiden looked at Josh's face and thought of backing off for a moment, but decided to sit down for he had already come this far.

"No." he stated flatly, before Aiden could initiate further conversation. "You don't need to buy me a drink."

"Oh, Alrighty then," Aiden said a little taken aback, "So anyway Josh, what do you do?"

"Why, is it any business of yours?" he replied churlishly.

Aiden wanted to leave the table just then but his mouth would not listen to his mind and decided to talk on.

"No, just asking if you study in some university around this place."

"Yeah, am an architecture student at Misoha." He replied not so ever glancing at Aiden but looking straight ahead.

"Architecture eh? Used to sleepless nights, A3 sheets and T-squares?"

"Why, are you an architect too?" he asked with an annoyed expression on his face.

"No, it's just that some of my very good friends are. I'm an engineering student."

The guy looked away once again. Aiden was not sure how to proceed any more. Should he try to talk to this guy one more time or should he just politely leave while he still wore his dignity. Was Tinka's guess right that this Josh was interested in him? Hardly seemed so. He would try to talk just once more and if things did not get any warmer, he would just have to leave this chap.

"So your submissions and viva's must be coming up right?"

Josh firmly placed his mug on the table and rotated to face Aiden. "Listen buddy, go play your homo games with someone else. I AM NOT INTERESTED. If you feel I was looking at you earlier, it's because you look a lot like my cousin, so please would you just get lost?"

Aiden looked him squarely in the face, "thanks for clearing that up." Not at all showing the hurt he felt inside on his face he got up to leave. Tinka Appeared behind the two suddenly.

"Hey you guys, what's going on?"

"Your ugly homo friend out here was hitting on me."

"And what makes you think he was hitting on you? Did he ask you for a blowjob or something?" Tinka knew how to put someone in a spot.

"No but he… just fuck off you two!"

"Not everyone comes from a respectful household I guess," Tinka stated as she grabbed Aiden by the arm and pulled him back over to where they were initially seated. Aiden felt like a pile of shit, and Tinka felt even worse.

"Shit, Sorry Ade, never meant to get you humiliated like that."

Aiden looked over at Tinka's apologetic expression. He tried to put a smile on his face but could barely muster the courage for one.

"It's fine," he squeaked and cleared his throat to get his voice out, "it's just that I looked like his cousin so he was giving me the look over earlier."

"It's all my fault, please let me buy you a drink."

Aiden looked at Tinka, thankful that even though he had no one to share his life with consummately, he at least had Tinka.

. . . . .

Not too far away from the booming music of the disco, in a dark alley, the view got nebulous as a naked human form gradually 'shimmered' onto the material plane. The deserted alley felt the presence of one of the most powerful dark Perpetuals. The form was crouched, the body wrapped into itself as if in a cocoon. Black had arrived into the human world. He slowly un-entangled himself and stood up to his full height. A towering figure with a forbidding presence. The thew of his torso apparent at just a glance with ridges along the abdomen descending into powerful pubes. The strapping arms appeared mighty but hardly showed signs of the superhuman feats they were capable of.

Sturdy legs lofted him to an impressive verticality. His back was sinewy and rippled with each muscular form palpating under the slightest movement.

The human encased dark Seraph extended one arm outwards with the palms facing upwards and slowly closed his palm in the shape of a claw as each muscle in the arm tensed.

"Stealth Ability 37; Shadowy Specter," Black voiced out. And as soon as those words left his mouth his form was morphed to a black velvet which burgeoned in all directions and then rapidly fell to the ground. The Stealth spell would allow Black to move about undetected as he searched for methods to blend into the surroundings and found his target. A dark blackness now moved about on the earth as it left the deserted alley and moved along streets in which people strayed.

The shadow soon glided along to the entrance of an edifice which possessed a miscellany of clothes displayed on a myriad of mannequins. The structure appeared to be isolated as was common for a facility of its kind for this time of the night. The shadowy form sailed under the locked glass doors. Black slid inside a clothing and accessories shop.

Once inside, the shadow resumed the form of a naked man; one in search of garbs. Black came over to a mannequin set adorned in the latest styles and looked over them. The mannequins were skinny and not up to his height. Finding an attire would be difficult. Just then he noticed a male species mannequin in the centre enclosed in a glass casing which appeared to be larger than the others. Adorned in dark denim with a cross gartering white string extending from head to toe on either side. Black shoes of leather of the most upmarket kind and a white gossamer shirt, diaphanous to some extent.

Black proceeded to disrobe the lifeless model as he put on each garment on his own body. He would have to do this manually as his powers were of no use in such circumstances. In fact, the extent of his powers would be greatly suppressed when he would be in this form. Just then black's realized he was not alone in the huge room. A security guard stood gaping at him as soon as he finished attiring himself. Black cursed himself in his mind. His abilities were restrained and would take some time to recover and even then would not return to their full efficiency till he assumed his original form. That explained how a security guard had gotten so close without him sensing it.

"Hey you!" the man in uniform bellowed. "What the fuck are you doing in here?"

Black knew he would have to take matters into his own hands. He extended his left arm forward, bending it into a V shape and placed his right hand across it creating a cross structure. He opened his mouth to cant.

"Internecine Ability 60; BlackFang Slash." Black rapidly moved his right arm across as if slashing the left with two fingers. Simultaneously A black streak appeared just above the nape of the security guard and slashed diagonally across the neck. A grimace remained painted across the victim's face as his head was severed off and a chunk of his body slowly slipped off from the bottom half. Both parts fell to the floor. Blood sputtered in all directions.

The security guard would never understand how this entity had managed to cut him in two from a distance of more than 40 feet.

Black reeled under the recoil effect of the mutually destructive 'internecine' spell. The recoil was immense for a spell of such low caliber, as the dark seraph was itself devoid of his powers. A few seconds later, Black, Shaking off the effects of the recoil headed towards the main entrance. Fully attired in clothes he could now proceed on his quest to find the Alchemist.

9 hours later, policemen and forensic experts would examine the macabre homicide of a clothesline store security guard. The body, in 2 parts, one consisting of the head, neck, a shoulder blade and part of an arm and the other part consisting of whatever else a human body comprises of, would leave them dumbfounded. What force could slice the human body like this, as if it were a mere vegetable?

. . . . .

Aiden stared into the mirror ahead of him. He was still at the disc, in the washroom. He had excused himself for a moment from Tinka to come to the men's restroom. The music thumped in muffled tones as Aiden sadly looked at his own reflection.

Was he that ugly? He sure had had his share of one-nighters, all thanks to the internet. He could meet guys who were not so blessed with looks and carry out his release with them. In fact the last 2 years had seen him indulge in many one night stands, owing to easy get away procedures from the frat rooms. But relationships were another world apart.

He looked at his scruffy black hair. Tousled. It was always like that. He never combed it. Did he need a hair-cut? Usually it was cut short and hardly required much combing but right now it was long and disheveled. It just looked un-maintained. His hair-cut was at least a couple of months overdue. Then he looked at his glasses. Did glasses make him look over-nerdy? Some of his one one-night 'Johns' enjoyed his nerdy look. They loved it when the nerdy guy turned into an animal in bed. And he had worn glasses all his life. Switching over to contacts or something would be a harrowing experience. He looked at his face. Ordinary; Painfully so. And right now there was a zit above his left brow which made him grimace even more. Aiden contemplated his own looks. He remembered Josh's words calling him, well, ugly. And that made him feel lower than a pug's testicles.

He scanned his eyes over his own body in the mirror. At least that was in good shape. He loved keeping fit. All the daily push-ups and tennis made his body streamlined and well proportioned, though he felt he was a little skinny. 5'11" was not a bad height either. His teeth looked okay as well. Thank God he had had braces for a year when he was 17. Aiden thought back to the days when his looks never mattered.

A toilet stall door swung open behind him with a clang as someone strolled out. Aiden quickly left the mirror to get back into the noisy bacchanal ambience. He was now in no mood to stay and would leave immediately, informing Tinka and the others. He would have to come up with some excuse for Chas and Aditi, but he was sure Tinka would accompany him out of this wretched place.

"Hey Tinka." He called out to her in a soft voice as he neared her, "I don't much feel like staying here. I think I'll leave."

Tinka looked at him sorrowfully. She knew most of this was her fault. She should not have coaxed Aiden to go and talk to that blonde asshole. Seeing the saturnine look on Aiden's face, she decided she would have to accompany him. She no longer felt like staying there either.

"You know what, I'm gonna come too. Let's just get away from here."

Tinka raised herself from the barstool as Aiden told her to wait a moment as he went over and informed Jason and Aditi who were now busy dancing away to the cadence, gyrating on the dance floor. Aiden felt a little better to see that at least Jason was having a good time. As Aiden approached the couple, he noticed that Aditi's movements suddenly got slower and she almost stopped dancing, her eyes fixated towards the entrance of the disc. Aiden followed her gaze, looking across the sea of people drinking, swinging and laughing till his eyes rested on Him.

He stood there, as if searching for someone, his face expressionless. A tall man with the looks of a comic book superhero. With a diaphanous white top that accentuated his perfect muscular torso and denim clad legs with lacings on the sides the man looked drop dead gorgeous. Aiden stood transfixed for all of 5 seconds. He had never in his life laid eyes on someone so strikingly handsome. Then he remembered the incident with that Josh character and sighed inwards. Aiden progressed towards Aditi who was apparently still gazing at 'Mr. Knock you dead with one look', as Aiden now referred to him in his mind. Aiden looked around to notice that by now, many people had their eyes riveted towards the new entry.

"Hey Aditi," Aiden screamed above the deafening music, shaking the girl out her staring stupor. "Tinka and me are leaving. You guys have a nice time."

"Uh… yeah. Ok." Was all she replied. Then she blushed and smiled and diverted her attention back to Jason who was still dancing unaware of what was going on around. That was just like Jason, to not be aware of such things, Aiden thought to himself.

Aiden made his way back to Tinka who had noticed the new arrival too. "Super hot guy eh?" she questioned, motioning towards the centre of more than half the club's attention.

"Yeah." Aiden muttered softly under his breath, not raising his eyes to look in the pointed direction. Tinka decided to not pursue this line any further. She felt a sudden rise of desire to stay back and try to approach the guy but then decided against it remembering the state Aiden was in. She quietly followed Aiden as he headed towards the door.

"Hey!" a voice called out to Aiden just as he was about to exit the club. Aiden whirled around to see if it was him being called out to. It was the white shirt hunky guy. And he signaled Aiden to stop as he made his way across the sea of people towards him. People turned their heads as he passed them, envious, fascinated and some openly drooling at the sight of such beauty. Aiden looked at Tinka's face with a questioning look on his face. She shrugged her shoulders and returned him a puzzled look.

"Hi! I'm Will. Can I buy you a drink?"

Aiden stood a little befuddled. Why was this Adonis type character approaching him, who had all but left the bar, asking to buy a drink. His thoughts were running even hazier as he realized that this guy had severe green eyes whose hues were even noticeable in the lights of the disc. He just looked at the guy's mouth moving till he realized the man had stopped talking a few moments ago.

"Uhh... drink?"

"Yeah sure! I'd love to buy you a drink, if you have the time that is!"

Aiden was flustered. Why was this guy so adamant to buy him a drink? Why would such an awesomely handsome chap be interested in him? Was someone playing a trick on him or something?

Unknown to Aiden, his thoughts were being read. His mind was rummaged along as Black, who had assumed the name of Will had found his target. Powerful Perpetuals often possessed the ability to read the minds of lesser humans. Black was presently scouring the Alchemist's mind perusing each and every thought that came up.

Aiden composed himself. "Hey man, I really appreciate the offer, but I was just about to leave. I have to drop my friend back too." He gestured towards Tinka

"Cool, can I tag along?" Will asked with an innocent expression.

"You? Err..." Aiden was dumbfounded.

"Of course you can!" Tinka interpolated forcefully. "We'd love to have your company...err, Will. I'm Tinka and this here is Aiden."

Aiden shrugged his shoulders in a 'sure-join-us' gesture and then headed outside with his best friend and the hottest dude on the planet in tow. A couple of girls entering the club in the opposite directions ogled at the new collection to the pair.

"Hey Handsome," one of them cooed at Will, "Wanna buy me a drink."

"No, I'll buy you one!" interjected the other. And then both of them giggled as the trio walked by, Will ignoring the tittering pair.

The three walked out into the relatively warmer temperature of the night; Aiden was finding it hard to keep his eyes of the man walking beside him but at the same time could not understand what to say to him. Tinka was trying to figure out the new person who was busy skimming along Aiden's thoughts.

Yes. This was the alchemist. There was a subtle difference in the way his mind and thoughts felt when compared to other humans. His task was now to win over the usage of the Alchemist's powers. Seduction was the easiest way, but as he combed Aiden's mind he realized that his prey was in an emotionally unstable state right now. It was too bad that his psychic abilities would only allow him to probe at surfacing thoughts and not allow him to delve into the mind as his Empress could. If he had her abilities, he would effortlessly have been able to plant the thought of sex directly into the boy's brain.

"Really nice Weather today." Will started sensing the awkwardness going through Aiden's head. "A good thing it rained in the afternoon; reallybrought down the temperature."

"Yeah A much needed respite from the relentless heat." Tinka added smiling.

"Easy for the two of you to say. I was outside and got caught in the rain in the morning. Got totally drenched." Aiden stated with a mock frown on his face.

"Sorry to hear that." Will replied.

"No, actually I love getting soaked in the rain. Just that I had my bag and all. My books were steeped."

"Then good riddance eh? Get rid of all the college books and all?" Will's smile widened and Aiden could not help noting his perfectly straight immaculate teeth. "Some people sure have it all", he thought to himself, and to Black as well.

"Yup, sure did, but I had one of my frat mate's books too. Boy was he furious!" Aiden was laughing hard as he pictured Jason seething with rage at him in the morning.

"Frat mate? You guys are students in one of the universities nearby?" Will knew that asking such a question would immediately give rise to thoughts in Aiden's mind which would give him a little more information to help his aims.

"Yeah," Aiden replied, I am an engineering student and Tinka here is struggling to become an architect."

"What do you mean struggling?" asked an irked Tinka. "Will, take note that Aiden here is the phoniest of engineers you'll ever get to meet. These engineers are all no good con artistes that dupe people out of their money in exchange for nothing."

"Don't even get me started on the bitchy work you architects do..." and the two were once again lost I their arguments, forgetting all about their surroundings.

Black pretended to enjoy their banter and plastered a smile across his face. Inside he felt absolutely revolted. These humans were so lowly and pathetic. Their pass times and habits were contemptible. Why did the alchemy powers only surface in a human soul? Black had a slight urge to use one of the Internecine Ability spells to wipe out both these pathetic creatures right there on the spot. Even this Alchemist boy seemed over vulnerable. He wondered if seducing him would work.

Nearing a coffee shop Black sensed that Aiden would like to enjoy some coffee.

"Hey you two, care for some coffee. I sure would like some."

The pair stopped arguing and looked at Will. Aiden was contemplating having some coffee himself. "Yeah sure." Was his reply, "If you also want some," he asked Tinka.

Tinka saw this as a perfect opportunity to clear her name for the mess she had caused earlier in the bar with the Josh dude. She also felt that Will was a nice enough guy from the conversations they had had.

"You boys go ahead. I have to get back to my sorority. Have some sheets to cover up on." Black immediately saw through the lie. So she was leaving so Aiden could spend some time alone with him. These pitiable humans sure did things in strange ways. But it suited him just fine.

"Are you sure?" Aiden inquired. He badly wanted to chat up the hunky Will, but due to the events that happened earlier he could still not think straight.

"Yes positive. It's not like I have to have a chaperone till the hostel or something."

"We could just go till your dorm, drop you off and …"

"Just go dammit," she growled, and then leaned in and whispered into Aiden's ear, "Have fun darling, you deserve it. And don't forget, I wan't ALL the details later."

Black smiled at her as she waved and trudged off.

A small golden bell above the door chimed as the door swung open and Aiden entered along with Will in tow. The café was sparsely filled, as it was expected to be, given the late hour. All eyes turned to see who entered and then remained fixed on the taller of the two men. Aiden noticed the stares and felt a tinge of jealousy within him. What was there to be jealous of he wondered. He knew next to nothing about this guy; other than the fact that he should be shooting for some major Hollywood movie rather than sipping coffee with a person as boring as himself. Aiden wondered if movie stars and models looked this hot from close but then thinking about the ones he had actually met face to face, he came to the conclusion that they did not.

Aiden settled onto one of the cushioned sofas glad that they were available and Black sat down next to him. Black sensed a hue of confidence arising in the Alchemist that was not there earlier. He left it to the boy to initiate the conversation this time.

Aiden paused a few moments enraptured by the beauty seated next to him. In the lights of the café, his features were clearly visible. The chiseled cheek bones, the strong muscular jaw, the soft pink lips, the dense black hair, the perfect complexion and his severe green eyes. This guy was the complete looks package and Aiden wondered if he could ever be in a relationship with a person of such beauty. "He maybe a complete idiot inside" Aiden reminded himself but still wondered why Will was interested in him.

"So Will, What do you do? I mean you know that I am an engineering student and all. How old are you first of all?"

"Why, how old do I look?"

"I don't know, 24, 25 years old?"

Black chuckled at this reply thinking his actual age was the number Aiden quoted, multiplied by at least 40. "I'm 27," he decided and stated the same to Aiden.

A young boy who looked to be about 16 interrupted them. "What will you both have?" the young boy smiled a little too much at Will who immediately interpreted from his mind that this young waiter had just quarreled with his friend, a brunette looking scornfully at him, as to who would serve the hot man candy. Apparently the curly haired brunette had lost.

"I'll have an Iced Eskimo," quoted Aiden.

"Make that two." Will smiled at Aiden.

"Anything else?" the young waiter asked, eager to stay on and talk a bit more. His eyes were still focused on Will. Aiden lifted his eyebrows thinking that the young waiter could not possibly be any more obvious in ogling at his companion.

"No that will be all, thank you." Will read Aiden thoughts and quickly dismissed the waiter who went back with a disappointed look.

"So Will, is your name short for William or is it just Will?"

"No it's just Will. Will Black that is."

"Will Black? So you don't mind me calling you Mr. Black?"

"Not at all. In fact many people do call me Black."

"No, just kidding. Will's fine."

"Suit yourself."

"And Mr. Will, what do you do? You already know I am an engineering student."

Scient Abilities and referring to Aiden's thought patterns allowed Black to come up with a reply to this one. "I am a social worker."

Aiden raised his eye brows at his reply. Black had just chosen a profession from the alchemist's mind which the alchemist really looked up to.

"No kidding. Social worker?"

"Well sort of. My grandfather left me in charge of this really huge retirement home and I take care of that."

"I thought you would probably be a model or something," and for some strange reason, Aiden himself was blushing after saying that. "So what kind of work does it require?"

"Taking care of the premises, the facilities, medical care, sometimes seeking sponsors and donations and in general, to just keep the place running."

"Really cool. You'll have to take me there sometime."

Black replied without flinching, "Definitely. Any time you want." He also immediately picked up the fact that Aiden was genuinely interested and he would have to make arrangements for the necessary.

Aiden, on his part, now looked at Will in a totally different light.

"So Aiden, how old are you and what's your full name."

"Yeah, sorry about that. Aiden Writer. That's my full name. Just turned 21 this March."

And with that the discussion soon shifted to various topics ranging from studies, weather, eating habits and sports. Black conveniently stated that he played the same sports Aiden did changing a few details here and there, in an attempt to not make it sound totally rigged.

"No kidding!" Aiden had burst out when he heard Will loved tennis and swimming. "I love tennis and swimming myself!"

Throughout their conversation Black searched for an opportunity to seduce the Alchemist and break him. The cat and mouse games were tiring him out more than any of the strongest Internecine Ability spells could, but he was aware of the fact, that anything happening between them would have to be totally consensual, that even the slightest of resistances from the Alchemist would ruin everything. If things went a little too awry and the Alchemist got unbridled control of his powers, even he could be annihilated.

Aiden was enjoying himself, really liking his the company of this new man that had sought him out. Not only was he 10 times a regulation hottie; he really seemed like he cared a great deal about people and was great to converse with too. Somewhere along the way Aiden was entranced by his looks yet again. He shifted a little to adjust his nether regions, and suddenly realized that the two had been chattering away since almost 40 minutes. He would have to get back to the frat soon; unless of course, he found some other place to spend the night.

Black understood the line of thought and at once picked up that the frat rooms were no place for him and Aiden to have a mating session. Maybe he could do the boy on the beach itself. There was no moon and it was pitch dark. No one would notice. But then the boy's thoughts shifted once more. He wanted this to be more than a one night stand. Black felt dark rage rising inside him as he perused the thought of a relationship cruising in the boy's mind. He had no time for childish games. But Aiden's next few words caught him completely off guard.

"Tell me Will, why are you interested in me?"

Black searched Aiden's mind but could not find a reply. Suddenly and abruptly, the mind that he had been reading like an open book was blank, and as hard as he tried, he could not find the answer to the question asked of him surfacing anywhere in Aiden's head.

"Why do you ask that?"

"I mean," Aiden paused, speaking every word slowly, "Hot like you, doesn't hang out with plain like me, unless for a very good reason."

Black would have to resolve this question on his own. He took a deep breath.

"You know, back at the bar, I just got a glimpse of you and was suddenly deeply attracted. I saw the melancholy on your face and immediately knew that I wanted to see that face smiling. But you were leaving from the bar, and I knew that I wanted to go along with you and get out of that stuffy place. And in fact, I think I made an excellent choice."

Aiden stared at him blankly, a slight smile on his face. Black could confirm his mind was blank too. In fact there were still no though signals he could pick up on.

"You're beautiful Aiden. And you attract me in more ways than billions of people can. I just had to be with you."

Aiden stared at Will not knowing what to say. Then he smiled and let his breath out. He had been holding it in ever since he had questioned Will and had not even been aware of it.

"Ok, I have to get back to my frat now, it's getting pretty late." Aiden arose from his seat. Black was confused. What the fuck had he just said? Was he going to bang the Alchemist tonight? Was the Alchemist angry or upset with him? Did he never want to see him again? Or worse, had his mission failed? Why was he not being able to read the boy's thoughts anymore?

"Can I see you again tomorrow?" asked Aiden in a timid voice.

Black took Aiden's phone number when Aiden asked for his, stating he would call him the next day. Aiden insisted on paying for his share of the coffee. It hardly mattered to Black actually, just that he would not get to spend the money he had pilfered from the long haired fat man before he entered the disco.

Outside the café Black shook hands with Aiden awkwardly. Then he took a step closing the distance between them and firmly planted his lips on the boy's. He pulled away 15 seconds later.

Aiden had just experienced the most mind-blowing kiss of his life.

The dark seraph walked away, promising to give a call the next day.

. . . . .

The troglodyte sorcerer advanced cautiously. It had taken him many days to complete his journey to reach Immaculata, the capital city of the Kingdom of light. But he was certain that the news he carried would grab the interest of the ruler. He was even certain that he would be handsomely rewarded.

The elephantine golden gates swung open slowly as he was allowed entrance into the Emperor's chamber. The troglodyte gazed all around, his one eye open with wonder at the grandeur of the Emperor's court. Sturdy edifices of spotless white marble with gold linings held up a ceiling which was too high to fathom. Azure fabrics swooped down as if from the sky and reached almost all the way to the ground. Courtiers in the most opulent fabrics absorbed the lowly troglodyte with interest. And towards the end, in the centre of this magnificent hall, elevated 20 feet from the marbled floor stood a throne rising high into the air. On it was seated the Emperor Witenhoem, who once used to be the guardian of the city of Immaculata. He was still more fondly known as the Keeper of the Light, White.

The troglodyte approached the throne his head bowed till he neared the steps leading to the throne and genuflected, bowing in reverence.

"Lift your head and speak please," a deep masculine voice called out. The troglodyte raised his head and drank in the sight of the Emperor with his only eye. Seated on the throne was a handsome Perpetual, his face radiating in the power he possessed, his prevailing body rested upon a robe of white tuft, and he wore robes of the same pure white himself.

"My lord, this humble servant of yours has stumbled upon a discovery that will pique your interest. It is with the news of this discovery that I arrive here."

"Pray, inform us. What is this discovery you speak of?"

The troglodyte paused, knowing this was going to have a dramatic effect. "The discovery of the presence of the Alchemist my Lord."

Immediately hundreds of voices started talking all at once. Every courtier started talking at the same time. The ruler raised his hand to thwart the hubbub. Instantly silence filled the hall.

"And what of the Alchemist?"

"He thrives on the material plane my lord, his powers concealed in a human body. As of now he is 21 years if age and possesses no knowledge of his capabilities."

At once the Keeper of the light rose and unfurled his great pearl wings stretching to more than 15 meters across. The troglodyte realized that these were the legendary white wings that the Emperor was seated on which had seemed like soft white tuft which he had assumed to be a robe at first glance.

The stentorian voice White boomed throughout the gathering, "If what you say is true, them I myself will descend to the material plane and find the alchemist. I will entreat him to lend us the use of his powers to defeat the Kingdom of the Void."

Two days of affluent comfort later, the troglodyte would return to his runnels, with enough riches for five of his future generations to fritter.

.....

Episode Two

"Steve," Aiden whispered to the sleeping form. "Hey buddy, get up."

Steve rolled towards one side opened his eyes halfway to see who was disturbing him.

"Hey C'mon, let's play some tennis."

"What's the time?" Steve inquired groggily.

"It's 5:40."

"And it's Sunday morning right?"

"Yeah, so do you wanna play?"

Steve opened his eyes with a sudden forced effort, thinking of how Aiden had never been one to get up early on Sundays. He shot up and sat vertical with a jerk.

"Ok, let's go!"

Aiden hurriedly got up and started to assemble his tennis gear. The previous night he had returned back to the frats after 1 and had hardly had four hours of sleep. Yet when he thought of Will and the kiss, he hardly felt tired. In fact, he felt pepped up like a hot fudge sundae with nuts. The world seemed like an awesome place to live in. At the same time, Aiden reminded himself at the back of his head to not get his hopes up too high.

"Will might never call me again, and it's not like I have any contact number of his." Aiden reminded himself to keep his exuberance under control or severe disappointment could be headed his way.

Aiden looked towards Jason's side of the room. Jason was snoring slightly, his lips shaped into a slight smile. Seemed like Jason had had a great time with Aditi too.

Three sets of tennis later, an exhausted Steve called it a game and slumped down on the benches adjacent to the courts, his lack of sleep finally catching up to him. Aiden was still prancing about, not even a bit debilitated. Steve had managed to beat him 2-1 but Aiden had almost beaten him in the last set losing 5-7. This was the farthest he had ever come in a tennis contest with Steve.

"So where did you suddenly get all this energy from?" Steve had a questioning look on his face.

"Don't know man." Aiden replied though he knew exactly where it was all coming from. It was the newness of discovering someone. The newness of being enamored by someone who was so out of league, but yet seemed very interested in you.

Aiden made his way towards where Steve had settled down, still swinging his racket and practicing his strokes till he too flopped down beside Steve.

"So how did it go yesterday night with Jason and that Indian chick and all?"

"It went pretty well," Aiden replied still smiling at the events of the day before.

"Jason handled himself well with a girl around?"

"Yeah, although with a little help in the start from me and Tinka, but I think he managed well on his own later on."

Steve gazed at Aiden, the former being able to make out from his demeanor that there was something more about the previous day that Aiden wanted to tell him about. Aiden cleared his throat.

"I sorta… um, met someone myself yesterday."

"Some guy?" Aiden was uncomfortable once more. What was it about Steve that could put him at unease so easily when it came to this topic? He was usually never unnerved about his sexuality being discussed.

"Yeah, his name's Will, Will Black. He's 27 years old." Aiden knew that this was all the information Steve would want from him. "And he's a social worker who runs a retirement home." Aiden quickly added the last bit, as if it compensated for his apparently aberrant tastes in men.

"Cool." That was all Steve replied. Aiden surmised that since Steve knew he had slept in the frat the night before, he would reckon that this was something better off than a one night stand. Somehow Aiden felt like he had passed a test.

"I'll go get some water," Steve stated as he rose up and walked towards the filters. Aiden sort of wished that he could make Steve meet Will. He was sure that anyone would be impressed by his personable self and he would get to show him off a little or something like that. Will was such an awesome person. His face, his eyes, his body, his personality, his manner; his overall bearing. "I just hope I am not a charity case that he had decided to please for an evening or so," Aiden was trying to calm himself. He wished he could talk to Will again, but then stealing a glance at his watch he realized that Will most certainly would not be awake at 7:30 in the morning on a Sunday.

Just then his cell phone buzzed on the bench beside him. Aiden lifted the set not recognizing the number.

"Hello?"

"Yeah Hi," replied a voice from the other side. Aiden at once knew who it was.

"Will, is that you?"

"Yup, Will here."

"Shit! I was just thinking about you!"

"I know!" replied a cheeky voice from the other end.

"So you're awake so early on a Sunday?"

"Yeah, awake and thinking about you!" Aiden tunred crimson, thankful that Will would not be able to see him blushing over the phone.

"Listen," Will stated, "Hey how about meeting up and going bowling or something?"

Aiden had hardly ever bowled in is life before. He knew he would probably find the sport interesting if someone would just push him a little into it.

"Bowling, er, yeah why not?"

"Cool, can I meet you at 8:30 at the same coffee shop then? We'll grab a bite to eat and then head towards the alleys. They open at 9 o'clock"

"Fine by me."

"Ok, meet you there then."

"Ok."

There was a pause on the other side before Will's voice stated, "I'm really looking forward to meeting you."

By now, Aiden face was positively roseate, the smile on his face bigger wider had been in a long time.

"Bye." The phone clicked. Aiden kissed his phone and leaped up in the air with joy screaming "Yesssss!"

An amused Steve was staring at the bouncing form of Aiden. Aiden immediately stopped hopping when he saw Steve staring at him.

"Err, that was Will, the guy I told you about."

"I guessed as much." Steve replied grinning. "C'mon, let's get back to the room." Aiden followed Steve out of the courts.

"And stop grinning so much. You're beaming like a house on fire!"

. . . . .

Old wooden floor boards creaked as a large Doberman padded across the room and settled down for a nap. It knew its master would not be back for quite some time from now. It shut its eyes and slowly drifted off into doggie dreamland. Suddenly its ears twitched as something awakened it from its vigilant slumber. The large canine opened its eyes and suddenly shot up. It stared into the atmosphere before it and let out a guttural noise. The air ahead started to slowly deform and turn turbid. The turbidity grew more and more intense until it exploded in white fumes.

Another powerful perpetual had just entered the material plane.

White's unclothed human form emerged from the white vapors. White looked down at his nude form. He would need to have garments to mingle with the humans and find the alchemist. Then he looked around at his surroundings.

Had that much changed since he had last been here? The last time he was here, these coordinates comprised of a deserted location. Now he was apparently in someone's home as he looked down at his canine friend growling at him, its mouth showing pointed white teeth. Suddenly the animal balked and fled yelping.

White smiled and spread out both his arms in a crucifixion pose and spoke out. "Assorted Ability 4; Fabric Habiliment."

Rings of white and azure lights appeared around both his wrists. The rings moved towards each other, expanding and contracting in shape as they hovered above the muscles beneath, leaving cloth in their wake. They reached till his biceps on either side and then suddenly frittered away. White stared at the cloth that covered his alms halfway up to the biceps. The spell had dispelled. He had just entered the material plane and it would be some time before his abilities recovered.

He firmly held his alms perpendicular to his body, concentrated within himself and repeated, "Assorted Ability 4; Fabric habiliment."

The rings of light appeared again and started their motion along his alms. They covered the muscles in his alms and moved towards the torso and neck, slowly floating over the ridges and contours on his abdomen and the taut and varied muscles on his back leaving a trail of cloth along. They moved across his nether regions and then to the doughty pillars that were his legs. Completing the entire path along his impressive frame, they reached his ankles, and then slowly dissipated,completing their task this time.

White now had to search for the alchemist. He brought his palms together in front of his chest, holding them about a quarter feet apart. "Ability of the Light 84; Quarry Seek." A narrow beam of laser-like white light emerged from his chest and pointed towards the South West, continuing through the walls of the house. This light would lead him to the Alchemist. White walked over to the door and exited the apartment. He wondered what he would say to the alchemist once he met him.

.....

Aiden was happy; happier than he had been in a long time. He sat grinning opposite Will who grinned back at him. Aiden had gone bowling with Will, almost a first for Aiden; he had never formally bowled in his life before, just accompanied friends who bowled. And Will had given him a time to remember. The two sat outside the bowling lanes, Aiden holding his arm which seemed to be burning, he had strained it too much; tennis in the morning and now this.

"What? Why're you smiling?" inquired Will.

"What me? And what about you? You're grinning too!"

"Well, let's just say I found your bowling abilities exceptional!" Will was referring to Aiden's bowling 'techniques', and in particular to the time when he had tried to get Aiden to improve his stance. Aiden, totally enraptured in the 'I-am-gonna-knock-all-those-pins-down-with-this-strike' mood had stepped forward and swung the bowling ball with force. The next moment Aiden slipped and crashed down to the floor beneath skidding to where the ball ought to have gone while the ball went flying two lanes to the left. Fortunately no one was hurt, except Aiden's pride. Will soon resolved his pride issues with a smile.

Aiden showed his tongue to Will and stated with a mock frown on his face, "If you're referring to the incident where I goofed up and slipped, it's not my fault that they tell you to take of your shoes outside and play only in your socks."

"They never told you to wear your socks and play! You should have taken them off too!" Will was guffawing by the time he finished. Aiden glared at him angrily.

"Yeah yeah, whatever!"

"Seriously! You should have seen yourself! I still don't understand how you and not the ball ended up in the lane!"

"Ok, ok, I get it; Very funny indeed."

Will continued laughing. Aiden was still staring at him, thinking how beautiful he looked when he laughed. Then he decided the guy was so damn good-looking that he would look drop dead gorgeous even in a bloated fancy-dress frog rubber costume.

Will finally stopped laughing. "So, you wanna hit the video-game arcades?"

Aiden continued to stare at Will for a few more moments, thinking wasn't this 27 year old dude a bit too old for video games?

"What? You think I'm too old for video games?" Obiously Black had been reading his thoughts, ever since they'd met that morning.

"No!" said Aiden forcefully surprising even himself. "Let' go to the arcades!"

At that moment Aiden's phone buzzed. He looked at the phone screen. It was Tinka. Aiden answered the call.

"Hey what's up?"

"Don't act all ignorant with me!" she yelled before he could get in one more word. "What happened with that Will dude yesterday night? I want all the minutest details."

"Hey, Tinks. Sorry, can't talk right now, will call you later." Aiden was eager to put down the phone. Tinka apparently had other plans.

"Can't talk? Omigod! You're still with him aren't you?"

"Not still," he stated looking at Will, thinking his cryptic way of talking would not allow Will to understand that he was their subject of discussion. Little did he know otherwise.

"You met up with him again today?" an incredulous Tinka asked.

"Yes." Aiden answered, "Ok now bye, gotta go!"

"Wait you moron… did you or did you not do the dirty with him?"

"No!" Aiden replied haughtily. Will was still standing in front of him, patiently tapping his foot.

"Ok, go for now, but you better have time to tell me everything later!"

"Sure, bye!" Aiden clicked off the phone and looked apologetically at Will for keeping him waiting so long.

"It's the girl from yesterday, Tinka right?" Will enquired.

Aiden looked at him dumbfounded. "How'd you know?"

"Lucky guess!"

"Yeah it was her. She was asking about how things went between, err, with us yesterday." Aiden admitted sheepishly.

"And you never told her things were rocking?!" Will was looking at Aiden indignantly.

"Yeah?!"

"Well anyway, let's head to the arcade!"

Aiden followed Will wondering what the hell he had done to deserve such a person. He hoped it was for real. That their friendship or relationship or whatever this was, was real. Then he tugged at his cargos to make himself comfortable. They were Steve's cargos. He had been exasperated in the morning after getting Will's call to meet up for bowling. "What the hell should I wear?" he had lamented. Bowling meant casuals and his favorite cargo's were in the wash. He had borrowed Steve's good pair but Steve was a size smaller than him. He was sure these cargos would leave grooves along his waist.

Will on the other hand, Aiden observed, was dressed smartly in black denim cargos and a green turtleneck shirt. "He looks gorgeous" Aiden had thought many times. Even as Will had been bowling his turns and Aiden had wistfully admired his posterior. Apparently the girls in the neighboring lane had noticed him too, and were clapping and applauding whenever Will bowled. But they had all suddenly disappeared when Aiden had started finding them irritating and things had been perfect after that.

Fifty minutes of frenzied video-gaming later, Will lead Aiden to a burger joint. The pair ordered their meals. Will haggled with Aiden for paying for his meal but Aiden declined it like always. The two settled down with their meals.

"So, what's the plan after this?" Will asked with his eyebrows raised.

Aiden instantly thought about all the work he had lined up for the day. And he thought about how Will could afford to just goof off like this, but then he surmised that since it was a Sunday, he was probably relaxing and enjoying. Before Aiden could come up with an answer, Will interjected.

"I have some work to be done during the day, but I'm free in the evening. I would love for you to come and see the retirement home."

Aiden was pleased. He would have time for his academic duties as well. This guy was just too perfect.

"Ok, so what time should I come?"

"No, I'll come and pick you up around 6:30. That fine with you?"

"Won't that be a little too late in the evening or something?"

"No, no. It will be perfect. It's a retirement home; it's not like the people are in a hurry to go somewhere," Will added smiling.

"Ok then, 6:30 is perfect."

"And we'll go someplace for dinner after that. But only if you'll allow me to pay for the both of us."

Aiden gestured at him helplessly, but before he could say anything else, Will interjected once again.

"We're just going for pizza, I got free coupons!" Will held out a pair of coupons in his hand, rubbing them against one another.

"All right then." Aiden finally relented. "That means I have breakfast, lunch and dinner with you today!"

"Yup, and I am really sorry I can't spend any more time with you." Will smiled as he said this.

Inside, Black seethed at the amount of effort he had already put into this endeavor. He was surely fucking the alchemist tonight, and hopefully his mission would be complete.

· · · · ·

Aiden looked at the address that Tinka had given him, The number on the building stated that it was the one she had asked him to go to, but there was no sign of the optician shop she hadtold him would be there. All he saw was a shop with a small sign saying "Horoscopus. Fortune Telling." Aiden made a weird face thinking of the lack of taste with the jarring black and red colors used in the signboard and strained his eyes to read the finer print under the main title. 'Future predicted for lowest prices.'

Aiden looked around helplessly. This was certainly not the place to consult an optometrist. Was Tinka exacting revenge for the toothpaste biscuits prank by sending him to a bogus location? Just then he looked up. There it was; 'Optical Palace'. This was the place Tinka had asked him to visit. "Cheesy names around here," Aiden thought to himself.

It had been just that morning that Aiden had decided that he had had enough of his bespectacled look. He would try wearing contact lenses for a while. "I can always revert back to my glasses if I don't find lenses any good," he had reasoned. Aiden climbed up the narrow spiral steps leading up to the shop and entered it. "Okay Aiden," he said to himself, "Time for a new you!"

8 feet below Aiden's feet, a petit Japanese lady was having great trouble entertaining a customer. The irate patron was annoyed as the fortune telling Japanese lady had been telling him to hold on for she was facing some psychic disturbances. After 10 minutes of petulant waiting, the customer stomped off cursing why he had ever come here in the first place. The Japanese lady was still trying to figure out what was wrong with the 12 sided dodecagon shaped board she used to predict her patrons' fortunes. She knew she was not very good at fortune telling; she would never be as good as her mother had been at it. But eve she could understand that something out of the ordinary was happening, and she could hardly understand it. Suddenly she saw a vision in the crystal placed at the centre. A vision of a strapping young man who was the devil. And a vision of a boy who would be used to serve the devil's purposes.

Aiden's nearby presence had triggered this reaction, though he and the Oriental lady would never know that. The fortune teller was witnessing the most vivid vision of her life. It worried her and made her sick to the stomach to look at the consequences of the devil's deed.

. . . . .

Aiden stole a glance at his watch as he reached the main entrance of his college. It was 6:26 PM. Will had said he would pick him up from the main gate of his university. Aiden made his way towards the granite benches to sit and wait.

Just then a black sleek car drove up and halted beside Aiden. Aiden raised his eye brows staring at the streamlined body of the car. Yup, it was a Lamborghini though Aiden had no idea which one. Who the hell was driving this beauty?

As if on cue, the door of the car disengaged from its position and rose up. Will sat in the driver's seat in a tight red T shirt that showed off his perfect body. He was wearing glares that made him look super hot to Aiden.

"So you wanna get in or not?" Aiden's mouth was still agape, speechless.

Aiden finally composed himself. "You own this car?!"

"Yeah, I do, now just get your butt in here!"

Aiden stepped into the svelte vehicle and adjusted hmself a little consciously into the leather seat. "Shit! Too much!" Aiden exclaimed, glancing all around at the design of the car. The dashboard, the seats, the glowing buttons. "I've never been in anything like this before!"

Will took of his glares and winked at him. "Well now you have."

Aiden was still staring wide-eyed at everything. "Ok, buckle up buddy, and we'll head towards the Joe Black retirement home." Will changed gears as they zoomed off.

Aiden was busy thinking about telling all his friends about the car and what their reactions would be when the thought hit him. 'Shit! this guy's loaded! Where the hell did he get all this money from?'

"So you're thinking, how a person like me who runs a retirement home, gets to own a car like this? And you're kinda charging me of embezzlement of social funds in your mind?"

Aiden looked back at Will with a deer caught in the headlights expression. "So you are eh?"

Aiden picked up on Will's humor and decided to play along. "So should I charge you with embezzlement of retirement home funds?"

"Well actually, this car was given to me as a present on my 21st birthday by my grandfather."

"No fair! How come I never get things like that on my birthdays?" Aiden harrumphed and folded his arms across his chest. "And to think that I turned 21 just this year!"

"But I do need to ask you one thing." Aiden added.

"Shoot."

"How come you walked with me everywhere before? If I owned this baby, I certainly would never walk to go anyplace in my life. Even if the distance is only a 100 feet."

"But if I would not have walked yesterday, I would not have met you, would I?"

Aiden blushed at Will's reply. It would take some time before he understood Will's fascination with him.

10 minutes of car journeying later, in which Aiden perused all of Will's CD's and tested the potent music system of the car, Will slowed down in a huge compound, in front of a 2 floor storey wide structure.

"Yup. Here we are!" Will stated braking to a complete stop in front of the entrance of the edifice.

"So this is the Joe Black retirement home?" Aiden asked, reading the golden letters above the foyer. He noticed the muted pastels of mauve and green that the building was painted in, giving the whole structure a serene and peaceful look.

"Yup. Joe Black was my grandfather," Will stated as he switched off the engine and the doors on either side slowly swung up. The two exited the car and walked up to the foyer.

"C'mon, let me take you on the grand tour."

Aiden followed Will as he pushed open the glass doors. A podgy receptionist with red cheeks greeted them.

"Good evening Mr. Black. We have a guest?"

"Good Evening Doris. Yes, this is Mr. Writer, who's interested in taking a look around the retirement home. I shall personally escort him."

"Very well, and should I arrange for something to eat, something later perhaps?"

"No that won't be necessary; Mr. Writer and I have plans for later." Will was smiling and looked at Aiden who smiled back. Aiden loved the fact that Will always seemed happy and smiled perpetually. He knew for a fact that he always had a dorky grin on his own face whenever he was around Will.

Will led him through a door at towards the right leading to a narrow corridor painted in white. "Let's start with the indoor recreation rooms." Aiden followed Will as the passage opened into a set of large rooms filled and bustling with people. There were cubicles one after the other that catered to different activities. "Wow!" he breathed.

"My grandfather constructed this five years back," Will stated referring to the room around him as he waved to a blonde girl to come over. "It's a recreation place for elder people to spend some relaxation time in and indulge in their hobbies." "We even have a home theatre system towards that side." Will pointed to a large TV screen with equally tall speakers on either side. No one was watching anything at the time.

Aiden looked around, taking in the sights of the rooms. Towards his left a room filled with stands on which white papers attached to clip boards rested. Two elder men were busy painting portraits of what appeared to be each other, while another elderly lady was giving shape to some wet clay. They turned around on hearing Will's voice greeting him good evening and smiled at Aiden. Aiden smiled back. On the other side was a larger room filled with more than a dozen tables on which were carom boards, chess and other board games. This section was rife with people playing games who all nodded to Will in acknowledgement. "Sunday evening is the ideal time for gamers," Will explained.

They strolled past a number of other rooms, Will casually telling Aiden about all the activities that went on around here. There was a smaller room in which soft music played as an elderly couple swayed gently to the music. The lady winked at Will as he passed. There was a reading section with shelves full of books. A few elderly people, some with thick glasses sat in easy chairs as they read them.

"And here we have Mr. Kimberley's piano," Will pointed towards the large object. "Mr. Kimberley would not enter our retirement home unless we guaranteed that his piano would come too. He is however banned from playing during the evenings when the most crowd gathers here. Our senior members complain that at their age, they have lost enough hearing and would greatly appreciate losing no more." Aiden chuckled as he sauntered beside Will.

A blonde girl about Aiden's age, who Will had initially waved to, suddenly appeared. "Mr. Black," she said, "How's your day going?"

"Perfect Rachael." Will introduced the girl to Aiden. "This is Rachael here. She spends her evenings here helping us in our tasks."

Aiden and Rachael said hi to each other and Aiden immediately felt that he too would like to spend some time with the people here. Everyday was hardly a possibility, but maybe once or twice a week he could come here. Everything had such a clean and salubrious feel. It would be really nice to spend an evening or two a week here.

Black did not at all like this line of thought.

"And here we have our gardens." Will stated as he led Aiden through an exit to an open space where there were lawns with a few tables and chairs arranged around. "Our elder people spend a lot of time gardening here and they are solely responsible for the number of prizes we have won for their gardening efforts." Aiden noticed three old ladies who were sitting at table playing cards under a lighted umbrella for it was dark. "Ah, that's Mrs. Montgomery and her card playing troupe. They never give it a rest." Black called out to them and asked them to go indoors and play. "After this game dear." The old lady replied. Aiden noticed the wooden u-shaped hoops and pegs that were sticking out of the ground for playing croquet.

Will then led Aiden to the Medical premises showing introducing him to the head doctor and his nurses. "We have the latest medical technology and appliances." Will stated. "We better have, for the price many of the people's children pay for their parents to stay here.

"This place is huge." Aiden said, after visiting the yoga hall and the sauna rooms. "It never looked this huge from the outside!"

"We currently house 283 elderly people here. It has to be huge for that kind of a number."

"Hey, can you wait a second?" Aiden questioned. "I need to visit the restroom."

"Sure, the restroom's that way," Will stated, pointing towards a long corridor. He had been wondering when the boy would ask him of the pressing problem that he had been getting signs of from his mind for quite long. "Towards the outside garden, there are a couple of doors to the right. I'll wait right here."

Aiden headed of to attend to nature's call. He hurriedly finished off his business not wanting to keep 'his hunk' waiting. He opened the door of the toilet and bumped into a small Japanese lady.

"Oh Sorry!" Aiden looked down and noticed how small the lady was.

The lady gaped at Aiden and suddenly shrieked, "It's you! It's you! I found you!"

"Who me?" Aiden asked bewildered. He noticed that the lady's complexion was as white as milk.

"Yes, I've been trying to track you since so long!" she said, completely dropping of the phony Japanese accent she would assume for her customers, it gave them an oriental feel when she did that.

"Uhh… I…"

"No, you don't know me but…" the lady stopped as footsteps were heard along the corridor.

"Listen!" she said, "There's no time! Just listen to me. The devil – he's with you and he's after you!"

"After me? What devil?"

The footsteps were getting closer, their soft thudding indicating someone just around the corner.

"Yes, he wants to use you, he wants to…"

Just then Will appeared around the corner. It took a fraction of a second for Black to read both the people's minds and understand what had transpired.

"What's going on here?" he boomed in a loud voice. Aiden noticed it for the first time; an angry expression on Will's face. The Japanese lady got a horrified expression on her face as she looked at Will. The devil of her vision stood right in front of her.

"I don't know… this lady…"

Suddenly the Japanese lady burst out into a string of Japanese, bowing again and again, as if apologizing. She got close to Aiden and discreetly slipped a card into the back pocket of his jeans. "Call me," she whispered. Aiden caught a glimpse of the card before she slid it behind him. A vibrant display of black and red colors that read something like 'Horoscope'.

But stealth was not something that could have fooled Black. He had already read the lady's intention and knew about the card she placed in Aiden's pocket.

Then as abruptly as she had entered the scene the lady bobbed off, away from the two. Aiden was still gawking in her direction, befuddled while Black looked at her retreating form with his face as black as thunder. Abruptly his face broke into a smile.

"Senile old people!" he stated, "C'mon, We've just been roaming around, let's involve ourselves with the patrons a bit." Aiden noticed Will had a large box tucked under his arm. He shrugged and followed Will, dismissing the incident as doting effects on an elderly person.

Will led Aiden to the residential quarters and knocked on a door with a label stating the room belong to a Mrs. Anderson.

"Come in." a mellow voice answered.

The two entered a neat room where a wizened lady sat on a chair at the side, accompanied by one of her companions on the bed. Both were knitting some kind of woolen wear. And judging by the number of balls of wool lying on the bed, Aiden surmised they sure did knit a lot!

"Dear child! Good to see you!" Mrs. Anderson called out with a twinkle in her eye. Black walked towards her, bend over and hugged her. He hugged the other lady as well.

"This is Aiden here," he stated introducing Aiden to the two ladies who mentioned what a fine man he was. "And we've come so I can oust you and Aiden in a game of Pictionary," Will stated naughtily as he placed the box he was carrying on the bed. Aiden looked at the box and smiled. He was very good at the game.

Aiden was teamed up with Mrs. Anderson and Will with Mrs. Green, the other lady. 5 minutes into the game, Aiden realized that both the elder players were really good at the game. In fact, compared to them, he sucked at it! However Mrs. Anderson was good enough to compensate for his flaws. She soon led herself and Aiden to victory.

·····

A boisterous pair stormed out of Pizza Inn. Aiden was laughing hard leaning against Will's shoulder who was himself howling with laughter, his eyes tearing.

"Well what else could she have done?" Aiden asked between laughs. "The sand was running out and I was not being able to guess the word."

"You dolt! How could you not come up with that word? It was one of the easier ones."

Will was referring to their Pictionary game when Mrs. Aiden had to draw 'PISTOL' to advance to the next block. Mrs. Aiden was relieved thinking she had an easy one. She drew a gun shape with a trigger and Aiden started guessing. "Revolver, gun, Policeman, robber, thief!" Aiden had cried out. Mrs. Anderson shook her head fervently and Aiden guessed further on; "Holster, err....trigger, bullet...um rifle, carbine!" Mrs. Anderson had stared at Aiden exasperatedly. The minute glass indicated their time was running out. Finally the old lady sketched a penis, with a pair of testicles hanging and drew a stream of droplets gushing out of the tip. Aiden looked up at the old lady's face not believing what she had drawn... "Piss??" and then realization dawned upon him. "Pistol!!" he cried out, a second before the last grains of sand trickled down. Mrs. Anderson had leaped into the air, an extraordinary feat for a woman her age, and hugged Aiden. An embarrassed Aiden smacked his head wondering how he had not come up with such a simple word.

And Will was laughing at the same incident now.

"Get over yourself," Aiden stated with a mock frown on his face as he playfully swatted at Will's butt. And then burst into peals of laughter himself.

Black was furious inside. He had been laughing along all this time, playing this game. This day had completely drained the Perpetual. With all the arrangements his mistress had to make to create an illusory retirement home and all the troglodyte Empaths she had appointed to stay in as elder people. Each one of those Empaths could read any human's mind. The Empress of Vand had commissioned them to carry out the extended charade.

"So what now?" asked Black, not knowing what the alchemist was going to think of for their next move.

"Ice Cream!" yelled Aiden as he dragged Will towards a small Ice cream outlet which read 'Frozen Palace'.

.....

White was close. He could sense it. The white laser-like light he was following was leading to a structure of some sort. 'Frozen Palace', it read. Would he meet the alchemist there? White was nervous. For centuries the Kingdom of Light had awaited the arrival of the Alchemist. And soon White would convene with him.

What would the Alchemist say? Would he agree to help out a distressed Seraph? He could refuse at once, after all, the Alchemist's powers were his to use.

White made his way across the crowded grounds as people stared at him passing by. It was his external beauty, he knew that. He would know it without even glancing into their minds. The humans were cretins in this matter. Judging things far too greatly from just their outside appearances. They had a lot to learn yet. He walked past a trio of girls that were openly ogling him. One of them whistled as his imposing form crossed them, nearing 'Frozen Palace'.

. . . . .

Back In the Kingdom of the Dark, the Empress of Vand was anxious. And that in itself was a rare thing. She had seen in the seven vision stone, the one she used to watch her Guardian Black and the Alchmest in, that her greatest enemy was in the vicinity of the former two. She had no inkling how her 'blessed' rival had found the Alchemist. But one thing was certain; he could in no manner be allowed to intervene right then.

The small girl sat between the 6 crystals she had assembled. She closed her eyes and started murmuring under her breath, her voice getting louder with every word. All of a sudden, the 6 crystals shone brightly, and a six-pointed star was etched on the ground, effulgent in black flames. The voice of the little girl was deafening now, reverberating across for miles. And as she approached the crescendo of her chanting, she abruptly stopped her incantations, opening her eyes. She had succeeded in her task.

"Pi, you will procure us some time." The pet chimera received her message telepathically.

"Yes, your excellency."

"You will engage White and prevent him from intervening."

The Chimera descended, as if bowing with respect as his eyes glowed icy silver. The fanciful creature then shimmered and disappeared onto the material plane.

"White cannot encounter the Alchemist or Black at this moment," the little lass stated to a nonexistent gathering.

. . . . .

White cautiously made his was towards the Ice cream parlor following the white light of 'Quarry Seek'. When he neared the structure, he realized that the laser light passed through the structure and went beyond it. Had he not sensed that the alchemist was near here somewhere? The light of Quarry Seek seemed to say otherwise. He shrugged his shoulders and walked past the glowing letters which stated 'Frozen Palace', following the light as it led him astray.

White walked on still wondering what powers the Alchemist possessed. Legends had it that the Alchemist would arrive and the battle between the Kingdom of Light and Dark would be over. Legend also stated that the Alchemist possessed powers beyond contemplation. He wondered what these legendary abilities of the Alchemist could be.

White realized that following the light spell he had been led astray from the crowd. He had been striding for more than 15 minutes and now he walked in an open stretch of land where not a single person was visible. Where was the light taking him to?

Abruptly a chill ran in the atmosphere. White instantly realized that something was wrong. Soft notes of music wafted in the air, steadily getting louder. White looked around rapidly, trying to understand what was happening. The melody resounding in the atmosphere, where was it originating from? It was the sound of a flute.

In the next instant came a crashing wave at a high speed, a sonic ice breaker that unexpectedly boomed from behind White and collided with the high Seraph, ramming into him at a high speed and thrusting him along before it impaled him into an iron fence.

White reeled under the blow of the impact and got up unsteadily. The deleterious wave had knocked him face forward into the iron fence. The fence now lay on the ground, mangled pieces of iron twisted beyond recognition, but white had suffered greatly from the blow too. His torso throbbed with the force of the impact and blood dripped from above his right eye brow, blurring his vision before it trickled to the ground. Any pain or pleasure experienced by the corporeal shell that encased him would impair his spirit directly. The attack had caught him completely off guard.

White raised his arm, wiping the blood from his eyes with the back of his palm so he could see clearly. Directly ahead at a distance of about a 100 yards he could make out a hazy shape flitting about, slowly approaching him.

"Who are you?" his voice boomed. White had no clue as to what force could lunge at him with such an inexorable capacity.

"Who am I?" The voice questioned back with mirth in the voice. The shadowy shape slowly evolved into a human form. "Don't disrespect me by failing to recognize me White!"

White stared dumbfounded at the small 10 year old boy standing 50 yards ahead of him. A boy with white hair standing vertically upright, adorned in a black robe. It was Pi, the pet chimera of his sworn enemy, the Empress of Vand. Only this time he possessed his true form, the one of a 10 year old child with an evil smirk on his face. He held a 2-feet long glass flute in his hand, the 'Flute of Frost', White recognized the device responsible for the icy sonic wave that crashed him earlier.

"You!" cried out White.

"Yes me," the child replied as he lifted the glassy flute to his lips and blew into the grooves, his fingers dancing proficiently up and down the transparent instrument. White tuned his senses to make out the presence of a spiritual cordon that had been placed around, encompassing a circular area with a 1 mile radius. Even the subjects of the dark understood the importance of remaining unknown to the humans. The spiritual cordon would isolate the circular region so anything taking place inside the caulked area would remain unseen from the material plane. So Pi, intended to fight him here? White wondered if the cordoned area would be large enough to withstand the mayhem that was about to take place.

Shrapnels of ice surrounded White's adversary Pi, as he completed a melody and gathered energy in the form of an icy orb levitating in front of his torso.

White stretched out both his hands and placing one palm over the other he aimed towards the child to spout a spell.

"Ability of the Light 21, Flaming Shot." A red fiery sphere materialized perpendicular to his palms.

White grimaced and fired the flaming ball towards the kid. Pi let out a battle cry as he swung his flute in an arc, hurling his iced sphere towards his opponent. The iced sphere hurtled towards White at an astonishing pace, burgeoning into the profile of an enormous icy wave that screeched an ear-piercing sound as it advanced. It collided with the fiery ball fired by White, causing an explosion leaving behind flames and fumes of boiling water which slowly dissipated.

The two adversaries stared fixatedly at each other, the child smirking and the man frowning.

"Well you countered that this time," Pi stated contemptuously, "Let's see you counter these." Pi lifted the flute to his lips again, playing a melody of higher note this time. The shrapnel of ice around his body glowed as more than a dozen orbs of ice and sound materialized around him. White raised his eye brows knowing he would not be able to counter these many with the flaming ball spell.

The younger fighter swerved his transparent flute into arc shapes, sending wave after wave of icy sonic blasts towards White.

White dodged the first wave jumping a high altitude. Just as he landed on the ground another wave came crashing towards him which he eschewed by skidding to his left. He looked in dismay at the number of crushing waves that were approaching him or being fired by Pi and decided he needed higher agility and greater movement faculty. He leaped into the air dodging a wave as it shrieked across, and closed his eyes while still in the air.

An assortment of miniature comet shaped lights accumulated behind his shoulders and took the shape of giant pearl white wings. His pinions were back. He flapped them and flew higher into the air.

"Trying to fly away little fairy?" Pi aimed his waves to the flying form of the angel now. Swiftly White avoided one wave after the other. He knew he would have to go on the offensive now.

He concentrated his energies and called out to his fighting companion. A brilliant light dazzled in front of White, radiating sparkling light that caused Pi to shield his eyes. White now held the most powerful weapon in the Kingdom of Light, the 'Helos Saber'. He let out a howl as he clashed his sword against an approaching icy sonic blast, a wave that was larger than his own form, frittering away the blast and dispelling it.

White swooped down to the ground and stood up magnificently, his White wings out and proud, brandishing the sword of Helos in one hand.

"My opponent gives me hardly enough time to draw out my own artillery."

Pi gritted his teeth, "The Helos Saber shall no longer be able to defeat the Flute of Frost." He once more played out screeching high pitched tones on his flute as more icy orbs resounded around him. "Die, you cursed creature of the Light!"

. . . . .

Aiden could not stop giggling as Will led him out of the ice cream parlor, holding him tightly with a hand around his waist. Aiden felt ebullient, as if he had had a glass of some exquisite wine. Will was having that effect on him.

Out of the blue Will pulled him into a dark corner beside the shop and slammed him against the wall. Immediately he smashed his mouth upon Aiden's kissing him fiercely. Aiden retaliated with equal intensity. Will was pressing into Aiden's body and Aiden could feel a rock hard penis pressing against his stomach. Aiden was sure Will could feel his own penis' joy as it was forced upon Will's thigh.

Will broke the kiss as abruptly as he had started it. His severe green eyes looked into Aiden's, his face reflecting a pure animalistic sexual urge. He slid one hand down and grabbed Aiden's throbbing member with it, rubbing it gently.

"Let's go to my place," he uttered in almost a growl.

Aiden only moaned and closed his eyes. Will was taking him further than he had ever been in many ways. Will jerked on Aiden's hand and half jogged to the black Lamborghini, dragging Aiden along.

6 minutes of frenzied driving later, Will pulled into the parking lot of an 80 storey building. Aiden gasped at the huge structure before him.

"You live…" Aiden's words were silenced by Will's voracious mouth crashed upon his own as it tended to devour Aiden. Will was bending towards the passenger seat and the two were jerking forward and backward as their mouths wrestled.

Suddenly Will lunged back on his seat with pain. "Oww! You bit me!" Aiden had no clue what had taken over him. He looked at a small cut on Will's lip as it turned dark red. Aiden lurched forwards and initiated the onslaught of hungry wet kissing himself this time.

The two finally broke apart as Will wrenched Aiden apart, both gasping for air. "Let's go up," he growled with pure sexual passion on his face. Aiden elicited another moan and followed Will out of the car.

The elevator witnessed another tongue fight as Will once again slammed Aiden against the walls, holding Aiden's face with both his hands. Aiden could hardly breathe but he was in no hurry to stop the kiss. Aiden would have probably died of suffocation if Will's floor would not have arrived, and a man in a black suit, waiting for the elevator, would not have coughed rather obviously to break up the two.

Once inside Will's apartment Aiden once again dived for Will's mouth who stopped him half way in his advance. Will placed his arms around Aiden's waist and rapidly lifted him up placing him on his shoulder as if carrying a sack of potatoes. Aiden was surprised at how effortlessly Will seemed to do that but he was getting a great view of Will's denim clad butt from being thrown across his shoulder. Aiden was still giggling. Will lead him to a bedroom that housed a king sized bed and dumped Aiden on the bed.

In one fluid motion Will stripped off his red T-shirt and looked down upon Aiden as a predator about to ravage his prey. Aiden stared at the glorious male body on display. Lean muscles and cuts at all the right places. How many hours of hard work could possibly attain one such a body?

Staring at Will's form, suddenly Aiden's rational mind came back. He felt embarrassed that such a God was going to have sex with him; he certainly would not be good enough for Will.

Black immediately picked up on this line of thought and softly plopped down beside an Aiden who was lowering his gaze.

"Hey? What's the matter?" he cooed. The split second change of mood in the room was palpable.

Will placed his fingers below Aiden's chin and lifted his face, till their eyes met. Aiden was hardly able to look into the emerald greenness of Will's eyes. "Will I be good enough for you?" Aiden asked, his voice sounding as if he had just flunked a major examination.

Will smiled, "Aid, you're the hottest thing that's happened to me in a long time. I want you so bad!" Will took Aiden's hand and led it down to his crotch making Aiden feel the hardness that was all for him.

"Fuck rationality" Aiden thought as he lunged forwards and took Will's mouth into his own.

. . . . .

White was dodging wave upon wave of icy juggernauts and was getting annoyed. Pi, was skilled and was not giving him a single opening to even get close to him. Further, even the glacial waves that he stopped by thrashing at with the Helos Saber would explode into frigid shards that pierced his skin and made his hand numb. He looked down to the bleeding hand that held the sword. "This has gone far enough," he thought.

White held his left hand perpendicular to his body and chanted, "Guardian Ability 7, Golden Sphere."

A translucent golden sphere appeared around White encasing his entire form in an impenetrable bubble. Pi's sonic icy waves rammed into the force field which absorbed the impact forming a bulwark; rendering the crushing waves ineffective.

Pi, paused his volley of attacks to take in the new development. "Your force field is useless White," he called out. "It is not mobile, so all you can do is stay there and maintain it."

White released the force field and dashed towards Pi, holding his sword to the side ready to strike. Pi was taken back by the sudden movement but recovered enough to resume firing his waves towards a charging White. White dodged a wave still sprinting towards the young fighter. He was enclosing the distance between them rapidly. All he needed to do was shatter the Flute of Frost and this battle victory would be his. Pi fired another wave which White dodged and lunged to close the final few spaces between him and his adversary. This was it.

White swung his sword forcefully and Pi lifted the flute to counter the blow as a reflex. A loud clanging sound pervaded the atmosphere as the two weapons clashed. White was befuddled.

The flute did not shatter. In fact Pi was swinging the delicate looking instrument back at him countering every blow he gave and was retaliating as a skilled fighter. White swung his sword around in rapid strokes only managing to strike the flute and not Pi. Finally Pi maneuvered away and flung himself out of reach. White paused.

"You thought you could smash the 'Flute of Frost' to smithereens with your pathetic sword? You are too naïve White!"

White had no reply. He creased his brow and decided to go ahead and fight Pi the old fashioned way, sword fighting with physical contact. Pi seemed to possess sleight of hand, but surely he would oust him in sword fighting.

Pi lifted his flute to his lips to begin another melody as White dashed forward. He would give Pi no time to complete these stupid melodies. Pi abruptly wrenched the flute off his mouth to counteract White's sword. White swung the Helos Saber a few more times moving swiftly, the pair dancing almost as if the scene was pre-choreographed. The Flute of Frost screeched each time the sword clashed against it. Yes, he could defeat Pi in this field. The kid was losing! Just a few more strokes and…

Suddenly White flinched and recoiled. What was the searing pain throughout his body? He stopped short and looked down at his body. Several star shaped icicles were etched into his body, jutting out at odd angles. Pi laughed a maniacal laughter noticing White's expression.

"You fool, you did not even notice the icicles the flute left behind in its wake while it fought the sword. Those are the icicles that it left in the path as you rushed headlong after me. The flute left those icicles as it glided along defending your sword, and those icicles pierced your body. And you notice them now after so many have penetrated your body. You deserve to die!"

Pi lifted the flute once more and played two dull tones. To White's dismay the icicles latched on to his body started vibrating and resonantly exploded.

White shrieked agonizingly as the freezing mini explosions blew out bits of his body. Small chunks of flesh blew out from his abdomen, form his left arm, from the left side of his body and even his legs. Tiny ice pieces dove into his skin and were embedded deep into it by the momentum imparted to them from the explosions. The great angel collapsed on his knees as a heap on the ground, heavily wounded as blood gushed out from everywhere. Bit's of his flesh lay strewn on the ground intermingled with feathers as his wings were torn at multiple places.

How could he have noticed the icicles that the flute left as it swung in retaliation to his attacks each time. The kid was a deadly fighter. Deadly and cold-blooded.

Pi was still laughing fanatically. "You pathetic insect. You are no match for me."

White's mind was reeling fast as the pain was overwhelming his body. How could he be losing to the Empress' pet chimera? Was this creature that powerful? The sting of ice was too much for him to bear. And he was being sapped of his strength as the blood gushed out and the icicles remained embedded in his body. "No! I will not lose." He thought to himself staring at the ground. He opened his mouth to speak, "Ability of the Light 29, Self Immolation."

White whole body was instantly engulfed in flames. He burned in the fire of his own flame, melting all the icicles that were entrenched within him. Pi stopped laughing and stared wide eyed at the white angel who dug the sword in the ground and forced himself up on it, still refulgent in his own flames. Slowly the flames scattered away.

White raised his head to scream, "I will not lose to you!" And with that the energies of Helos were awakened. The sword burst into golden flames, the heat causing Pi to back off. Pi ran sideways along with White, who despite being severely crippled was lunging at him with the golden flaming sword. Pi realized he would have to use stronger abilities himself if he was to fight White.

White lunged at Pi and pierced the flaming sword into the boy's body. But what was this? The body suddenly shattered and fell to the ground. It was an illusion.

"My opponent gives me hardly enough time to draw out my own artillery." Pi quoted a former dialogue of White.

White swirled around to see Pi standing 200 yards from him, balancing himself on the iron fence.

"I don't know how you got there Pi," he stated calmly. "But you will be defeated by my sword now."

"We'll see," Pi stated before he played on the flute again.

"Damn flautist," White voiced to himself.

The sounds of Pi's flute reverberated across the open land. White noticed that everything suddenly began to change. Dark clouds rapidly covered the night sky and the moon. The ambient temperature dropped 10 degrees. Pi himself was glowing like his ice shrapnels. The melody was getting more high-pitched, unbearable for a human ear. White braced himself for what was about to come. He knew in light of the injuries received earlier that he would net be able to fight for much longer.

Pi's body turned into ice as frigid waves started swirling around the flautist. The waves got higher and higher and consequently swallowed the whole boy.

"Fight my inherent form you insect!" Pi's voice called from amidst the icy conglomeration.

"The ice dragon!"

With a blinding flash of light, the entire icy mass rose up into the air. White was startled as a snake like outline with the head of a dragon slithered into the air, its body more than a 100 feet long.

"Great," White thought as the dragon lurched towards him. Pi had turned himself into the icy mass that was the dragon and swooped down as thousands of gallons of near freezing water and ice towards White. White let out a battle cry as the flames of his swords flared and engulfed his entire body. He leaped at the icy dragon, swinging his sword.

A huge explosion resulted and the shock of it shook the earth for miles. Vapors and sparks of fire floated everywhere and nothing was visible for a minute. White examined himself. He had been injured once more, below his shoulder blade where a deep gash caused blood to ooze out. But where was Pi?

The settling fumes answered White's question. Pi lay on the ground clutching his foot, a deep cut visible on his foot. He had deep bruises elsewhere on his body and he hardly looked happy anymore. White looked at the sight and took a deep breath. It was a 10 year old child grimacing with pain.

"Beg forgiveness now and I shall let you go. If you don't then the next blow will be much more powerful."

"Beg? I shall never ev..." Pi's words were interrupted as he heard his mistress' voice in his mind.

"Come back. You've bought us enough time!" the lass uttered into his brain.

Pi growled "No, I shall not come back now!"

"Come back immediately!" the voice ordered.

"No!" Pi spat out. "I shall defeat White!"

"You fool, you…" but Pi had shut out his mistress' voice from his head. He was determined that he would defeat White. He lifted the flute to his lips one last time as he stood up.

"I have one last move left," he stated before he blew into the grooves of the glassy instrument. The melody was long this time and was reaching a crescendo. It was a rhapsody, White realized. However he would not interrupt the child this time. He would let him prepare his move.

A ring of frost surrounded the flautist as he played on, the tune getting faster and faster. His fingers were dancing vigorously along the flute. It was getting even colder now. The earth cracked open below Pi, as if the ground was witnessing an earthquake with the child as the epicenter, and a large platform of ice lifted him off the ground.

Pi stopped playing. The move's preparation was complete.

"This is the ultimate move of the 'Flute of Frost'" he explained. "The flute calls forth water from the ground and saturates that present in the atmosphere. The water from the ground freezes as it reaches the surface. The frozen water then surges upwards into the air in the form of giant icicles. These icicles then collect the saturated moisture in the atmosphere and explode into thousands of icy shards."

White hardly needed an explanation as he witnessed the move himself. The ground was being cracked everywhere as frozen stalagmites of ice burgeoned from it. Large icicles suddenly popped into the air and stopped at eye level, pausing for a few seconds as if wondering what to do. Abruptly they exploded as hundreds of tiny needle shaped ice shards flew in every direction at a high velocity. Pi himself was enshrouded in a translucent icy orb that White guessed would protect him from any damage. Icicles burst forth everywhere in the air as stalagmites rose around for hundreds of feet in every direction.

White used a move used earlier. "Guardian Ability 7, Golden Sphere." The golden sphere appeared around him but he knew it would not be of much use against these millions of needle shaped icicles that were ricocheting everywhere. He would have to use the flaming fires of Helos.

The white angel Witenhoem was at his limit now. The damage he had taken throughout the battle was overwhelmingly severe. He had no more energy left to keep swinging his sword around. The outcome of the battle would be decided with the next strike.

White invoked all the strength that he could muster in the state he was in. Large golden circles appeared directly overhead him, thousands of meters above in the dark clouds. The circles revolved and let out a streak of golden lightning that fell upon the white angel and engulfed him. His entire body and sword emanated powerful spiritual pressure.

And then he ran forward, screaming with all his might. One powerful swing and everything collapsed. The Flute of Frost had been shattered.

·····

When White had recovered enough to stand up he headed towards the body that lay on the ground. It was the slain body of his child enemy Pi. The scene looked gruesome; the body of a 10 year old with a big slash across his torso, lying in a pool of his own blood. The mighty battle was over.

White bend over and looked more closely at the child's skin.

"Fish scales," he muttered under his breath referring to the scales that subtly covered the boy's body, scales that related to his chimera form. White heaved a sigh of relief. He had vanquished a mighty enemy but was severely injured in the process. He looked down upon his once beautiful body that was mangled and mutilated beyond recognition now. He felt all energy sapped from his body as he slumped to the ground with fatigue. He would require at least a couple of days to heal himself.

He watched as the boy's body slowly froze to ice and melted away.

Back on the throne of Vand, a little girl cursed the 'Dark Stasis' curse upon her that prevented her from entering the material plane at night. If only she could have intervened and saved her pet. She wailed for the loss of her pet. She screamed and swore her enemy would suffer.

·····

Black had been containing the rage within himself for far too long. The boy had been having fucking him with his eyes every single moment. Playing this pitiable game with the Alchemist, this charade of love and attraction and lust. Constantly having to keep his attention, constantly having to try and woo him and constantly having to clear off his bitching insecurities about himself; telling him how attractive he found him. He was getting sweet retribution for all that now.

Black was riding the boy hard. His sex buried deep inside the boy as he vigorously pistoned in and out of the boy's hole. It was not all Black's doing, the brutal fucking. The boy wanted it hard and he was giving it to him. He could feel the waves of pleasure as they exploded across the boy's brain; he had his eyes closed and his lips apart moaning in ecstasy. The bed squeaked violently, as if it's legs were about to give away. Black ploughed the boy harder.

Without warning the boy convulsed shuddering, and finally orgasmed, spewing white cum between the two bodies. Black would force his own orgasm immediately but then he read in the boy's mind that he did not wish him to. He wanted 'his Will' to take his own time and derive the most enjoyment. The boy somehow derived pleasure in this fact. Then he would derive his own pleasure, Black surmised, as he continued to thrust into the boy for a few more minutes.

Finally he exploded, his dick spewing it's 'Perpetual cum' inside the condom that clad his member deep inside the boy's chute. That was surely some savage fucking the buy had indulged him in. How did this shy and reserved boy, who's only notorious streak was passing a sarcastic remark here and there, turn so vicious in bed?

Black slumped onto the boy, his muscular defined body resting upon the young youth's. He lifted his face and looked at an expression of contentment on the boy's face. Glowing with serenity. And then he realized it was happening again. He could not read the boy's thoughts at all. The human mind was in constant turmoil, thinking a hundred irrelevant thoughts every few minutes. This boy obviously had thoughts running in his head right now too. So why the fuck could he not read them? His brow furrowed as he tried to extract the boy's thought. No use, he could not pick up a single trace. This was the same thing that happened in the coffee shopthe previous day.

Then the boy slowly leaned forward and kissed him completely. Black lowered his hand to grasp the erect penis of the boy and just like that the thoughts were back. He could suddenly read all the boys thoughts again. They surfaced as abruptly as they had vanished.

The boy now wanted to fuck him, and was finding it hard to tell him that. He had hoped that one fuck would tire the boy out but this boy was insatiable. Very well, he would have to give into the boy's needs for now.

"I want you inside me." He whispered ending the boy's struggle with his own thoughts.

Aiden smiled widely as he heard that. He raised himself and Black along with him as he opened a condom packet and readied himself to enter this godly creature.

. . . . .

The boy was finally asleep breathing heavily. Black had spooned him and had his arms around the boy. The boy had pushed himself further into Black before he went to sleep.

The Alchemist had displayed an unquenchable appetite for sex once they hit the bed. He had explored every inch of Black's body and had bitten and sucked on every single centimeter of his body. He had fucked the Black angel and had been savagely fucked by Black in return several times. More than 2 hours of constant activities had left marks everywhere on Black's body and several on the boy's body too. Black's skin was sore everywhere, even his asshole was sore. Who would have thought this boy would turn into such an animal in bed?

But now Black had work on his hands. He slowly disentangled himself from the boy's form, no easy act considering the intricate way the boy had intertwined their bodies. Black slowly stood up still naked and headed to where the boy's jeans were lying on a chair. He probed the back pocket and picked out a black and red rectangular card.

'Horoscopus' it read. This was the card slipped into the boy's pocket by that small Japanese lady. It held a contact number and an address.

"Internecine Ability 12, Black Cinders," Black stated. Black fumes of smoke emerged from the card burning with sooty flames till it was completely incarcerated. The Alchemist would never find this card. The recoil for such a low class internecine spell was small, and it hardly stung Black.

Black had one more task. "Ambulatory Ability 7; Shimmer Teleport." Black's form steadily disappeared from the room and a few seconds later appeared in the room of a sleeping Japanese lady. Seeing her sleeping form, Black intentionally dropped a flask on her table onto the floor. The lady woke up with a start as the flask crashed onto the floor.

She stared terrified at the naked man in her room; the devil himself. She opened her mouth to scream for help but no voice left her throat. Black lifted his left hand and closed his palm except for the index finger and the middle finger which he held sticking out. "Internecine Ability 94; Psychic Implosion." Immediately the Japanese lady's brain exploded inwards inside her skull, turning all the cerebral matter into pulp. One of her eyeballs popped out of its socket as the other turned towards the far up right corner, resting at an odd angle. She fell back on the bed, dead, trails of blood trickling down from her nostrils and her ears.

This time the internecine spell was powerful and Black flinched at the recoil. He however had no time to recover completely as he heard footsteps coming towards the door. Black swiftly cited the Teleportation spell and was transported back to the room in which the Alchemist slept. He looked at the peacefully sleeping form of the boy. For now his job was complete. The Empress would later inform him whether he had succeeded in bending the Alchemist to his will or not.

Staring at the sleeping form, he suddenly recollected those moments when he would not be able to read the Alchemist's mind. It terrified Black, and he knew not the reason for it.

He slowly slipped back into the bed beside the sleeping boy who moaned a little in his sleep and shifted a little to adjust him back into their previous position.

. . . . .

Episode Three

In the Kingdom of Light, far away from the material plane, White opened his eyes awakening from a deep slumber. He was immediately surprised at the form of a woman angel bending over his body as he lay. Frigeria was still there? How long had she been healing him?

The beautiful form of the raven haired angel turned her attention towards her Emperor. "Finally the white angel Witenhoem rises." Her voice reverberated as the tinker of muted bells across the chamber in which White lay.

"Frigeria, how long have you been healing me?" White was slowly trying to raise himself and Frigeria helped him in the task. His colossal wings opened up as he sat upright. He still felt enervated, but all the pain had vanished. There was no longer a single bruise on his body.

"I have been healing you, but two nights. The wounds of battle you possessed were of a draconian nature."

"Yes," White grunted as he sat himself upright. "I was led into a battle with a small child; the kind that was the son of the devil himself."

Frigeria nodded her head in understanding. "So it was Pi that you fought. I reckoned as much when you appeared and collapsed onto your throne. My fear knew no bounds when I saw the injuries you bore and the icy shards embedded deep within you. Even your wings were torn and ragged. I almost thought that we had lost our ruler!"

White smiled at the worry expressed by the greatest healer in the Kingdom of Light. "Fear not Frigeria, it will take more than a chimerical creature to conquer me. I returned to you with wounds of a draconian nature you say, Pi did not return to the Kingdom of Void at all."

"So he was defeated." Frigeria took a deep breath absorbing the news.

"Defeated and destroyed."

"And yet, the involvement of Pi suggests that the Empress herself is involved in this matter of the Alchemist."

"Indeed it does, all the more reason for me to hasten and reach the Alchemist."

. . . . .

In the Kingdom of Void also far away from the material plane, another angel, albeit a dark one, was crouched in reverence under his ruler. The undersized ruler shook her head from side to side, her golden yellow tresses, which reached all the way to the ground, swaying as she swayed.

"He is not yet ready," she stated. "The alchemist will not lend us the use of his powers in his current state."

The doughty black angel lifted his gaze to meet the eyes of his mistress.

"And in fact," the Empress continued, "It might be quite some time before the Alchemist will be prepared. You Arangyunus, will have to keep wooing him till he reaches that stage."

Black nodded understandingly. This task was proving to be diabolically difficult. The dark Seraph had been putting in all his efforts for four continuous days and the mistress only stated that converting the Alchemist would take much more time. Black had been constantly endeavoring, and in the process had lost himself several times, lost his finesse and he was feeling like he was losing his sanity. He felt as if the young boy was gradually pulling the ground from beneath him rather than the other way round.

But this was no time to founder, and certainly not the time to possess a weak mind. The most important task he had ever been bestowed was upon him, and he would have to complete it consummately.

"I understand," The dark seraph finally whispered back.

"Slowly poison his mind. Seduce every pore of him. Completely overwhelm him with yourself. And when he is ready to do any task you ask of him, it is then that he will be ready." Having lost her pet, the Empress was more determined than ever to thrall the Alchemist. The Alchemist would grant her the ability to extirpate all her enemies, and one in particular; one that would allow her to exact sweet revenge for the death of her pet, and revenge for a matter that went far deeper into time, one that very few knew of.

White would suffer for his chicanery.

Black nodded once more accepting his orders.

"Empress, where is Pi. It had been some time since I have seen the chimera." Black had never been fond of the fanciful creature himself but was used to its sessile presence with his mistress. It was strange that the past few times he had taken audience with the Empress in the Kingdom of Void, there had been no signs of her pet.

The little lass steeled herself. She would not inform Arangyunus that her pet had been defeated. Annihilated at the hands of her adversary. Destroyed by White while her own guardian frolicked with the alchemist. Black would not know of this.

"I have sent him on a task to the dark glaciers of Void. I am afraid it will be some time before he returns."

Black acknowledged the fact and raised himself. It was time to go back to the material plane. Time to return to the boy who was so infatuated with him but was still not ready to do as he desired. Back to the boy that he had been seducing. The same boy who now sometimes scared him.

·····

Aiden was a little nervous while entering his class. He ran a hand through his hair for the umpteenth time. This was the first time Aiden had gotten his hair styled in 21 years of his life. He had finally gathered the courage to change his hair. He had gone from shaggy uncombed disheveled tufts to sleek middle-parted hair. He was unsure whether of what others would think when they saw it. But he had liked it when he saw himself in the mirror. And now his fellow budding engineers would see it for the first time.

Aiden took a deep breath and entered the lecture hall through the front door. The crowd was boisterous as usual, as they would be when no lecturer had yet entered the class, and a few took notice of Aiden's changed comport. Aiden looked across to where he normally sat on the last row with Dominic and Storm. Yup, they were there as usual, seemingly engrossed in some type of an argument.

Aiden made his way towards them as someone commented how weird he looked in his new hairstyle.

Dominic had been the center of Aiden's universe for more than two years, in fact, ever since he had entered the university. According to Aiden, Dominic was a persevering, extremely good natured person who always tried to keep everyone around him happy. Dominic was smart when the situation demanded him to be, he was sincere and basically the embodiment of Aiden's ideal. He studied hard, involving himself in a million college activities and organizations and was always busy. He was good looking with his West European aristocratic face and though Aiden knew that there were at least 3-4 other guys in class that looked better than Dominic, he would never place them in the same category. Dominic possessed an athletic built that gave the impression that he worked out and played a lot of sports. Aiden knew otherwise, the guy would not touch a sport if his life depended on it.

The other one of his close friends was Storm McDonald. True to his name, Storm could eat up a storm anytime he wanted. With his 6'4" frame and weighing more than 290 pounds, Storm was everyone's teddy bear. But Storm was hardly lazy or sluggish. He was energetic, hard-working and sincere, the kind Aiden always associated with. Storm completed the trio who were often referred to as the beavers of the class, owing to their industrious natures.

Aiden came over to Dominic and Storm as the two looked up. Both got a puzzled expression on their faces seeing him.

"Hey, wadyou do to you hair? You look like a clown!"

"Thanx Randy." Aiden sneered at the commentator feeling a little let down.

"Hey cool!" It was Dominic this time. "Your hair looks good!"

Aiden immediately felt a lot better. Dominic had said it looked good, and that overwrote what everyone else had to say, well almost everyone. He still had to show Will his new hairdo.

Aiden settled in next to Dominic and Storm as the professor entered the class.

Dominic asked in hushed tones. "Where you been lately, I don't see you at all nowadays?"

Spending all his free time with Will, who somehow mysteriously always seemed to be free when Aiden was, it was expected that Dominic had hardly caught a glimpse of him outside class in the last few days. In fact he was sure that he was going to have trouble staying awake in class owing to the overnight workouts he was having with Will.

Just then Aiden's phone buzzed on silent mode. He looked at it to find a message from Will. 'MISSING U. WANNA B WITH U' it read. Aiden felt a surge of joy within him. He wanted to scream out loud and tell Dominic and everyone in the whole damn class that he was in love with the most amazing person on the planet. The hottest hunk who also had an awesome personality and heart. He wanted to tell Dominic about his sexuality, about being in love with him for so long and then meeting the most awesome guy on the planet; Will. He somehow felt that Dominic would be happy for him. But Aiden knew he did not have the guts to blurt all that out.

"Just busy." He whispered back.

Aiden adjusted himself and concentrated on the lecture being delivered ahead of him. It wasn't long before his eyelids became heavy and he started slumping down in his seat. Dominic nudged him and finally started glaring at him after 3 failed attempts to wake him up. Between his nightly marathons with Will, his college lectures and the sports time he spent with his roommates, Aiden was having a hard time covering his shut-eye time needs.

"What the fuck are you so sleepy for?" Dominic burst out at him once the professor had left. "You know that was our HOD's lecture and he saw you sleeping! You're lucky our HOD is of such a great nature. Any other teacher and you would be hung by your balls for dozing off like that!"

Aiden smiled back sheepishly and said sorry. He felt guilty for sleeping during class, the professor being amongst the only ones he actually liked. He would have to catch up on sleep somehow or he was going to be in bad shape.

"Ok listen sleepyhead," Dominic began, "We are assembling a robot for the upcoming TechFest. You interested in joining the team?"

Aiden knew he hardly had time these days, but it was Dominic asking.

"Yeah Sure! Who else is on the team?"

"Me, you and Mr. hyperactive here," Storm interrupted, referring to Dominic as the hyperactive dude.

"So we are going to an electronics specialist who'll give us pointers for a few days and help us get started. We'll meet him for our first meeting tomorrow evening at 6." It was just like Dominic to have everything already planned out.

"At 6?" Aiden raised his eye brows and folded his arms across his chest. He realized his time with Will would be choked if the consultation were to materialize and take place everyday.

Dominic sat on top of their table and huffed. "Yeah, after college, at 6. Every day at 6 till the TechFest."

Aiden immediately understood that the robotics deal was something time-consuming that he had involved himself in; something that would last quite a while. He wondered how he would keep his commitments and still meet up with Will daily. All he felt like doing right now was to get into bed with Will and spend the remainder of his life there.

"You guys coming to the cafeteria? I wanna grab a bite to eat." It was Storm rubbing his tummy.

"Shit!" Aiden exclaimed. "I have to meet Tinka there. Almost forgot. She'll kill me if I don't reach there on time!"

The three headed towards the cafeteria, Aiden rushing them along. On reaching there he immediately left the other two and headed towards what was commonly referred to as the 'Archi area' by architecture students or 'The big mess' by others. A section of the cafeteria that was always bustling with architecture and interior designing related students. Tables overpiled with A3 sheets, 32 inch folders and .1 mm microtip pens. The Architecture students stubbornly refused to complete their work elsewhere, much to the chagrin of the mess in charge; he had given up on getting them to do their work elsewhere, leaving that section of the cafeteria a sight to behold on submission days.

Tinka was furiously inking sheets as Aiden hurried over to her. She had 'commanded' him to meet her and help her complete her work before the submission.

"You're 7 minutes late!" she growled and then paused to take a better look at him. "Omigod! What did you do to your hair?!"

"Howzzit look?" Aiden beamed and waited for her response.

"Looks cool! How did you get it into you to…," Tinka paused as realization dawned upon her, "Oh, so Will is having this influence on you?"

"No of course not. I was planning all along to…" Aiden paused only to find Tinka looking at him with a 'yeah-rite' look, tapping her foot on the ground. "Yes he is." Aiden finally admitted sheepishly.

"It really suits you. You look all cute and all. "

"It better look good for the amount of time and money I put into it." Aiden muttered. "That bloody hair dresser put some burning cream in my hair to straighten it, and then kept me there for 3 hours. Never had such a lengthy haircut in my life."

"Ok, stop goofing around and grab those pencil colors. Start scribbling in these tiles in this manner." Tinka pointed him towards the sheets that were overflowing from all sides of the table. "And be neat," she added menacingly.

Aiden mock saluted her, "Yes Sir!" and hastily got down to coloring the floor tiles in the weird mosaic pattern Tinka wanted it in.

"How come I am the only non-Archi student that has to do Archi work?" Aiden grumbled after 2 minutes of frantic penciling. All around were frenzied wannabe architects trying to complete their sheets. He glanced at the patch he had colored and groaned as he compared it to the vast expanse left. This would e one hell of a task.

"Cause you are the only boy from the engineering side who bears some semblance to a person who can draw and color." Tinka answered.

"So you get to be all your colleagues' envy for having additional help from outside, and all I get is ink stains and pencil marks on myself?"

"You also get my brilliant company!" Tinka replied bend over her work still busy limning straight lines with her T-square.

"Yeah rite!"

"So did you collect your contacts from that eye-shop?" Tinka was referring to the contact lenses that Aiden had recently ordered.

"Nope; will do it tomorrow. Have my first half free tomorrow," Aiden replied finishing a green patch and looking satisfactorily at it. His mind immediately thought about how similar Will's eyes were to the shade he was using.

"So new hairdo, getting rid of spectacles, getting contacts and that glow on your face. Will sure seems good for you."

Aiden stopped coloring and placed his pencil on the sheet. He waited till Tinka looked up at him. "He's perfect!" he stated triumphantly.

"He's just too great, forget the fact he looks ultra-hot. He's always so sweet and caring. And he always spends an enormous amount of time with me but still leaves me enough time to get all my academic work done."

Tinka stopped her inking and stood upright smiling, waiting for Aiden to finish.

"And the sex rocks!" Aiden added.

"He is remarkable." Tinka finally answered and took a deep breath before adding the next bit; "Isn't he a bit too perfect?"

Aiden was taken aback. Was Tinka stating that Will was too good for him, way above his league? Was she saying he had hidden vices? He knew Tinka would be happy as long as he was happy. Maybe it was just her way of asking him if he was not telling her something. Aiden opened his mouth to answer when his cellphone buzzed in his pocket.

Aiden fished out the set from his pocket to find another message from Will. 'MISS U LIKE CRAZY. U BETTER BE FREE IN THE EVENING.'

Aiden instantly forgot all of Tinka's worries as he flashed his cellphone showed her the message and started thumbing his keypad to send Will a reply. Tinka smiled at an effervescent Aiden, hoping things turned out perfect between Will and Aiden.

·····

White stood atop a building as the sun was setting. So he had finally found the Alchemist. He looked down to where he could see an unassuming lad dressed in blue jeans and an orange sweatshirt leaning against a wall, apparently waiting for someone. So this boy was the Alchemist. And he had finally found him. The moment had come. But now he no longer felt nervous at having to accost the Alchemist. It was because he was not going to.

Instead he was going to ask the Alchemist for help without the boy knowing he had done it. He would enter the boy's mind and search for the answers to all his questions, searching through his beliefs. He would dive in and scour his mind and ultimately get the answer he was seeking; would the Alchemist lend the Kingdom of Light his powers or not? And it would take all of five seconds. He would have his answer and the alchemist would never catch a glimpse of him.

White braced himself and concentrated for plunging into the boys mind. The next instant, his mind was in. Zooming across the thoughts and desires, through beliefs and faiths, through secrets and sorrows, seeking only the answers to the questions he had in mind. Zig-zagging through the meandering reflections, the welter of labyrinthine thoughts. Seeking his answers through the kaleidoscopically human mind. And seconds later he exited forcefully, his consciousness back inside his own mind.

White had received his answer. The Alchemist had refused to help.

·····

Aiden had arrived at the coffee shop he was supposed to meet Will at. Whenever he would plan to meet up at a certain time, Will would always already be there waiting for him. Being extremely punctual himself, Aiden had admired this quality in Will but then felt guilty that he himself would be the one to arrive late. This time Aiden turned up earlier than the set time and was waiting for Will outside the coffee shop. The same coffee shop that they had been to on the first night they had met.

Aiden noticed the arrival of the black Lamborghini that signified Will's entry. Yup, Will was there before time but Aiden had beaten him. He knew it would be a minute or so till Will parked his car and came up to him. He smiled with anticipation; he could barely wait to see his lover again.

Suddenly Aiden witnessed an excruciating strain. He felt dizzy as a million thoughts ran through his head. Aiden lost all control and staggered unsteadily bracing himself against the wall for support. And just as abruptly as it had started, the strain was gone. Aiden steadied himself, wondering what the hell had happened.

"Ade, relax buddy what's wrong?" It was Will who had come rushing to Aiden's side as he had seen Aiden suddenly look dizzy and start swaying about.

"I… I don't know." Aiden finally managed to squeak out. He felt as if he had just spent 20 straight hours preparing for his Microprocessors exam. He wiped a trail of drool from his mouth with the back of his hand

"You Ok? What happened?" Aiden saw Will's expression of care and worry and his uneasiness dissipated.

"Yup, perfectly fine!" Aiden smiled and straightened himself. He still felt a little mentally exhausted.

"Should I take you to my place or something?"

Aiden looked into Will's eyes. Will had on a black leather jacket, a bit like the biker kind. His chest definition was visible through the thin white T-shirt he had on under. Aiden thought he looked ravishing. He could feel his hormones surging at the sight of Will. "One quick coffee and we're outta here" he thought

"No, no. Just felt a little dizzy suddenly. Its gone now; am fine. Let's just go and have some coffee"

"Your hairdo looks great." Will suddenly chimed in. Aiden blushed. Will had liked his hair makeover. The entire haircut investment was worth it now

Aiden grabbed Will's hand and led him inside the coffee shop wondering what had transpired a few moments ago. He had no clue that a powerful Perpetual had entered his mind and had rummaged it to find answers to his many questions. He had no clue that he had in fact subconsciously denied lending his help to this Perpetual.

Aiden entered the coffee shop and immediately let go of Will's hand when he noticed who was inside. It was Aditi, the Indian girl Jason had had the hots for. And sure enough, Jason sat opposite her with his back to the entrance. Aiden would recognize the red Nike cap anywhere. So Jason had hooked up with Aditi after all. And it was a wonder that Jason was sacrificing his 'sports time' to be with this girl.

Aditi noticed the two and waved to them. 'More to Will than to me' Aiden thought. He frowned thinking his time with Will would get a little spoiled. But then it would give him a chance to spend some time with Jason as he had hardly done so in the past few days. Aiden guided Will towards the pair. Jason upon noticing Aiden's arrival, immediately raised his hand in a high five; his standard greeting.

"Hey wazzzup?" Jason was all smiles as Aiden high-fived him. Jason paused and creased his brow, taking a closer look at Aiden. "What the hell did you do to your hair?"

"Just something a bit different." Jason then glanced curiously at Will.

"Hey Aditi, this is Will. Will these are my friends."

Will greeted the two warmly, Aditi retuning his greeting in a prolonged seductive manner, annoying Aiden.

"So should we sit down and interrupt you two?" Will asked.

"Sure." Aditi answered before Jason could say anything. "Just join us."

Will and Aiden sat opposite each other with Jason and Aditi on either side of them. Aiden would have much preferred sitting next to Will on the comfy sofas the cafe offered. Looked like this would have to do for now.

"So Will," Aditi started, "What do you do for a living?"

"I run a retirement home," Will continued as Aditi raised her eye brows at his reply. "It's called the Joe Black retirement home, just off shore towards the pier."

"Cool and how do the two of you know each other?" she asked swishing her manicured finger between Aiden and Will.

"He's just a friend," Aiden blurted out but the girl paid him no attention. She was waiting for Will's reply. Aiden looked at Aditi busy eyeing Will and felt a tinge of jealousy. Aditi continued asking Will questions, trying to keep his entire attention on herself. It was then that Aiden noticed Will. Will was looking straight at him while he answered Aditi, not taking his eyes away even once. Aiden stared back at the unblinking acute green eyes. He was madly besotted with this man.

Aiden broke his gaze as an annoyed Jason tired to interrupt the conversation and get a few words in. Jason was apparently not happy at Aditi's obvious ogling. Aiden smiled as he thought about how Aditi was struggling to capture Will's attention as Jason strived to capture hers.

A young boy arrived and introduced himself as the waiter. Aiden immediately recognized him as the waiter who had been an overeager server to Will on the first day when he had come here. Poor chap was still vying for Will to take notice of him, albeit with no results. Aiden thought for the hundredth time how lucky he was to be the one that commanded all of Will's attention.

The two new arrivals ordered for coffee while Jason stated that he had already had some. He shot down Aditi's suggestion to order some more. Aditi finally ordered a pastry for herself which Aiden was sure, looking at her figure, she would never be able to finish.

5 minutes of conversation later, in which Jason scowled and frowned at Aditi, Will perfunctorily answered flimsy questions and Aiden adjusted his crotch three or four times under the table, Aiden noticed someone he was not at all prepared to see. It took a moment for Aiden to register who this guy was.

It was the blonde guy Josh, getting up and heading towards the exit; and he would cross their table. The same Josh who had rudely turned him down in the bar 4 days ago and humiliated him. Aiden tried to look elsewhere as Josh squinted his eyes staring at Aiden as he neared their group. Will immediately turned to see who was the person he was reading about in Aiden's thoughts.

A loud crash was heard as Will stealthily slipped his foot out, tripping Josh who landed on his face with a splat.

"I'm sorry," Will leaped up and offered his hand to a dazed red-faced Josh who was trying to raise himself off the ground. He grabbed hold of Will's hand through the leather jacket as he gradually got up. Meanwhile Will intentionally tipped the coffee mug he had in his other hand and spilled its contents over him.

Josh shrieked as the hot liquid splattered all over his torso. "You asshole!"

"Shit, sorry. Really sorry. Didn't meant to…" Will continued to apologize though he felt none of that at all. This boy had hurt the Alchemist's feelings and would have to pay for it. Will felt the rage inside him tending to flow out when suddenly he picked up Aiden's thoughts.

The Alchemist did not want this boy to suffer, nor did he wish for anything bad to happen to him. Even after all the pain this boy had caused him. Even though all he had said during the entire episode was "Oh shit!" as the coffee spilled on Josh, Will read through his thoughts that he intended no harm to be caused to the boy.

Those thoughts of the Alchemist acted like a few drops of cold water, sprinkled onto boiling milk overflowing from a container. Black immediately simmered down.

A couple of waiters rushed over to help a screaming Josh up and Will himself helped him for real this time. He cursed himself thinking of the way he had acted. Why did the alchemist's thoughts influence him so much? And why had he felt so angry at this boy in the first place? The waiters escorted an agitated Josh towards the restrooms to get him cleaned up.

The four looked at each other as Josh and his profanities faded away.

"What was that all about?" asked a bewildered Aditi.

"Don't know, but…" Jason could take it no longer. "Let's go, I gotta get going."

Aditi flinched, but she knew she was not having any luck here. "Yup let's go." She stated as she got up.

"See you guys later." She added as Jason possessively put an arm around her and hastily led her out.

Aiden heaved a sigh of relief and Will grinned at him.

"Whew! Good riddance with that female!" Will spoke out.

"Good riddance indeed."

Aiden had another thought on his mind. He couldn't shake the feeling that Will somehow knew what significance Josh held in his life recently, and was somehow getting back at him for that.

"That guy you just spilled coffee on, did you know him from before?"

"Who me? No." Will replied truthfully.

Aiden decided to accept that and forget about it. The big-eyed young waiter appeared and started cleaning the mess beside their table. The same one Aiden had despised on an earlier day for ogling at Will. But this time Aiden felt pity. Will was downright hot. Any sane person would be attracted to him. But Will would not even give the young waiter the time of day. Maybe Will could just…

"Hey kid!" Will called out to the young waiter who immediately perked up when he realized it was Will calling out to him.

"How was the show?" Will was referring to the episode with Josh that had just occurred.

"Nice show! I hate that prick. He's a total dick." the kid was smiling wide, all his front teeth showing. Finally this hunk of the first water had paid him some attention.

Will winked at the kid and playfully swatted his butt as he passed by. Aiden almost choked on his own coffee when he saw Will slapping the waiter's butt but kept grinning at Will who grinned back evilly at him.

Will had just made the young waiter's day.

Internally, Black wondered why he wanted to fulfill this boy's every wish, however small it might be.

Not too far away from the coffee house, an irritable Aditi finally wrenched her hand and jerked herself away from Jason who was speedily dragging her along

"Hey easy, easy," she said slowing down. "Chill tiger!"

"What chill?" Jason asked agitatedly. He was peeved to the core at Aditi's behavior back at the coffee house. But he was not going to tell her that.

Aditi started laughing at his petulant expression.

"What's so funny?" Jason demanded.

"Well it's you and your jealousy, God you males are an envy-filled species!"

"Who's jealous?" Jason was still not going to admit his anger was arising because he was jealous of Will. Will, who so easily grabbed Aditi's attention.

"Jealous of me flirting with that hottie Will." Aditi had a triumphant look on her face. Jason looked at her knowing she hit the nail on the correct spot but unsure of what to say.

"But you needn't worry about a damn thing." She added. "They're both gay anyway."

"Who's gay?" Jason had a flustered expression on his face. He was clearly not understanding what Aditi was saying. He cursed girls and their way of communication.

"Your friend and his hunky boyfriend Will. They're both gay," She clarified.

"Aiden's not gay!"

"Of course he is! Didn't you know? I thought he was your roommate."

"He is my roommate. And he's not gay."

"Uh-uh he is" she replied shaking her head. "You're such a doofus. Can't you see the way they look at each other. Aiden's as gay as a goose!"

Jason stared at Aditi with a shocked expression, his mind hardly able to register what was going on. "And so's Will." Aditi added with a sigh.

Jason was left repulsed at the thought that his roommate might be gay.

. . . . .

Frigeria entered the chamber where her ruler White sat in loneliness. The same chamber where she had spend 2 days healing the great white angel. Only this time he was in no need of any physical healing.

The great angel sat on a flat marble top in a pensive mood, his right elbow resting on his thigh as it supported his chin with the fist of his hand. His gigantic wings drooping behind, depicting his state of mind.

Frigeria settled down beside her ruler on the white floor, her velvety sequins swishing as she did so. She looked wistfully at his face. "What occurred?" she asked, her voice reverberating across as the dulcet tinker of bells.

White lifted his countenance to gaze upon the beautiful raven haired angel.

"The Alchemist declined to assist us." A simple assertion, yet the tone that White used conveyed that the weight behind those words was indeed not imponderous.

"You yourself asked him this?"

White hesitated before he replied, "I obtained the answer through sub conscious ingress."

Frigeria understood immediately. The mighty guardian of Light had been nervy when it came to matters dealing with the Alchemist. He had asked the boy for help and had been refused. And the boy had no inkling of it. A mere boy intimidated the courageous guardin who wished to remain anonymous in case something negative happened.

"But what were his reasons?"

White took a deep breath. This was going to be difficult to explain.

"As I raced along the insides of his minds and created a virtual world, I played out the entire scenario where I broached the Alchemist."

Frigeria swished around and made herself comfortable, knowing this would be a long explanation

"At the onset when I told the boy of the ancient legends and the power of the Alchemist, the boy thought I was asinine. He would not believe of the Kingdom of Light and the Kingdom of Void and the powers that watched over them. He thought of me as an imbecile. Then I showed him my true form and stretched out my wings. That's when the boy was left perplexed."

"The boy accompanied me to Immaculata and I crossed him over to this plane. He stayed on for about a day and after taking in the surroundings and seeing everything around, he came to the conclusion that he would not help us."

White paused looking directly at Frigeria. She waited for him to go on.

"The boy soon understood the conflict between the Kingdoms of Light and Void and realized what it was that I was asking him to do. That was when he refused."

"The boy understood that I was asking him to extirpate our enemies, wipe out an entire other kingdom. He completely refused to do so. He said that this other universe contained two Kingdoms that balanced each other out and the entities that lived in it had different mindsets. He said that the powers of Black and White offset each other and it was not his to intervene. Especially if intervening meant killing thousands of entities and taking their blood on his own hands. He would not under any circumstances be responsible for wiping out an entire Kingdom and slaughtering thousands, just to fulfill a prophecy."

Deep melancholy filled Frigeria's eyes, melancholy filled with understanding and wonder as White continued.

"The entire royal court begged him to facilitate the Kingdom of Light. Me and you Frigeria; we fell to his feet and cried. We beseeched him stating that he was the one who was designated to fulfill the prophecies and end the war between the two rival Kingdoms. The Alchemist's heart ached to see us distressed but he still refused to be the one to carry out the ponderous sinful task."

"I clearly remember the words he used before he asked us to return us to his home. 'Good and bad are variations of the same Karma. And you ask me to hoard such enormous bad Karma so that your Kingdom can crush the adversary. I cannot do that.' And with that the Alchemist asked us to forgive him for he could be of no help."

Silence reigned in the room as White finished; both angels absorbing what had just been said. Finally Frigeria opened her mouth to speak.

"The Alchemist is of far nobler thought than we are."

"Yes indeed." White nodded and rose from the marble top. "And such nobility will need to be safeguarded."

"So what does the great one plan to do?"

White unfurled his wings once more. "Protect him."

. . . . .

A naked Aiden was plopped onto the large bed as Will dumped him there. Will carrying the boy over to his bedroom and dumping him unceremoniously had become a sort of ritual for the two. Aiden straightened himself on the bed still looking lustfully at Will. He was stark nude and Will still had all of his clothes on, including a very sexy leather jacket which made him look like the cream of all gay men's fantasies. Will grinned evilly at Aiden and teasingly took the jacket off, showing of his broad chest and shoulders, sparingly covered by a thin white T-shirt that attached itself to Will's torso like shrink wrap. Aiden's dick stood out in full glory, throbbing in anticipation.

Will caught hold of the ends of his T-shirt and started gyrating as he tantalizingly lifted the thin white material. Aiden waited in anticipation to see that perfect masculine musculature once more, but Will was in no hurry.

"Tease, aren't you?"

Will replied by licking his lips seductively and pulling off the T-shirt in one stroke. Aiden stopped breathing for a few seconds as his entire being was riveted onto the slowly disrobing body.

Will stepped closer to the bed and unbuckled his jeans still gyrating to the imaginary music in his head. He bend down and lowered his jeans revealing powerful legs that any person would kill to own. Now he was clad only on tight black boxer briefs which were straining under the pressure from his erect member, protruding obscenely from the band.

Aiden raised himself and reached out to grab Will's crotch who torturously swung out of reach.

"C'mere you tease!" Aiden wanted nothing more than to touch that solid perfect body.

Will instead bend over and lifted his jacket and put the leather garment back on. He was now clad in only his leather biker jacket and black underwear. Aiden moaned as Will stretched his arms and pulled out a muscular pose, the contours of his abdomen prominently sketched.

Will slowly advanced once again towards Aiden who this time managed to hook his finger into the band of his underwear. Aiden slowly pulled him closer, putting his other hand on Will's muscular butt. He ran his hands along the insides of Will's thighs feeling the shape of the hard musculature until he reached Will's crotch which he cupped in his hand, feeling the weight of his balls, admiring the colossal sex god towering over him.

Slowly Aiden pulled away the underwear as Will's large rock hard member stood straight sticking out, pressed rigidly against his belly. Aiden licked his lips and smiled. This was the powerful tool that had been pounding him since the last 3 days, the tool that had caused him to have sore anuses, reminding him of Will throughout his college lectures.

Aiden stroked the huge phallus a couple of times and then took it into his mouth. Will groaned in pleasure and inched closer towards Aiden, clutching at the boy's hair as he pulled him closer. Sexual bliss was not restricted only to the humans after all.

Aiden continued sucking on the thickly veined rod, trying to take in a little more each time. He relaxed his throat muscles so he could take it in even further, but it was of no use; he could never reach the hilt. Either he was not skilled enough, or more obviously, Will was just too large.

Aiden withdrew partially and grabbed the base of Will's cock, stroking it while still sucking on the head. Will was moaning Aiden's name and cooing, telling him how good it felt.

Abruptly Will bend down pulling Aiden's lips off his cock, smothering them with a kiss which Aiden returned with heated passion. Will gradually lifted him up and turned his body over, resting him on the edge of the bed. Aiden was about to be fucked from behind while using the bed for support.

Will finally broke the kiss and reached out for a condom. He found no use of the item for himself, but the Alchemist wanted it to be used so it would be. He slowly slipped it on and stroked it till it stretched out encasing his massive organ. Will pressed his weight on Aiden and started kissing and sucking the back of his neck as he loosened Aiden's anus with his fingers. Aiden was experiencing celestial pleasures, moaning like only Will could make him moan.

Will lifted himself and positioned himself to enter the boy, holding his hips on either side. He managed to get the head inside as Aiden's sphincter muscles relaxed and gradually slipped more of his member in. The whole time Aiden was writhing in agony and ecstasy, having no intention for Will to stop. Soon Will was in. Aiden felt complete.

Will slowly started pulling in and out causing Aiden to moan even louder. He worked to a faster pace and then started pounding the Alchemist's ass the way he wanted it. Will was furiously humping him, the bed squeaking wildly, Aiden moaning loudly and the sheets which Aiden had clenched with his fists coming off a little from the bed each time Will slammed his pelvis against the boy's butt. Will still had his leather jacket on and Aiden could feel it's velvety coarseness against his back.

Aiden was moaning like a sore pig now, enraptured in the animalistic fucking, lost in celestial bliss. He could feel the beads of sweat dripping of his forehead, dropping onto the white sheets that he had clenched and was tugging at each time Will slammed into him. Aiden felt the whole world around him rocking. He could feel his own steel hard dick flopping between the sheets and his belly. He could smell the smell of Will's leather jacket intertwined with his sweat and Will's own masculine scent. And each sensation was pushing him over the edge. He was very close now.

He felt Will gasping as he plunged long and deep within him climaxing with the last thrusts. Simultaneously Will grasped his cock and stroked it hard and long. The sensations were too much for Aiden who was immediately inundated with the pleasure of the Gods as he fell of the precipice of orgasm. Thick ropes of semen spurted out from his dick as he screamed in elation.

Will slumped down on his back pressing his weight against him as he sucked on the back of his neck once more. Aiden lay complacent, reveling in post orgasmic bliss, wondering how he could still cum so much even when he was involved in so much sexual activity.

Will gradually exited and freed himself from Aiden, then lifted him up in his arms. He gently placed him on the bed as the boy looked at him with a sated expression on his face. Will got rid of the condom and joined Aiden in bed kissing him softly, who reached out his hands and gently kneaded Will's powerful butt.

Aiden placed one hand on each solid pectoral of Will and pushed him back against the bed. He got up on his knees and swooped down to attack one of Will's nipples, but Will caught him halfway.

"It's time for you to be complacent, not complaisant," he stated firmly.

With that he pushed the boy back onto his back and straddled him; placing one knee on either side of the boy's torso. Instantly he swooped down to the boy's chest and started ravenously biting and sucking along it. Aiden gasped as Will slowly reached one hand across the boy's once again erect cock and tantalizingly teased the area around his sore anus.

"Should we try it once more?" he asked knowing what Aiden's answer would be.

"Yes!" Aiden managed to squeak out between gasps. "But harder this time!"

· · · · ·

Aiden awoke groggily as he felt some sort of weird sensation. The morning sun streamed in through the windows as he noticed the gorgeous form of Will on top of him, breathing heavily, not snoring at all. His entire weight was on Aiden and the hard and lean looking body was apparently warm and soft to touch. Then Aiden realized why he was feeling weird. Will's dick was still inside him. Had he slept off like that? "This is definitely a first for me" Aiden thought a little nervously.

Will started getting hard as he opened his eyes and gazed at his lover pressed below him. "Hey beautiful!"

Aiden took a deep breath not knowing how to say it, but Will's penis was steadily elongating inside him.

"You know you're still inside me."

Will raised his eye brows and immediately perked up, pulling his almost erect penis out of Aiden. The penis was still condom clad and had the remains of Will's cum on the tip.

"Not that I didn't like it." Aiden grumbled making Will smile.

"Then let's get it back in there." Will said getting off the bed and frantically searching for condoms while he disposed the one that had stayed inside Aiden's ass all night long.

Aiden giggled as Will scurried about in the room and then in the bathroom. He preferred to top when he had sex, but with Will he was bottoming most of the time. And he was relishing it. Will always insisted he top whenever Aiden felt the least bit like it. Somehow Will would always understand what Aiden was in the mood off. '100% sex compatibility' Aiden happily thought to himself as Will finished his distracting chores jumped in the bed next to him.

Will slowly kissed the boy as he fumbled with his own dick, trying to gain entry. Aiden was always worried about his morning breath cause Will never had any. But if Will was noticing it, he sure was not complaining. Will finally found the right spot and pressed against it, still kissing Aiden who had him tightly enveloped in his arms. He slipped in easily through a comparatively loose anus ring.

10 minutes of hot morning sex later, Aiden raised himself from the bed eager to visit the loo. He knew all that pounding would give him some trouble, but he would happily bear it. He blissfully sat on the toilet seat, thinking for the thousandth time how lucky he was.

Slowly his thoughts drifted from early morning post orgasmic bliss to his college and friends. Tinka and Steve were still the only ones who knew about Will. What would Jason and the others think if they were to find out this hot property was his boyfriend; and that he banged him every night? What would Dominic think? Would they severe all ties with him? He pushed the thoughts out of his mind as he thought about the work he had planned for the day. He had to go and collect his contact lenses and catch up on his college assignments. Apart from that he had also promised Dominic for the electronics robot assembling Techfest thing. And he had lectures throughout the afternoon. Thankfully he had the time before lunch free so he could wrap up all his chores and play a little tennis with Steve. Steve who would be peeved that he hardly played any tennis with him these days. He was certain that Steve would instantly agree to accompany him to the courts and bunk all his lectures. Nothing could stop Steve from a game of tennis.

He flushed the toilet and came back to the room to find Will lazily grazing his hands across his body as he lay on the bed.

"Hey Will, gotta leave now. Could you give me a lift back to campus?"

Will continued to distract Aiden by rubbing small circles on his abdomen with his fingers. "You could go or…" Will paused as he seductively licked his lips, "We could just stay here and have some more fun."

Aiden was adamant though he knew he was getting hard and had no clothes on to hide it. "No stop it! There's tonnes of work I have to finish today."

Will replied by swiftly getting off the bed and enveloping Aiden's thickening penis with his mouth.

Aiden managed to put in as he panted for breath, "Ah, ok… so you'll… you'll drop me after… uhh… this, won't you?"

Will nodded his head still continuing to suck on Aiden's penis.

"And I…uhh…I'm kinda busy today and won't… ahh… won't be able to meet you till nighttime."

Will nodded again, his head still bobbing along Aiden's shaft. Aiden was not telling him that he had free time today. But Will had long understood that this boy was a workaholic; he would never be happy if you gave him a 100 million dollars and nothing to do. Aiden liked to slog his ass all the time for he felt incomplete if he did not constantly work on something. Will knew that Aiden would spend all his free time catching up on his friends and work.

. . . . .

Aiden smashed the ball hard and out of Steve's reach which the latter did not even attempt to reach out to.

"Good shot!" Steve commended from the other side.

This was it, Aiden thought. A few more good shots like that and the set would be his. This was definitely going to be the best he had ever played. Now if only his serve would click in the next round.

Aiden was playing a vigorous game of tennis with Steve. And he was in the best form he had ever been. He positioned himself to serve as he bounced the fluorescent ball a couple of times on the ground; gauging the length and power he had to put in. A lob of the ball and wham!

"Fault." Steve called out from the other side.

Aiden cursed and took another ball out of his pocket and gauged the serve length and line again. One more lob and wham!

"Double Fault." Steve called out.

Aiden muttered angrily under his breath. Why the hell was the damn ball not falling into the correct area at least? Aiden cursed himself using his favorite mantra for tennis; 'I suck at this game.'

9 more minutes and Steve officially won the game. Aiden was still peeved and refused to quit playing. Steve was however enervated.

"Firstly I hear that you are so groggy nowadays that you sleep in your HOD's lecture," he shouted from his side of the court, "And now you possess so much energy that you literally bounce on an air cushion when we play tennis. What's going on?"

"What do you mean bounce?" Aiden shouted back.

"Well, by bounce I mean what you're doing right now; look at yourself!"

Aiden instantly stopped his prancing footwork and sheepishly realized what Steve was talking about.

"So it's all because of that Will dude eh?" Aiden was glad that Steve at least remembered the name.

"Ok, just a few more shots and I'll call it quits," Steve called out tugging at the collar of his T-shirt. "I'm pooped! After's, you can play against the wall!"

Steve stretched out and served towards Aiden. But his opponent was no longer looking at the ball nor in it's general direction. Aiden stood mesmerized by someone who had just entered the courts.

"You Nu.." but Aiden did not hear the rest. All he realized was sudden throbbing pain as the ball smacked his head and he slumped to the ground holding his head.

Steve ran over to Aiden's side and heard footsteps alongside as someone else rushed to the 'serve victim' who sat on the ground dazed, his spectacles resting on his nose at an odd angle.

"What the fuck were you zoning out for?" An agitated Steve shouted at Steve as he cradled his roommate in his arms. "Are you ok?"

"You ok buddy?" Another voice asked.

Aiden could barely process anything, He felt as if his skull had been split into two. The intense ache on the side of his head felt like a 100 bowling balls inside his skull banging the insides to get out. What had caused him to zone out? Oh yes, It was the vision of a God. A god wearing tennis togas and wielding a racket that had entered the courts. But Aiden realized through the pain that someone other than Steve was bending down next to him.

White had been the person Aiden had caught a glimpse of before the ball rocketed into his head. The human form of his. And unknown to the players, White leisurely hovered his hand over Aiden's head, healing him of his pain. Humans were easy to heal.

Aiden was confused; the pain in his head was dissipating, and fast. As it faded exponentially he could hear Steve continuously asking him whether he was all right.

Aiden finally lifted his head and was immediately captivated by the presence of this new comer. "I'm fine," he managed to squeak out.

Squatting down was the most beautiful sight he had ever seen. Or was it the second most beautiful? The first thing Aiden noticed were the deep sapphire eyes; a mesmerizing blue; eyes that belonged to another world. And then he noticed the strong noble face; a face that bespoke of divinity and warmth. A strong square jaw attributed to the most masculine roots one could possess. And lastly Aiden noticed the golden blonde hair, hair that reflected the sun and refracted its beams. Aiden could hardly move.

Steve wore a perplexed expression, confused why Aiden's face registered no signs of pain; instead he had a dorky look on it. He swung his head sideways to see why and himself paused at the sight of this new man. It was a few moments before he realized that the effect that this man had on him for just a few seconds, was the same Aiden was under, only more severe and prolonged.

Steve leaned over and whispered into Aiden's ear, "Get up you dork!"

"Uh, yeah." And then Aiden realized how foolish he must be looking. "Why the hell did you slam the ball into me?" he asked his face turning red as he raised himself with the help of the two people, immediately feeling where the new guy grabbed his arm to lift him up.

"What the fuck? I served only to find you suddenly zoned out in the middle of the tennis court."

"I was not zoned out!" Aiden stated indignantly. "I was just…"

Steve ran his hand over the side of Aiden's head, "You took it pretty hard, are you sure its not hurting?"

"It's not." Aiden said, running his own hand over where the ball had smacked him. "It really isn't."

Steve stared for a couple of seconds wondering whether to attribute Aiden's lack of pain to this new arrival, then finally decided that the pain would have been too intense for Aiden to hide if indeed the ball had hit him the way he thought it had.

Finally the new arrival spoke, "You guys still playing?"

Aiden was still entranced a little by this new angel. He noticed his tall built and obvious physique under the flimsy tennis wear and eyed his well-developed strapping legs. Immediately Aiden felt embarrassed of his own legs. 'Should have worn full length tracks' he thought to himself.

"No I'm pooped." Steve stated.

"I'm still playing!" Aiden hastily added with a goofy expression on his face.

"I'm sorry," the man stated as Aiden hung on to his every word staring at how his deep red lips moved, "I'm Scott, Scott White." Scott extended his hand.

Aiden quickly extended his hand and shook it before Steve could reach out his.

"I'm Aiden, and this is Steve." Aiden could feel the tingling warmth of Scott's hand.

"So, are we playing?" Scott questioned as Aiden continued smiling, showing no signs of leaving his hand. Suddenly images of Will came crashing through Aiden's mind. What was he doing; drooling over some stranger? He had his own hunk that was hotter than this guy, or maybe equally hot, but was there harm in looking? No, he could not make such an ass of himself after all that Will did for him. Will was now the centre of his everything, and he would be the only eye-candy he ogled at.

Aiden averted his gaze from Scott as he spoke, "Yeah sure, I'll take that court." Aiden paced towards the other side of the net.

Steve shrugged once looking at the new guy and then headed towards the benches to assemble his gear. He was sure Aiden was going to make a dork of himself in front of someone who looked as hot as this guy. He collected his gear and headed out of the courts, whispering to Aiden as he passed him.

"I'm sure this one's hotter than your Will."

"No way, he's not." Aiden replied knitting his brow, but Steve had already passed by. Aiden looked at his new opponent, knowing he was going to make a mess of himself in front of this new guy. What had he gotten himself into?

Scott placed himself to serve as Aiden readied to face him. Wham! Aiden was not sure what had happened. Had the ball gone by?

"Err, I think that's an ace." Scott called out.

"It is?" an incredulous Aiden asked.

"Yup, you missed it."

A few more serves later Aiden realized Scott was brilliant at the game. And he understood that he was even holding himself back. 'This guy's a real pro', he thought.

"You serve," Scott called out. Aiden was already worried that his adversary was out of his league, and now he would also get to witness his miserable serve. 'Great' he thought to himself.

Aiden readied himself and bounced the ball against the ground, praying the ball would at least land in the designated area. He smacked the ball hard as Scott called out 'Fault' from the other side even before the ball touched the ground anywhere. Aiden was nervous as hell in front of this new chap.

A few more serves later Aiden thought to call it quits, thinking he must be wasting such an ace player's time. "You know, you should find a better opponent, I'll be leaving now."

"No, no stay." Scott pleaded. "You ARE a good opponent."

Aiden walked towards the net and leaned against the pole on the side. "Yeah, tell me about it."

"Your serve is pretty good, a little timing will turn it into a juggernaut!"

Aiden raised his eyebrows at the comment. His serve and timing; he knew he could hardly use the two in the same sentence, but was that all that was wrong with his serve? Nah! His whole form sucked. But yet, Scott did not sound like he was making fun of him.

Scott walked towards Aiden's side, "Here, serve with me."

. . . . .

Aiden led Scott toward the sideshop to 'recharge on fluids' as Scott had put it. The latter had offered to help him improve his serve, and he actually had. He had prodded him to time his lobs and swing at the ball at the correct height. Had it been that simple? How come he had never seen it before? But Scott had also posed severe problems in his tennis shorts when he leaned against him to correct his stance. Aiden had cursed his hormones seeing how genuine and polite this man was. 'He actually did want to help me out and was not at all condescending,' he thought. Otherwise, most of the time whenever someone tried to correct his tennis, his ego would prevent him from learning.

White on the other hand was about to embark on another mental dive. He was curious to know the mental state of the alchemist and the import of things in his life. Only this time he would dive subtly, skim over cursorily; the Alchemist would not even realize that his mind had been perused. White caught his breath and dived in.

His consciousness raced through the insides, as a spectator and not as an active involved entity this time. And suddenly White realized a cornucopia of feelings that overwhelmed and saturated him.

The Alchemist was drugged on newly discovered love. And it felt exciting and satiating at the same time. The Alchemist was sharing his heart with someone, and White was left dizzied by the feelings that flooded him. Love that was solid and which felt oddly familiar. When had he ever experienced something like this before?

"Scott, what will you have?" Aiden questioned for the second time from the counter.

White blinked and his consciousness jumped back into his own mind. He had lost himself in the tender feelings of adoration and affection that beleaguered him inside the boy's mind.

"Uh, Yeah, just any Oj type of thing." He finally answered. He noticed the alchemist looking at him with an odd expression. He would have to be very cautious around this boy.

Aiden asked for two Gatorades which an eager girl behind the counter fetched, all the while smiling goofily at White. White immediately offered to pay the trivialities but Aiden refused to accept, paying on his own. The two settled down on a table with their drinks.

"So what do you do Scott?" Aiden asked. "As in, how come you get to play on the university courts?"

White sipped his drink before he answered. He never fancied human food. "I organize some courses outside campus, just behind your back entrance."

"And that allows you to play on campus?" Aiden had an incredulous expression on his face.

"Yeah they do. The coach is an old friend of mine."

"How come I've never seen you before?" Aiden asked before he could stop himself.

White was having a difficult time with this boy. The great Angel might be a God who performed Herculean tasks, but lying and deceiving this innocent boy was not one of them. "Don't know. Timings don't match I guess."

Aiden seemed content with the answer as he resumed sipping his drink. White wanted to try one more thing. He mentally projected the thought of his having sex with the boy into Aiden's mind, and waited to gauge his reflections.

The boy was initially excited by the thought, but the fluttering feeling lasted hardly a second. Instead he reacted violently, foisting the thought out of his head, clearly repulsed and accusing his own self of infidelity. His face had turned a little crimson in those few moments. White was impressed.

'Very Well,' White thought to himself. 'If this boy is indeed so steady and noble, I shall never ever enter his mind again unless a dire situation comes along.' And with that White pledged never to read Aiden's thoughts, nor enter his mind again.

·····

A human shape dashed across the irate walkers apologizing as it sped by.

"Sorry," Aiden called out as he raced towards his destination. He was heading over to collect his contact lenses though he hardly had 20 minutes before his next lecture commenced. He knew he was cutting it close, but he could delay this task any longer. He wanted to wear his lenses the next time he appeared before Will. He could hardly wait to see how Will and his friends would react.

He finally reached the alley panting for breath and looked up to where the shop was. He was hoping his order was ready and would be delivered promptly.

And then he saw it; immediately remembering as he noticed it; the shop below with a flashy sign in black and red that read 'Horuscopus'. This was the card that the old frantic Japanese lady had slipped into his pocket the other day when he was with Will. Well he didn't know where that card was any longer but the lady had sounded desperate. He had forgotten all about it till now. Hadn't she insisted he call him?

Well he was going to have to do it later, if he did it at all, he had no time right now.

Aiden dashed up the spiral staircase cursing the fact he could not climb them any faster. Huffing for breath he entered the shop fishing a receipt out of his pocket, towards the immaculately dressed woman with her hair in a bun that sat at the counter.

"Hi, I'm here to collect an order," Aiden stated collecting his breath. "I was here on Sunday for some contact lenses."

The lady took the proffered card and put on a pair of reading glasses, reading it carefully. "Ah, yes of course. Have a seat, I'll just get your stuff."

Aiden was in no mood to take a seat, he frantically looked at his watch. 17 minutes left. It would take him about 10 minutes if he ran all the way back to university. He could make it to his lecture in time." He calmed himself and took a seat.

13 minutes of impatient waiting later, an irate Aiden asked the preened lady for the fourth time where his order was.

"It's just coming," she answered reassuring him and then called out to someone in a louder voice, "Charles! Get this young man's order pronto!"

Aiden was peeved to the core. He would never get to his lecture on time now. He might as well forget about it. He huffed and went back to sit on the uncomfortable waiting chairs. As soon as he sat down the lady called out, "Ah it's here!"

Aiden thanked the lady in a mordant tone and collected the goods. He had missed a lecture on account of their inefficiency. He walked leisurely out of the shop knowing there was no rush to go anywhere now.

As he descended the spiral stair case he noticed the sign for the Horoscope shop again. Well he could go there now, since he had the free time. Or should he?

After contemplating for half a minute whether he should enter a place with a banner like that, Aiden finally decided he would; he had glanced around and made sure no one who could recognize him would see him entering the store.

He pushed the black glass door open as wind chimes above the door jingled signaling his entry. Aiden found himself in the most colorful room he had seen in his entire life, filled with ominous masks and ornamental bands hanging across the walls. A Japanese girl, who Aiden estimated to be his own age, watching television turned to see who had entered.

"Can I help you?" Aiden noticed her white milky complexion and was reminded of the lady he had encountered having the same complexion.

"Uhh, I'm looking for a lady." Aiden stated unsure of what to ask for.

"The shop's closed, we don't cater to any customers any more."

"The sign outside…"

"We closed shop 3 days ago," the girl interrupted sharply as she muted the television and Aiden realized she had no accent. "The sign outside will be hammered out in a day or two."

"But I'm not here to get my fortune, uhh, future predicted…" The girl pursed her lips and waited for Aiden to continue.

"I'm here to meet an old lady who I met a few days back." Aiden finally managed to say. "Look, this old lady gave me a card to this place and asked for me to call her. I think she runs this place or something" Aiden regretted calling the lady old in front of her probable relative.

The girl's face went blank. "When did you meet her?"

Aiden recalled the day he had come for his lenses earlier, the day he had gone with Will to the retirement home. "On Sunday."

The girl bit her lower lip. "That's the day she died."

Aiden was taken aback. He had hardly dealt with death in his life before and was not sure how to react. "I'm sorry, I'll leave if you want me to."

"No wait, that old lady was my mother. Tell me where you met her." Aiden looked at the girl unsure of what to say. This girl had lost her mother 2 days ago and was talking about it so normally. She registered no signs of shock on her face, only one of determination.

"I met her near my friend's retirement home. She came after me and told me about some danger sort of thing."

"She told you of the devil that was after you," the girl stated flatly.

"Excuse me?"

The girl swiftly got up, switched off the television and turned towards Aiden. "My mom went nuts on Sunday. That was the day she died. In fact she was murdered. A demonic force killed her!"

Aiden was trying to follow what the girl was saying, but made little sense of it. The girl noticed Aiden's expression and stepped closer to him.

"Listen, you may think I'm out of whack, but my mom was psychic. And on that bastard day," she clenched her teeth, "My mom saw some sort of a vision and went nuts. She kept saying something like 'A devil would consume the boy!' and drove everyone else in the house mad. Finally she left the house to seek the boy or whatever."

Aiden scrunched his face and creased his brow. He had no idea what to make of this girl or her story.

"She returned later in the evening but was still inconsolable; she said she had not been able to warn the boy even though she had met him. We managed to get her to go to sleep after a big ruckus." The girl paused to add the next bit, "And thenthe devil murdered her!"

"She was?" Aiden asked not at all believing what was being said but having no inkling on how to react to a girl who spoke of a dead mother and supernatural phenomenon with such a straight face.

"Yes, she was. When we found her, her eyes had popped out of her head and blood was seeping out through her nose, through her ears, even through the sockets in her eyes." The girl's tone was getting louder and louder and she was almost screaming as she said the last bits.

"Uhh, I …"

The girl lashed out at Aiden, "You don't believe me do you? But you would believe the forensic reports that showed that her brain had exploded inside her skull, turned to mushy pulp, and all while she lay on her bed alone."

Aiden was having a hard time processing the situation. This girl was getting angry as her entire face had turned from white to red. Suddenly the rage on her face disappeared and tears streamed out form the corners of her eyes as she tried to wipe them with the back of her hand. Aiden stepped away from the girl as if she was a time bomb, ticking to go off.

"I'm sorry… it's just…" the rest of her words faded in the sobs.

"It's ok, I'll just leave." Aiden was feeling miserable.

"No, no, forgive me for all that anger."

"No, no it's ok."

"No dammit! Listen to what I have to say!" the girl burst out again. Aiden flinched ready to run off if she took the slightest step toward him. He was terrified of this girl now.

"You are the boy mama was trying to protect. You are the one the devil is after."

Aiden chewed at his lips.

"You are the one mama gave her life for."

. . . . .

A confused boy left the Horoscope shop. Aiden's head was spinning. What did the girl mean by insisting for him to believe in the devil? Why was she so adamant? And there was one thing that she said just before he left her that made him queasy; be careful of new people in your life.

Aiden was terrified. Did she mean to refer to Will? No, that was impossible! Will was the kindest person he had ever met in his entire life. Will was a new person in his life after all. And then he had met another person lately; Scott. These were the only two significant recent additions in his life lately. Or the girl might have been referring to scores of lesser important people that he encountered everyday.

Finally Aiden felt sick at himself for thinking about such things. He came to a conclusion; he had been a fool who felt for a girl that was so traumatized at her mother's death. For all he knew, the girl would scream and cry at anyone who entered the shop since her mother died. There was no reason to believe this obviously disturbed girl.

Then how did the lady who came after him in the first place fit into all this?

. . . . .

Dominic was tapping his fingers against the table waiting impatiently. He was a prompt person and disliked having to wait for anyone. And right now he was waiting for the most punctual person he knew.

Dominic looked up as he heard footsteps, his face registering surprise at seeing Aiden.

"Dude, where are your glasses?"

Aiden smiled feebly though he hardly felt like it at that time. "Oh, I switched to lenses."

Dominic raised his eyebrows and tried to say something but no words left his mouth. He started again, "What the hell do you mean lenses?"

Aiden's smile accumulated some joy. "Contact Lenses."

"Shit!" Dominic exclaimed. "First you change your hair, and now you dumped your glasses? I mean look at you! Who the fuck are you? I can barely recognize you!"

"So how does it look?" Aiden asked hesitatingly.

"It looks nice." Dominic thought for a couple of seconds before he added, "In fact it suits you pretty well."

Aiden was happy. Dominic had said he was looking good. He had been distressed throughout the afternoon, immersed in anxious thoughts, and had forgotten about the lenses till Dominic pointed it out.

"So what are all these changes for?"

"Uhh, just like that."

"Are you hiding something from me?"

The two were interrupted as a new person entered the room. Aiden stared wide eyed; it was Scott.

"So should we begin?" Scott asked smiling at the pair.

"Begin what?" Aiden asked confused. "Scott what are you doing here?" He was immediately aware of his contact lenses again but reckoned that Scott had met him just once before when he had been wearing spectacles. Scott would not know of the switch he had made; the switch that had been so dramatic for Aiden.

"I'm your guide for robot assembling. Didn't I tell you that I take some courses behind college?"

Aiden stared dumbfounded. Scott was wearing a half sleeved striped shirt and black jeans. And he looked seriously hot! Aiden was watching Scott's lips move as he spoke and was having a hard time concentrating on what he was saying. 'Shit'

Aiden thought to himself. 'If this hunk is gonna be my teacher here, I can safely say buh-bye to robotics with the amount I'll be able to concentrate with him around'.

"So shall we begin with our Micromouse?" Scott asked.

Scott disappeared into the adjoining room as the budding engineers followed. "You know him?" Dominic asked as they followed Scott.

"Yeah, sorta. Just met him today and played some tennis with him." Aiden entered a larger room where he found Storm already waiting, sitting on a tiny stool that threatened to give away any moment.

"Okay everyone." Scott clasped his hands as he waited for the trio to settle down. He took a deep breath before he started. "You all have the university TechFest coming up in 4 weeks time and are wanting to submit an entry for the Micromouse contest."

"We want to win it." Dominic interrupted.

"Yes definitely." Scott continued. "Your contest rules are here with me. The maze design and dimensions are categorically defined. What we will need is knowledge in microcontrollers, knowledge of basic assembly language, knowledge of a few electronic devices and a little knowledge of design dynamics."

Aiden was impressed through the little he heard when he was not distracted by Scott's looks. This guy was hot, hunky, smart, and polite. Weren't drop dead gorgeous people supposed to be snobbish and dumb? He now knew of two people who could shatter that theory now.

"What I require from you guys is your dedication and hard work. We don't have much time before the contest and we will have to make the most of the time we do have. I will be starting off with some basic circuits that are not actual components of the Micromouse robot. However these circuits will help you understand what you're doing and impart you important knowledge that could otherwise be left untouched even after completion of the robot."

Aiden stole a glance at his engineer buddies. They were looking up at Scott with respect and awe. Scott's dynamic personality had clearly swept them off their feet. 'He probably has this effect on everyone' Aiden realized.

The group split up into different tasks; Aiden was handed a bunch of circuitry material to complete a PCB and interpret what it did. Aiden started his work, surprised that a simple circuit could be so challenging when you had to work backwards with it. After some fiddling he called for Scott to find out why it was not working.

Scott lifted the board on which the circuit was mounted and glanced at the components.

"There's a tiny problem here." Scott finally stated. "Observe your green LED."

Aiden narrowed his eyes to observe and then cursed himself. He had soldered the LED in reverse polarity.

"Shit! what a dork!" Aiden muttered cursing himself as he slapped his forehead.

Scott smiled at Aiden. "Happens to the best of us."

Aiden was smitten. This man was so polite. He loved the manner in which Scott made you realize your mistakes and was not at all patronizing. This man was actually making him understand all the heavy circuitry he had been involved in for the first time. Otherwise Aiden's knowledge was bookish and pedantic. He could feel his heart warming next to Scott. This man exuded comfort and also some sort of intoxication.

Aiden watched as Scott went over to Storm who was busy fiddling with tiny electronic components with his large bulky fingers, a sight to behold. The two laughed at Storm's attempts to insert a thin wire into the breadboard grooves. Aiden noticed as Storm got up that Scott was nearly the same height as him. But whereas Storm possessed a lot of bulk and looked generally large, Scott was in perfect shape; perfect arms, broad back and shoulders, and the most perfect butt. Aiden scolded himself, 'Ok, finish your work first!' and forced himself to look down at the circuit.

"He's probably straight anyway!" He reasoned to himself. "Plus I have Will now."

· · · · ·

It was later in the evening when the trio left Scott and his gadgets. Aiden was feeling much better than he had been all afternoon. But as soon as Dominic and Storm left him he got lost in his own thoughts as he walked towards Will's apartment.

With the advent of the robotics project, he would now be meeting Scott on a regular basis. 'Scott White', he voiced to himself. He chuckled thinking there were two handsome men in his life who had last names of colors. 'Black and White'.

Scott was immensely likeable, other than the fact that he could almost make Aiden cum in his underwear. He was attracting Aiden like a moth to a flame. And Aiden was having a hard time stopping himself from being lured. But why did he even have to think about anyone else now?

Now there was Will in his life. A person who seemed to desire him as much as he did. And he was absolutely fantastic. Then what was bothering him. Wasn't all the things the Japanese girl and lady said crap? 'What devil drivel?!'

He suddenly remembered Tinka's question. 'Wasn't Will too perfect?' Why had his best friend said something like that? Aiden knew it was a harmless question, asked in care, but something like that from Tinka really affected him. Was Tinka feeling there was something wrong behind Will's façade? Why the hell did she have to feel that way? Just when he was so happy.

So now there were two alpha males in his life. Two men that both looked that they just stepped out from the cover of a romance novel. Men so handsome that they were difficult to fathom. So why was he so distressed?

Aiden reached Will's building, surprised he had not realized where the journey started and where it got over. He was way too washed out mentally. He was crestfallen and insecure. And he did not know a proper reason to assign for his worries.

. . . . .

Black opened the swung the door open knowing it was Aiden who had arrived. He was immediately flooded by Aiden's thoughts.

Aiden stood there in the hallway, trying to smile at him. But Black knew otherwise. He felt the pathos of unanswered questions overwhelming him. Black stepped forward and hugged Aiden, enfolding him within his arms. Aiden immediately closed his eyes and rested his head on his lover's strong shoulder.

Black gently stroked Aiden's back, swaying gently, purring sweet nothings in his ear. The boy was insecure and had only him to hold onto. He started analyzing Aiden's thoughts.

There was the worry of a fortune telling lady's daughter that had distressed his lover by telling him of a devil. So killing the old lady had not been good enough? There was nothing more that could be done about it now. If he tried to wipe out this daughter now, and Aiden found out, the consequences could be cataclysmic.

Then there was the matter of doubt and uncertainty a friend had expressed. The same girl he had met earlier. There was certainly no manner in which he could intervene there.

And then there was the matter of a new man that confused his lover's senses. Black decided to root out this man if he posed a problem again.

Black was till swaying with Aiden, still out in the hallway. He gauged Aiden's worries, fears, anxieties and doubts and felt melancholic himself. He would do anything in his powers to make Aiden feel better. All he wanted was to see this boy smile. No one would be allowed to harm his lover.

Black gently rubbed his cheeks against Aiden's, still purring soothingly as the boy stood still, holding onto, fearing to let go. Black knew what the boy wanted.

He gently lifted the boy in his arms and carried him inside, ever so slightly shutting the door. Reaching the bedroom he placed him on the bed softly and carefully removed their clothes before joining his lover.

Back made soft and tender love to Aiden, long and slow, completely losing himself in the tender passion and feelings of affection that inundated him. He wanted nothing more than to please this boy. To fill joy in his heart and rid him of his anxieties. To make him understand that everything would be ok. He climaxed the lovemaking, for the first time feeling sated himself.

He lightly ran his hair through Aiden's hair. He knew his next words should never have been uttered.

"Don't worry about anything. I'll always be with you."

And with that he quietly dozed of with his lover, knowing that the human feelings he was experiencing were going to land him in trouble.

. . . . .

 Fifteen minutes later Aiden groggily got out of the bed. He stepped over to where his jeans lay and fished out a tiny double sectioned box. Stretching the skin below his eyes he popped the contact lenses out and placed each one of them in the small compartments marked L and R.

Having finished the task, he moved back into the arms of his lover, cursing the fact that lenses needed to be removed before sleeping.

. . . . .

Episode Four

"See you in the evening then," Black said to Aiden who was busy tying his shoelaces, getting ready to leave his apartment.

"Yup, got tonnes of work to do before that." Aiden replied.

Black knew that since it was a Saturday, Aiden had few lectures in college and intended to cover up on his studies as well as do work on some robot project; this Aiden had informed him. He also knew what Aiden had not informed him about; that he planned on visiting the so called 'Joe Black retirement home'. Aiden meant to spend some time there and later tell him about it. Good thing he kept track of Aiden's thoughts; arrangements would have to be made to ensure that the old age home did exist and would be filled with patrons when Aiden got there.

"Why can't you just get bring along your work and do it here?" Black questioned, much to his own surprise. But he did not want Aiden to leave yet.

Aiden tightened a lace and stood up grinning. "Because, we both know that if I do get some of my assignments here, I'll never lay a finger on them with the way you keep me occupied."

Black showed Aiden his tongue and walked him to the door.

"Bye Will." Black replied by kissing Aiden on the lips, a kiss Aiden cut short, leaving Black needing more. He watched his lover make his way to the waiting elevator and waved to him before the doors of the elevator slid shut. Black took a deep breath as Aiden disappeared from view. He wondered if he had been spending too much time in his lover's head.

．．．．．

"You know I've never come to a place like this. You'll have to tell me what to do." Tinka was a bit queasy as Aiden led her inside a building painted in subtle hues of mauve and green. Large golden letters above the foyer claimed it to be the 'Joe Black retirement home'.

"There's nothing you've to do, stupid. It's not like we're here to juggle knives and jump through hoops of fire to entertain elder people."

"No but still; How should I behave and that kind of stuff."

"Just behave like yourself." Aiden stated and then pretended to think about what he said. "No wait, that would be disastrous, act as a normal polite girl."

Tinka swung her handbag and smacked Aiden across the head as the two entered the reception. Aiden's 'oww' was cut short as both realized that they were inside now and would have to put on some semblance of decency.

"Good evening Mr. Writer!" a chubby lady with red cheeks behind the reception desk boomed as soon as she looked at Aiden. Aiden frantically tried to recall the lady's name.

"It's Doris." The lady chimed in before Aiden could come up with anything to say. "I see you've come with a friend."

"Yes this is Tinka." Aiden referred to with his hand; who politely greeted the jolly receptionist.

"So you want to spend some time here? The oldies sure could use some younger company." The receptionist was beaming, all her 32 teeth showing to Aiden.

"Yeah, that's what we had in mind."

"I see, Mr. Black's not here to escort you today."

"Yes, I intended to come on my own. Please don't inform him, he'll go to a lot of trouble and come all the way here worrying unnecessarily."

"Sure thing, don't tell the boyfriend eh?" Doris lifted her eye brows suggestively as Aiden blushed.

"You kids go on ahead and give those oldies a time to remember," she said, swiftly getting up and ushering the two into a passage that Aiden remembered led to the recreation rooms.

"And remember," the jovial receptionist called out, "Don't do anything I wouldn't do."

Aiden and Tinka glanced at each other with a 'what was that all about' look on their faces.

· · · · ·

Tinka had been having a good time; though she had not expected it. She had been involved with Aiden and 6 elderly people from the retirement home in a card game called 'Uno', which she had just learned. Now 8 people were laughing and joking around a round table, including two aged men in wheelchairs, all throwing cards on the table with oomph, merrymaking as long known comrades.

"Draw Four!" Tinka squealed as she slammed a card on the table making Aiden grimace. "And I change the color to blue!" she added as Aiden's grimace turned into a frown and he lifted four more cards to add to the already loaded collection he possessed. Everyone on the table clapped and cheered at the girl.

"You're gonna get it from me sooner or later you know." Aiden mock growled at his friend.

"That's only if someone uses a reverse in their play. And I think I'll finish my cards till then." Tinka rubbed the two cards she had in her hand to emphasize her point.

Aiden groaned knowing he would never get a chance to trounce Tinka in the present game. She would have won long before he even got a through a fourth of his cards.

2 rounds later Tinka triumphantly thumped her last card on the table yelling 'Uno'. She was ecstatic that she had not only won the game, but ruined Aiden's position in it too. Being the first person to finish the game, she was the absolute winner.

As the game continued without her, Tinka glanced at her watch and realized it was over an hour since they had started the game. She was 'whipping Aiden's butt' as she put it, but she had something else in mind; she yet had to exact revenge on him for making her eat those 'melbies' filled with toothpaste in the coffee shop a week ago; and she had the proper apparatus in her handbag.

"Hey Aiden, I need to visit the restroom." Tinka whispered into Aiden's ear. She had won that round of the game and would have to wait till the next round to rejoin.

Aiden looked around and signaled to a blonde girl who's name he correctly recalled as Rachael and asked her to point Tinka towards the restroom.

Tinka entered the restroom, though she had no intention of actually using it. She shut the door behind her and took out a set of undersized black plastic binoculars from her handbag. This would be her method of taking revenge on Aiden.

The vengeful female then dipped into her bag once more to retrieve a stick of mascara and then proceeded to generously apply the mascara to the region surrounding the eye-piece; the mascara getting applied as a soft black shine, barely discernible to the human eye. All she had to do now was to get Aiden to use the binoculars once. And she would have the perfect opportunity on the way back when they passed the wharf area above on yellow bridge; and revenge would be hers. Of course she would not let Aiden know what had happened, and why people were staring at him till he himself realized the mascara smeared over and under his eyes.

As Tinka completed her nefarious deed, she perked up as she heard some intermittent humming-grunting sounds. There were some weird noises coming from somewhere, reverberating as a hum across the confined room. She knitted her brow wondering what the hum could be, and where it was coming from.

Tinka began placing everything into the handbag, placing the maligned binoculars in a plastic Ziploc. The noise suddenly got louder and more continuous. Her curiosity got the better of her. She walked towards the door swinging it open and immediately the sounds were amplified, indicating that the noise was resounding from an adjacent room. Tinka glanced around and realized that it was coming from a room adjacent to the restroom she was in, and the door was slightly ajar.

She quietly tiptoed towards the door and positioned herself against the open slit. 'Just a peek' she told herself.

What she saw left her astounded. "What the fuck?" she said before she could stop herself.

Inside the room were some 6 feet tall swarthy squid like beings; each having only one eye. Their tentacles were sliding about smoothly as they hummed and groaned.

Instantly Tinka felt someone appear behind her. She whirled around to find Will upon her and opened her mouth to let out a scream. But Will's hands moved with lightning pace to cover her mouth and stifle her shrieks.

The binoculars she had been holding in her hand fell to the ground with a thump.

. . . . .

Aiden was cursing the cards he held in his hand; he would surely end up being last at Uno unless he got hold of some fantastic cards; still he was enjoying himself. That's when he heard an abruptly cut-off noise. He immediately perked up.

"What's that? Is that Tinka?" he asked aloud.

Rachael face turned pale. "I'll go check it out." she stated, and quickly exited the room before Aiden could object. "She probably saw a cockroach or something." Rachael called out as she was leaving.

Aiden settled back down into his game.

· · · · ·

Black was present in the retirement home, though neither Aiden nor Tinka had known of it. He had been watching his lover and his friend. And then he had reacted instantly when he comprehended that his lover's friend had encountered something unusual.

He immediately focused on her and appeared directly behind her using an 'Ambulatory Ability'. The girl screamed in shock and fear as she saw him but he thwarted her din with a firm hand placed over her mouth. The girl writhed under his hold, but it was no use, his grip was far too tenacious for a fragile human.

Black held out one arm and hovered it above the girl's head as he opened his mouth to use a spell.

"Ability of the Shadows 34; Stasis Coffin."

Instantly a velvety black stasis field surrounded the girl, encapsulating her and cutting her off from all time and happenings. The girl would remain in the dark stasis, frozen in time, wrapped in a dark cocoon, unless Black would release her.

Black glowered at the two empathic troglodytes; the two that had not concealed their true forms and had caused the scene. He beckoned the two to follow as he placed a hand on Tinka's form, now encased in black fustian covering.

"Ambulatory Ability 7; Shimmer Teleport." And as soon as those words left his mouth he disappeared from the material plane, taking along with him the frozen form of Tinka; back to the Kingdom of Void.

The petite Empress sat on her throne, her countenance emanating rage that seemed unnatural for such a little girl. The space before her turned hazy as her guardian Black and the two miscreants, along with the 'coffinized' form of a human girl appeared in front of her.

"I have witnessed what had occurred on the seven vision stone." She stated angrily before anyone could say anything.

Black immediately bowed before his mistress. "And what should ensues then?" Black asked.

"Deracinate the perpetrators." A simple assertion from the little girl would end the lives of two troglodyte empaths.

Black rose from his position and stretched out both his arms, placing one palm on the back of the other, pointed towards the shuddering form of two careless troglodytes. "Internecine Ability 57; Ineluctable Disintegration."

The squid forms shrieked as their bodies started disintegrating, thousands of tiny particles slowly separating from their bodies, till their screams were curbed as their forms exploded in a cloud of dust and particulate matter. They had been consummately wiped out.

Black fell to his knees in pain, recoiling at the massive internecine spell he had used. But it had been befitting; the troglodytes would not be punished in any milder manner for their carelessness.

"Release the girl," the Empress ordered. She knew there was no time to waste as the Alchemist was waiting on the material plane.

Black reached out an arm as the stasis cover collapsed under his will. He was still holding himself in pain.

A bewildered Tinka blinked rapidly, trying to comprehend her surroundings. No words left her mouth as she looked around the dark chamber she was in; sparsely lit by opalescent multicolored gems studded in the walls that gave her surroundings an eerie feel. She was frightened and shocked at 'just' having been curbed by Will and witnessing two 'aliens', and all those feelings were interlaced with confusion as she saw her best friend's boyfriend writhing about on the floor with apparent pain.

"You girl, have witnessed too much." Tinka turned sideways to see the speaker. An adorable little girl, she noticed, with crystal blue eyes and long golden tresses that touched the ground.

"Don't hurt her." Black called out in the midst of painful agony. The Empress glowered at her Guardian with anger and contempt, but just for a moment. Then she turned her attention back to the intruder.

Tinka suddenly cradled her head in her hands as she felt a piercing pain through her skull. The Empress was expunging her memories.

. . . . .

Rachael led a dazed Tinka back to the recreation room where Aiden was still laughing and joking with his new found friends.

Aiden noticed her arrival and turned towards her.

"What happened?" he asked, with concern over his face, all his laughter and joy abruptly vanishing.

"It was a spider." Rachael explained and immediately Aiden relaxed. It had been some time since Tinka had disappeared.

"Creepy Scary eh?" Aiden asked Tinka, wiggling his eye-brows, smiling.

"Uh?" was all Tinka managed to eke out. She was confounded; she had no idea what was happening. Wasn't she in the restroom or something? And then what happened? Why was there a throbbing pain at the back of her head?

"Are you ok?" Aiden asked with concern once more as he rose up from his chair and headed towards his friend.

"She's fine." Rachael interjected. "Aren't you?"

Tinka hesitated before replying. "Yeah I'm fine." But she knew she was not. Something was wrong. Something had happened back there in the restroom. Something that shocked her to the core. But she could not recapitulate on the happenings. And all she had now was a spitting head ache.

"Listen Aide, I don't feel too well. Can we go back to campus?"

Aiden looked disbelievingly at his friend. What happened to her suddenly? He shrugged as he agreed to leave.

·····

"You servant…" a little girl spat out, "Seem to be harboring unnecessary human feelings that are clouding your judgment." The amorous feelings that she could sense in her guardians mind enraged her to no end. The same feelings had surfaced in Black once long before, and the consequences had been catastrophic.

Black was kneeling before his Empress, barely recovered from the recoil of his mutually destructive spell. But the anger and disdain he felt at himself overshadowed any physical pain he might have been experiencing. He knew why the Empress has summoned him again after deporting the Alchemist's friend back to the material plane; it had been his earlier outburst to not harm the girl.

"I evidently understand that the girl could not be erased because of her closeness to the Alchemist, and you obviously were apprised of that." The little girl was livid with anger at her guardian.

"And still you opened your wretched mouth to bid me?"

Black hung his head low. He could not gather the courage to look at his ruler.

"Human feelings are nothing but falsifying ephemeral tragedies that certainly seemed to have surfeited my abysmal servant. What have you to say?"

Black raised his head slightly, still not lifting his gaze to the enraged four year old. "Forgive me your Excellency, It shall not happen again."

"Obviously it will not," the Empress stated, her eyes burning with anger. "I shall be keeping a careful vigilance on you as well as on the Alchemist from now on."

. . . . .

"Now can you tell me why you made us leave from there?" an irritated Aiden asked his friend for the umpteenth time. "You totally made a scene out there."

Tinka tried to compose herself. Aiden was being difficult; or was she the one who was being difficult? She was confused before, but irritated now. Why the hell could she not recall what had happened? She went into the restroom and then whap! Blank. Every time she tried to strain herself to recall what had happened back there, her head would start throbbing painfully. But something was definitely wrong, and there was a feeling inside her which made her stomach churn and would be difficult to express to Aiden.

"Tinks, what's wrong? Talk to me!"

"Uh, yeah, just seem a little dizzy." Tinka stated, not knowing anything else to say. She was nervously biting her lower lip, trying to sort out things in her mind.

Aiden raised his hands exasperatedly as he ascended the acclivity of the yellow bridge from where one could see the ships. He was having no luck here. He had taken Tinka to the old-age home with a partial intention of showing her Will's work so she would do away with any aspersions and feelings of doubt she had for him, however subtle they might be, but things were seemingly back-firing. Looked like it was not working and in fact, Tinka had shut him out.

Suddenly Tinka stopped short and started fumbling through the contents of her handbag, rummaging madly through its contents as Aiden stopped beside her, giving her a look that asked 'Now what?'

"It's gone!" Tinka squealed. "It's not here!"

"What's not there?" asked Aiden hoping Tinka would not accuse the aged patrons of the retirement home of stealing her money.

"The binoculars. I had them earlier! They should be here!"

"Ok, ok, hang on a second. What binoculars?"

Tinka paused, knowing revealing about the binoculars would divulge classified revenge operation information, but this was not the time to be thinking of such things.

"Listen Aiden, I had a pair of black plastic binoculars I took to the restroom where I applied mascara on it." Aiden stared at his friend as if she had gone mad.

"They were going to be used to play a trick on you. And I had gone to prepare them in the restroom. And now they are gone!"

"What are you trying to say?" Aiden was exasperated as well as annoyed.

"What I'm trying to say is..," Tinka suddenly stopped. She knew what she wanted to say, and she knew Aiden would hate her for this. But she would have to do this.

"What I'm trying to say is that something happened while I was in there. I clearly remember going into the restroom and preparing the binoculars. And then something happened which I can't remember for the life in me, something bad. And something that threw me off completely."

Aiden was confused. What was Tinka's point?

"Aiden listen to me; you're gonna hate me for what I am going to say next, but I'm gonna say it anyway." Tinka prepared herself, carefully picking her words.

"There is something wrong about Will. He's not who he appears to be. There's something hiding behind that semblance of his, and it's not at all good."

Tinka looked sorrowfully at Aiden; he was speechless and the hurt was raw on his face.

"Listen Aide, I don't want to hurt you but I don't want to see Will hurting you either. I don't know what to say, but I know for certain that something is dead wrong!"

The two stared at each other, standing still on the path of the bridge, each hurt at the other's pain.

"But he said he would always stand by me!" Aiden sputtered finally. He felt all whiny and impaired.

Tinka stepped forward and hugged Aiden who stiffly resisted and kept his hands at his sides.

"Why won't you be happy for me?" Aiden had finally asked the question that had been playing in his mind for over 3 days now. Why would his best friend not be happy for his joy?

"I'm sorry Aide." Tinka finally whispered into his ear. "I don't know what this feeling I have is, but I promise I'll try to understand it and get over these differences with my feelings with Will."

Aiden relaxed into the girl's embrace. He hoped things would be better in the future and that everyone would get rid of their insecurities.

.....

Aiden sat waiting in the coffee shop he now considered his third home; his first being the frat room and his 'new' second being Will's apartment. But these were the last thoughts in his disconcerted mind. He felt restless and uneasy, unable to understand why things were happening as they were. He had met the greatest guy anyone could have ever known and now unknown obstacles had stymied his path to happiness. Why could he not just be happy and stop worrying about things? People would change and adapt automatically, wouldn't they?

"A penny for your thoughts mate!" Aiden looked up, jolted out of his reverie by Scott.

"I don't know anyone who used that line since the 70's," Aiden snorted, trying to make light of his mood.

"Ha ha." Scott said dispassionately as he settled down into the chair beside Aiden and immediately put on a business like demeanor. "So here's the PCB layout for the motor circuit, and I think you'll find it easy to understand now."

Aiden took the sheet of paper from Scott's hand and glanced at the circuit. 'Yep, it's a partial circuit' Aiden thought to himself. 'Scott really wants me to understand it in parts before I assemble these components'.

"So why such a glum face?" Scott asked.

Aiden took a deep breath. He had been distressed since the morning, and getting anxious about everything was becoming his second nature. He glanced at Scott who looked so hunky and so sincere. Should he have met Scott first? "Bah! Don't flatter yourself' he rebuked his mind. 'Just because he's bothered about me does not mean he's interested in me, and on top of that he has to be straight'.

"So what's going on in your mind?" Scott asked. White wanted more than anything to enter the boy's mind. This gracious youth who looked so distressed even though he was trying his best to hide it. No soul should be given the right to worry this boy. It would be easy to dive into the boy's mind and soothe it. He would also easily understand what was bothering him. But he had pledged to not infiltrate the boy's thoughts.

"You know when things seem perfect and then something small like a feeling comes along and totally wrecks your mind?" Aiden stated.

"Yeah." Scott nodded. He had no idea what the vague words Aiden used referred to. Patience would get him the answer.

"Well I really really like this person but things seem strewn with uncertainties; all of which are only playing around in my head."

Will nodded once more, waiting for Aiden to continue.

"I mean this person is the most awesome one I've ever met, I can never be luckier than to have… this person."

Will acknowledged Aiden's statement. He could obviously see the usage of 'a person' other than a 'he'. Why did humans try to hide their true selves?

"And instead of celebrating and reveling in the relationship, all I'm doing is worrying about inane things which I don't know a damn about. Why the hell do I have to be so screwed up?"

Aiden waited for Scott's reply. He had just blurted out nonsensical things to Scott, who probably thought he was nuts after hearing all that. Aiden stared at Scott's face whilehe waited for him to speak. The man looked absolute fireworks; the great face structure, the awesomely blue eyes, the golden blonde hair. Why the hell was this guy just an instructor who dealt in electronic circuits? Wasn't that for geeky guys like himself?

"Aiden, I don't fully comprehend your problem," Scott started, "But I can tell you certain things I've learnt. Your worrying incessantly, your being happy, your being sad; all of it is just a state of mind. Whatever happens around you, it's ultimately you who decides how you are going to react, and how happy or unhappy you are going to be."

"Apart from that, it seems you're with an incredible person. A person who would be very easy for you to fall in love with, and yet you are being held back by your own insecurities. If you really like this person, you should completely surrender, and with a person like you, I'm sure anyone would be more than willing to return the affection."

Aiden stared at Scott with warmth in his eyes. Everything Scott had said somehow applied to him. How could Scott be so wise and affable?

"Besides, I'm sure he's a remarkable person." Scott stated.

Aiden jerked up. "Er, who's remarkable?"

White immediately realized the revelation he had inducted in his speech; he had used a 'he'. There was no way out of this now.

"The guy you're falling for Aiden, I'm sure he'll be good for you."

Aiden was shocked. Was he that easy to read? It must be all the staring and gazing he had subjected Scott to. 'No wonder he thinks you're gay' he thought to himself. But Scott appeared to be taking it comfortably in stride.

"You don't mind th…"

"Of course I don't mind Aiden," Scott cut him off. "And I also know that any guy would be extremely lucky to have you."

Brian interrupted the pair before Aiden could say anything more. Aiden had gotten to know the young waiter that always served him; Brian, the waiter who had been eyeing Will before. Aiden had gotten a tad friendly with the boy.

The young waiter took their orders and stooped down to whisper into Aiden's ears. "How come you get the hottest guys on the planet?"

Aiden smiled at Brian. "And the looks aren't even the best parts of them you know."

Brian sighed before leaving to get the two their orders. He would never understand Aiden and his 'boyfriends'.

"Ahem!" Scott coughed as Aiden diverted his attention back to his companion.

Aiden smiled goofily at Scott. He realized that Scott was a person he would want by his side forever, even as a friend. And he was sure that nothing would get in his and Will's way now. He was going to pour everything he had in him, into being with Will.

"Thanks Scott. I mean, thanks a lot. Your words really make a difference."

"No no, I'm glad if I could be of any help."

The two sat smiling at each other, Aiden happy that he had not only found a great lover but also a great friend and White taking joy in the fact that he could do away with the Alchemists worries by just using his words.

The pair was distracted as someone crept close to White. Aiden looked with a puzzled expression as a timid old lady, totally crouched into herself came up to Scott.

"An angel!" the lady cried as she put both her wrinkled hands on White's cheeks and lightly stroked them.

"Uhh.." White uttered knowing what was happening. This aged human lady could see his true form.

"A beautiful golden angel." The lady reiterated. Aiden reached out his hand to stop the lady, then realized that Scott was not discomfited and the lady looked way too fragile, with her face skin wrinkled like parchment paper, to be threatening.

"Why doesn't the angel spread his wings and fly?" the lady asked in a sad manner as she leaned closer and embraced White in her arms.

Aiden watched smiling, finding it amusing that Scott was being compared to an angel. He did not understand the significance of the old lady's words.

. . . . .

Aiden nervously stopped outside the black glass door and contemplated what he was doing.

"This is it, he told himself. I have to do this." He tried to push the door open but it would not budge. 'So it's really not a shop kind of place anymore' he thought to himself as he knocked. Even the sign outside that read 'Horoscopus – Fortune Telling' was gone, and he was back there though he was not sure what he was doing.

The door swung open as the Japanese girl that had scared Aiden earlier, opened the door, and he once again noticed how pale white her complexion was.

"Oh," She uttered, clearly surprised to see Aiden. "It's you."

"Yeah it's me." Aiden replied, not sure of whether his trip here was a good idea.

"Listen if you've come to talk about the other day, I'm really sorry but I was an ass that day, I didn't mean to…"

"No, no, it's not a problem. I can understand," Aiden cut her off. Then he swung his hand forward to reveal a bouquet of a dozen white lilies he had been holding behind his back.

"I, err, got some flowers."

The girl stared wide eyed and then looked at the flowers and then back at Aiden's face, speechless. Aiden extended the flowers towards her.

"Thank you," she replied as she took them.

"Just my condolences for your mother; I can understand what you must be going through now."

The girl and Aiden stared awkwardly at each other for a few moments.

"I'll be going then." Aiden finally stated as he turned to leave.

"Listen," the girl called out. "I don't know what your name is, but this means a lot to me."

"Uh, no big deal. I just felt I owed you at least this much."

"And, uh." The girl hesitated. "Be careful."

Aiden smiled and nodded as he walked away. He had a warm feeling in his heart that told him he had just done a good thing.

. . . . .

"Yeah I'll be there in 30 minutes!" Aiden yelled into his phone before he disconnected the call and hastily started stripping his clothes. Steve was already at 'Escape' and was demanding Aiden get there fast. Escape was an amusement park, replete with rides and roller coasters and quaint food stalls and games. It had been

Steve's idea to go there with Aiden, and with Will. Aiden was excited that Steve was finally going to meet his boyfriend. He quickly ran through the things in his cupboard, unsure of what to wear.

"Dammit, there's nothing to wear!" he cursed. He had been wearing his best clothes everyday, along with some of Steve's and had rummaged through the best of both their wardrobes. "Will have to repeat this." He said as he pulled out a pair of jeans and a sweatshirt. He craned his neck from where he was standing, covered by the cupboard as the door swung open.

"Hi Jase." He called out as Jason entered.

"Hi." Jason said barely audibly without glancing at his roommate.

Jason had been avoiding him since the last few days, and Aiden couldn't help shake the feeling that he had come to know about him being gay. Jason would never come to the room when Aiden was there and would evade him in the college corridors. Or it could be just Aiden's overactive imagination. He hoped the latter was true.

"Hey Jason, Me, Steve and Will are going to 'Escape.' You wanna join us?"

"No, I gotta go."

"You could get Aditi along," Aiden advised as he stepped towards his roommate. Aiden had only his underwear on and he noticed Jason stepping backwards as he stepped ahead. Being roommates, they had never been modest before.

"NO!" Jason cried out suddenly. "I gotta go." And with that he hastily exited the room with a basketball under his arm which Aiden realized he had come to collect. Aiden stood there dumbfounded.

. . . . .

Aiden and Steve stood watching as Will took position and pulled his hand backwards, carefully aiming with the red painted tennis ball. With one swift motion he hurled the ball towards the target and smacked it bang in the centre.

"Bull's eye!" he yelled as the stall owner handed him over a pink teddy bear as his prize, glaring at him to give him an idea that this stall was meant for people much younger than him. Will took the proffered soft toy and made his way towards where Aiden and Steve were watching, leaning against a railing.

"Here, this if for you." Will handed over the fluff pink toy to his lover, smiling cheekily.

"What the hell am I gonna do with that?" Aiden asked indignantly as Steve burst out into peals of laughter.

"I dunno." Will replied innocently. "You could decorate your frat room or something with it."

Aiden hmmphed and pushed the teddy bear back into Will's hands, storming off to the stall where his boyfriend had 'won' him a teddy bear. He handed over a token to the irate vendor and took the 3 balls offered. 2 missed shots later he finally hit the mark and knocked down the target.

"Here! Your prize." The vendor scowled at Aiden as he handed over yet another pink fluffy teddy bear to a winner. The stall owner's face clearly showed his distaste for the likes of people their ages knocking down targets, and winning pink teddy bears. Aiden collected his 'hard earned' reward and strode towards his waiting friends purposefully, where Will was trying his best to put on a frown as Steve laughed maniacally.

"Here, this is for you!" Aiden reiterated with triumph on his face.

"And what am I supposed to do with that?"

"I don't know, put it into your car or something; I guess black Lambos and pink teddy bears look good together."

Will was not one to admit defeat. He purposefully walked back up to the game stall and handed over one more token to the stall owner, who was glowering at him with burning eyes this time. Will took the three red tennis balls and assumed his position to aim.

"This is for that one!" he called out to Aiden, pointing to a massive 4 foot tall pink teddy bear with a sign under it stating it as the grand prize. Will would be required to knock down targets on all three shots to win it.

Three glorious throws later, Will returned to his mates with a colossal pink bear; Aiden scowled as Steve held his sides which were by then hurting for he was laughing so hard.

"Well thank you!" Aiden stated angrily as he took the large teddy bear. "This is gonna be my new boy friend!"

"Oh no he's not! I'll whip his ass if he tries to be!"

And with that the trio burst out guffawing like a pack of hyenas, each laughing till their sides hurt. The stall owner was cursing the two pink teddy bear winners as the teddy bears were pushed onto Steve who handed them over to an excited 6 year old girl. The girl screamed with joy as her parents allowed her to accept the pink fluffy bear family.

"So where should we have dinner?" Will asked as the three finally restrained their laughter.

"Oh there's a diner just outside the main entrance where 'lots of grease' comes at no extra price," Steve interjected. "Scott will be joining us there."

Aiden looked questioningly at his roommate. "You called Scott?"

"Yeah Scott, the same Scott who played tennis with you the other day."

"Of course I know Scott!" Aiden replied. "He also happens to be my robotics guide, but when did you meet him?"

"Oh, he plays tennis with me in the mornings, now that you never have time for a game." Steve leaned in and whispered in Aiden's ear, "And he's always asking on and on about you. I think he's in love with you or something."

Will cleared his throat as Steve pulled away from Aiden who stood there with a confused expression on his face. Black could discern what was going on and knew all that had been discussed; he was not at all pleased. He knew of the Alchemist's fidelity but could not contemplate anyone else even touching his lover.

"Ok fine!" Aiden stated. "Let's go there and meet Scott then."

Aiden thought about how this would be the first time the two alpha males, Scott and Will, would be meeting each other; finding it a bit amusing for no particular reason. So Scott would meet his lover finally, and just when he had informed him about Will. This would be an interesting meeting to witness. His thoughts shifted to how Scott had learned that he was gay and had been completely supportive; and how contrary it was to Jason's behavior after his roommate probably learned about him. He would have to inform Steve about both these cases later.

A few minutes later the three settled down into the uncomfortable wooden chairs of the diner Steve had mentioned. Aiden glanced at the prices in the menu, happy that at least things were affordable here; he had been splurging too much money with Will nowadays and would never let Will pay for him anywhere. His self respect was burning a large hole in his pocket.

Will barely took part in the conversation while they waited for Scott and ordered a few appetizers. He was distressed. He felt restless, saturated with jealousy, though Aiden's mind assured him that there was no need to be. Who was this man that could prove a match for the mighty dark angel Arangyunus? He would tear this man apart if he ever lay a finger on his 'Aiden'.

Suddenly Black started feeling uneasy. He was sick with jealousy, he knew that. But there was some sort of other overwhelming feeling that was making him queasy. And it was getting stronger. No, this was not an emotion. It was something else. It was a powerful spirit force that was clashing with his own, and it was heading towards them. Something was drastically wrong.

"Ah there's Scott!" Steve stated as he yelled and waved a hand to direct Scott there.

Black swirled around, partly dazed by the proximity of this oppugning spirit force. And their eyes met.

The two arch rivals Black and White stared at each other, their faces enraged and black as thunder.

. . . . .

Episode Five

Aiden sat facing Steve in the uncomfortable wooden chairs. The two of them sat across the table, waiting. Aiden had looked forward to the junction when the two new people in his life would meet. It seemed like that moment was temporarily delayed. His thoughts went back to momets earlier when the two had confronted each other.

Scott had stopped short when he came towards the table, his face livid for some reason. He fetched out a glowing cellphone from his pocket as he signaled to the group that there was a call waiting to be answered; he walked away holding the phone to his ear. Aiden looked back at Will and noticed a raging expression which was slowly suffusing into a deadpan face. Aiden opened his mouth to say something but Will abruptly got up, pushing the chair out form under him; he stated he needed to visit the washroom.

And that left only Aiden and Steve sitting on the table for four. Aiden wondered if Scott and Will knew each other from before, but then let the thought slip. The antagonistic atmosphere that had suddenly materialized must have been his imagination. And with the two of them gone, it was just Steve and him at the table.

"You know, I think Jason found out about me," Aiden stated suddenly.

"Uh?" Steve looked at his roommate with a confused expression on his face.

"I think," Aiden reiterated clearing his throat, "Jason found out I'm gay."

"What? How's that?"

"I don't know how, but he's been acting weird since the last few days. He's been avoiding me everywhere."

Steve stared at Aiden with a credulous expression on his face. "Do you know for sure that he knows?"

"Yes I'm sure."

Steve waited for Aiden to continue.

"Today he went all red when I was in my underwear in the room. He bolted when I tried to talk to him, but it's not only that; he's shunning me everywhere else too. I'm spending every night at Will's place so I'm not in the room with you two at night, which is a good thing or he might have been sleeping in somebody else's room as well." Aiden was babbling; his mind became a jumble of thoughts when he thought about Jason.

Aiden sighed deeply and bit his lips nervously. Steve, on his part, had a sorrowful expression on his face. The two sat in silence absorbing the implications of the words.

"Well yeah, usually he's extremely warm and friendly," Steve finally broke the silence between them, "but when it comes to matters like this, he's totally insular."

"So what should I do?" Aiden was exasperated. He could not think about how life woulc be if Jason ceased to be one of his best buddies.

"Look Aiden, Jason's like a spider in a web. He knows of nothing other than the universe he's in. He will be forever merry in his own happy-go-lucky world, but if something from outside his realm disturbs him, he will shut down and avoid it. I think you know this as well as I do."

Aiden nodded, acknowledging the fact. He had always known that Jason was one person who would have severe trouble accepting his sexuality, if it ever came to light.

"I don't think there will be much point in approaching him, he'll probably block you out, but you can give it a try."

Aiden was terrified at the thought of approaching Jason with such a matter. What in the world would he say to him?

"Actually, it's a good thing he got to know of it now," Steve continued, "With Will around so much, he would have gotten to know sooner or later anyway."

"I'd prefer later than sooner," Aiden muttered under his breath. Here was a close friend of his who would balk and flee at the mention of his sexuality and there was a new friend he had made that had so casually accepted him.

"You know, Scott also knows that I'm gay."

"What?" Steve was dumbfounded again at the same matter. "Shit! Really?"

"Yeah, in fact he himself broached the subject and sorta outed me, and he's perfectly cool with it, in fact even supportive of it."

"Wow!" was all Steve could say after opening and closing his mouth a few times. "When I play tennis with him in the mornings he's always asking about you and somehow involving you in the topic. I thought he had it for you or something."

"No he doesn't!" Aiden exclaimed before his mind could let him think otherwise. The possibility that Scott was interested in him was titillating, but he had Will now, didn't he? "In fact he knows that I'm involved with Will."

"He knows Will?"

"No, he was going to meet him for the first time today, but Scott knows that I am involved with some other guy, and he knows that his name is Will."

Steve paused before he put to words his next thought; "Shit Aiden! How the hell do you suddenly have such mind-blowing guys after you?"

Aiden coughed mockingly as Steve used the term 'mind-blowing' to describe guys. He wondered how his life over the last few days had been absolutely dreamy, mixed with a few bumps. He had changed the way he looked, with the new hairdo and lenses which were a bitch sometimes, but he liked it. It was exactly one week ago that he had met Will, and was already so completely involved with him. How far would they go? He knew that he would try to always keep Will happy and go as far as it was possible to go with him. Maybe they would even…

And then there was Scott. He had really hit it off with him as well.

These two men that had added brilliant multicolored strokes to his black and white life. Two men that always tried to make him smile. Two men he was going to try and keep happy in return.

Aiden wondered where were those two men were now?

· · · · ·

White stood on the deserted path at the entrance of the wide black building. A sign that would be lit in flashing red and yellow neon lights during the functioning hours of the amusement park announced that this structure was the 'Hall of Mirrors'. And the strong oppugning spiritual force oozing from inside indicated that his adversary was inside.

'So the battle takes place here', he thought to himself as he climbed the two raised steps to enter the building and at once noticed that the chain that was supposed to be tied to two iron bars at the entrance was lying in two pieces on the floor. He pushed the sliding door and slipped inside.

White walked towards the increasing gradient of his arch opponents spirit force. He was finally going to fight Black. He could not remember if he had fought him at all before, but he had, hadn't he? He must have. It was strange then that he could not remember. He walked across the zigzag paths between the multitudes of mirrors which formed innumerable kaleidoscopical images of his form, reflecting images and after-images, some deformed and some perfectly upright.

He turned around a corner, only to be immediately confronted by his titan opponent. Black stood in a centre clearing with a grim expression on his face. The passage was lined on all sides with an arcade of mirrors at various angles, between which were reflected hundreds of images of the mighty dark seraph, channeling all the way to the extremely last glass mirror.

"So, we meet." White stated icily as he stepped closer to his rival. The mirrors all around were rapidly changing colors and shape to accommodate and reflect the new entry into the passage.

"Yes we do." Black replied as his hands swiftly fell to his sides and black mist enveloped his palms and slowly dissipated till the evanescent forms left behind two rigidly straight long sharp edged black swords that reached all the way to the ground, one in each hand. White immediately took note of the fact that Black had wasted no time in summoning his most powerful fighting companions; the 'Twin blades of Alacrity'. The thin savage black pair of swords were rumored to be capable of cutting through anything.

Instantly White concentrated his energies as a brilliant white light dazzled in front of his hand and he called upon his own battle comrade; the 'Helos Sabre', the almighty sword that had defeated Pi. But this battle White knew would be no where as 'easy' as the previous one.

Unknown to White, the telepathic voice of a little girl was booming inside his opponent's head, ordering him to come back. Black paid no heed to the voice, ignoring the commands of his Empress.

Eliciting a battle roar Black lunged towards his opponent as hundreds of mirror images everywhere changed locations rapidly. Wasting no time White swung out his sword which clashed resoundingly with the twin blades and black and white sparks scintillated from the impact. Black moved around rapidly and swung both his blades in wide circular arcs; one after the other as White countered each blow and counterattacked in return.

A mighty sword melee began as the two sworn enemies danced about in a hall of glasses, swords were clashing in hundreds of locations in the vicinity, as images copied out the scene in front of them. Shining white and misty black sparks flew in all directions.

White was astonished at the speed, skill and savagery of his opponent, he could barely keep up with the tempo with which the fight was progressing. He realized that if things continued like they were, he would have no time to cast any spells; but then neither would his adversary.

White was steadily losing ground as his redoubtable foe pushed him backward with a series of double strikes and precise cuts. He had been nicked with the stinging blade twice already and was nowhere near even touching his opponent. He swung the sword of the sun around defensively and helplessly as Black pushed him into a narrower passage filled with mirrors of all types.

Out of the blue white noticed an opening to strike as Black pulled back and seemingly rested his sword low. White lurched forwards to attack as Black chanted, "Ability of the Shadows 95; Image Replication."

White stopped his attack at the last moment. What was this? Standing ahead of him were four, no five maybe seven images of a dark angel with thin long blades in both hands. The innumerable images on the mirrored walls of Black and his illusive image forms made it almost impossible to tell the real one apart from the juxtapositions.

'Impossible but not quite', White thought to himself as he focused on a particular image and lunged forward with his sword. A lunging silver arc and sharp pain across his torso informed him that his chest had been slashed at. White screamed in pain as he skidded across the floor and crashed into a mirrored wall. The glass shattered and slivers of it sprinkled all around him. He had made a mistake. The real enemy had not been correctly identified.

"What's the matter Witenhoem?" Black asked with a contemptuous smile on his face. "Can't you tell which one of me is real?"

White gritted his teeth as the pain as blood oozed out of a deep cut in his chest. He pressed his hand against his torso to stop the flow of blood which continued its incessant flow. He would have to go on fighting, and he would have to be more careful.

White got up and steadied himself scowling at his adversary. With a howl he lunged forward and brandished his sword in long strokes as Black counterattacked and dodged. A few swings later he finally got his first touché on his opponent as he left a streak of blood across his shoulder.

A myriad of images and reflections on the hundreds of mirrors could be seen dancing around in a frenzied manner as the two warriors clashed their swords to prove their sleight of hand. Black reprised with powerful blows, matched by his opponent till suddenly White was left confused by a dazzling set of 'Blacks' that somehow joined the ruckus. Had Black not send away the images of his spells yet? White continued concentrating on his first opponent knowing that the images were just illusions and he had to somehow beat up only this one dark angel. A couple of strokes later he lost his opponent in the myriad of reflections, after reflections and doppelgangers that Black had created. He slashed around frantically dispelling a couple of the illusory forms of Black that vanished in fumes as soon as his sword touched them. But his real opponent had managed to evade him. Where was the real Black?

This time the blow of blades came as two punishing cruel streaks across his back as the cloth tore apart and the blades of Alacrity left behind ugly ragged lacerations. White grimaced and whirled around only to find Black's right foot connecting with his jaw as his body was flung across the air and plummeted against mirrors that shattered and fell clinking around him. Slivers of glass were embedded within him in several places now.

"You are really bad at this you know." Black simpered evilly as he examined his shoulder where White had left a mark. "You should possess much more skill if you want to fight for the Alchemist."

White looked disgustingly as his opponent as the dark Seraph stated, "The boy is mine," The dark angel voice was heavy with conviction. Conviction interlaced with determination that went unnoticed by White.

White got up once more unsteadily as shards of glass fell around him. The right side of his jaw where Black's foot had connected was throbbing with pain as blood trickled out from the corner of his mouth. He was having no luck with the mirrors and images; all were illusory deceptions for him. And all were contributing to give him a sound thrashing. The ruler of the kingdom of Light would not lose in such a derogatory manner!

White balanced himself on his feet as he raised himself up and to face the several images of Black that were standing menacingly around him. He held out his left palm and opened his mouth to chant, "Ability of the Light 3; Fusillading Shards."

Dozens of small crystal shaped glowing embers materialized in his palm which he flung in the space ahead of him before Black could react. The numerous crystals scattered in all directions, hitting Black and his replication images. The shards were insignificant in causing, damage but easily dissipated the images leaving only the lone dark angel standing with his two dark sleek swords by his sides. White immediately lunged forward towards Black, his sword had burst into golden flames. He would put his entire being into defeating his enemy.

. . . . .

Aiden glanced around the restaurant expecting either Scott or Will to turn up any instant. It had been over 10 minutes since they both abruptly left him. Where were they now?

He smiled apologetically at Steve before he fished out his phone to try and call Will, reckoning that to be better than going into the washroom and checking up on him. A recorded message informed him that the phone was switched off. Aiden 'humphed' as he excused himself from Steve and headed towards the washrooms.

. . . . .

The Empress of Woe was furious. It was night time; a time that prevented her from crossing over to the material plane; owing to the midnight curse that had once been placed upon her. And this was the second time during the 6 days that she needed to desperately cross over to the other side, this time to prevent her Guardian from fighting her greatest foe; at least for now. She had been commanding her dark warrior incessantly to give up the battle and return to her, but it had all been to no avail. Arangyunus simply ignored her.

It seemed like the dark angel was giving her sworn enemy a sound thrashing, but the outcome to the battle could change any instant. And she was not prepared under any circumstances to lose her Guardian to White now. She had lost Arangyunus to White a long time ago, though in a very different manner, and would not condone something like that happening again. She cursed the air around her as she etched a hexagon of blood on the floor of her chamber and knelt down at its centre to begin her chanting.

She would have to forcibly bring back her warrior.

. . . . .

Black was taken aback at the swiftness and sudden outburst of his enemy. White had cleverly destroyed all his after images with the fusillading shards and had destroyed several of the mirrors in the hall as well. They would serve to lessen his state of confusion as the two fought.

White was on a power surge, his entire body was iridescent in a golden sheen as the swords was flaming in bright golden yellow; a sign that the Keeper of the light was in a state of heightened power. The three swords swung around and clashed as the Blades of Alacrity met with the Helos Saber but Black was losing ground this time. The sheer heat his opponent was emanating form his form was scalding him. He could counter his White's heat aura with a spell but White's tempo and savagery rendered him devoid of any time to do so.

In his mad rage, White charged at his opponent as a juggernaut and several massive swings of the Helos Saber later, he had managed to severely injure Black across the abdomen. Black flinched at the slash across his abdomen as he staggered backwards into a thinner passage filled with mirrors. 'This was it!' White thought to himself. A perfect opening!

White pulled back his left hand as he hurtled forwards towards Black; one powerful punch to the face and his opponent would reel under the blow. Black whirled sideways and a horrified expression came across his face as White's extended fist came like lightning towards him.

Crash! White cursed himself as colossal pain recoiled through his arm and body. His fist had connected with a mirrored wall which now stood cracked open. He had mistakenly attacked a mirror thinking it to be his adversary. He swirled around to find his opponent but reacted too late as Black's leg swung out at his stomach and send him flying through the air for a second time.

White crashed heavily against a wall as he slumped down to the ground, still wielding his sword in hand. He had been fooled again. Was he that inefficient? His knuckles had been split open where he had pounded the wall with them and his stomach hurt to the point where his entire body was queasy with pain. He would not be able to fight for more than a few swings anymore.

"Confused again?" Black asked, standing upright with his two swords. "Won't you ever learn?"

Black's skin was searing everywhere due to the heat radiating from his rival. His abdomen had been cruelly slashed across as the cloth gave away and blood spilled out in a gruesome manner. But he was going to win this battle now. He brought forward both his swords till they formed a plus sign in front of his chest and chanted. "Ability of the Shadows 80; BlackMist Aura."

Instantly a wispy grey fog surrounded his body enveloping it and making it seem hazy and translucent. This mist would protect him from the heat of his opponent and at the same time increase the acuity of his dual swords.

He looked at his opponent who was once again groggily lifting his self up. "Do you think you can defeat me now White?"

White stood grimly with his gaze lowered toward the ground. His opponent was very powerful, with the correct combination of speed, power and precision. This was the Dark Angel after all, his own counterpart. On top of it all, his opponent could tell his real self from the since he carried a sword only in his right hand. Black carried two swords and the application of the linear inversion laws on the mirrors would not give the real one away. But he could not lose now. Losing to him would mean losing the Alchemist, and he had sworn that he would protect such nobility. It did not matter if he had to part with his life, he would protect the Alchemist with his last bit of energy.

"Ability of the light 19; Raging Inferno."

As soon as those words left White's mouth, columns of flame shot of in various directions. Black raised his hand to shield himself but his mist aura was enough to fend the burgeoning flames. Fire coursed through everywhere as profiles of red flaming waves spread through all directions. The whole Building was filled with flames seeping through every corner. 'Why had White wasted such a massive amount of spirit energy in such a pointless spell?' Black wondered. These flames would not even singe him once and not even provide him cover.

As the flames died down Black received his answer. Every single mirror in the hall had been shattered. Pieces of glass, some melting, some intact lay as jagged pieces on the floor strewn everywhere. So White did not want to get confused with the mirrors and reflections anymore? But he had had to pay a high cost for this.

Black found his opponent with his hands extended in front of his torso. "Ability of the Light 21, Flaming Shot." A red ball of fire materialized in front of his palms and White send it flying through the air towards Black who easily dodged it. Black noticed a perfect opening and flung one of his twin blades out at White. He had got him now!

The sword went hurtling towards White's form at an astonishing pace and struck a mirrored surface. "What?" Black cried out as the glass shattered. This meant White was behind him!

Black turned around just in time to stop White's sword swinging out at him with his single blade of Alacrity. White was on a massive power surge, his entire form was effulgent in golden flames that formed a wild golden sphere around him.

A power sphere that was threatening to engulf Black and steadily eating his 'Black Mist Aura' as the two swords strained against each other. Black was now face to face with White and saw the determination in his eyes.

White smiled through the golden flames, "What's the matter? Can't you tell which one of me is real?" Black realized how foolish he had been. He had been tricked by the only mirror that had been left standing in the hall. And now White was drastically increasing his emanations as the golden flames accumulated more and more power. White gritted his teeth as he called out to his own inner powers. But it was of no use. White was already high on his and Black would be finished before his entire strength was summoned. He was losing gradually and soon these Golden flames would engulf him and char his entire being. There was no escape. The fallen angel would cease to exist, defeated by his sworn enemy.

"Your tail ends here Arangyunus!" White yelled from amidst the flames.

Black closed his eyes and images of Aiden flashed across his mind. Images of the boy smiling, of them making love and all the events he had been through the past week raced through his mind. 'So this is goodbye to the Alchemist' Black thought to himself as his skin started peeling off from White's energy radiation. "I will always love you Aiden," he mouthed before the blinding golden energy became overwhelming.

And then there was a flash. Black's body was shrouded in fog as he suddenly disappeared from the material plane. White crashed through the fog and went plummeting towards the wall. What had happened? Had he not won the battle? Where was Black?

"Not so easy now!" the voice of a young girl reverberated across the hall. White let out a scream of agony as he realized that the Empress had pulled her guardian through from the material plane. He had been so close to destroying his arch-opponent. And with that scream he collapsed onto the floor possessing no more energy.

. . . . .

Aiden was perplexed. He had checked the washroom and there had been no sign of Will. He was standing outside the restaurant trying to catch a sign of either Scott or Will but there had been none. He was calling Will's number continuously but was getting a message that stated that the number was switched off. He could not even get through to Scott's number. It was more than 20 minutes since both Scott and Will had disappeared. Where were they?

Steve stepped out of the restaurant as Aiden's phone buzzed. Aiden glanced at the display which informed him it was Will calling. He pressed the button to answer.

"Where are you?"

There was silence from the other side till a feeble voice answered. "Hey Aide, sorry ran into some important business."

"But where are you?" Aiden asked exasperatedly.

"Really sorry." Will's voice was quivering. "But can't meet up with you right now. Will meet up tomorrow. Need to go now."

"Listen wait," Aiden almost shouted into the phone. "Are you ok, you sound like you're in pain or something."

There were a few seconds of silence on the other side before Will's voice replied. "No, I'm fine."

"Ok then should I…"

"I'll call you tomorrow Aiden." Will stated cutting him off before the phone clicked and Aiden got the dead connection tone. He looked at his phone's display worriedly which informed him that the call had lasted 37 seconds. There was a message waiting too. Aiden clicked on the message icon to find a message from Scott.

'SORRY, HAD 2 LEAVE. SUM IMPRTNT WORK.'

"What happened?" Steve questioned as Aiden looked up at his friend with an expression of disbelief. He had no clue what to say to Steve.

.....

White opened his eyes to find the form of a raven haired angel bend over him. He immediately raised himself and grabbed Frigeria by the shoulders. This was the second time in recent times that the raven haired angel had had to heal ruthless wounds inflicted on his body.

"Aiden, where is he?" he asked with frustration etched in his voice.

"There is no need to worry my King," Frigeria answered in her dulcet voice. The boy is safe and far from any harm."

"No, Arangyunus has seduced him; he has unknowingly fallen in league with the devil!" White raised himself completely from the flat marble top his body had rested upon. Immediately a shooting pain ran through his chest as he placed a hand upon it to realize that there were still deep lacerations there. And if the whiplash pain across his back was any indication to go by, he was sure there were astringent welts there too. He fell to the floor on his knees, barely able to contemplate anything around him.

"The boy is safe for now." Frigeria answered and then gathered conviction in her voice. "And you need to rest for now."

"No! I must get to Aiden!" the great white angel bellowed as he raised himself using his hand as support on the marble top. He had his fist and teeth clenched at the excruciating pain he was experiencing.

"No you will not." Frigeria stated flatly as she waved both her hands in a circular motion around White's face. All the White angel saw were dozens of silver butterflies fluttering before he lost consciousness and fell. Frigeria stepped ahead to allow the colossal angel to fall on her shoulder. She knew that the spell she had used would not last very long on this powerful angel. But she had no choice.

"We cannot lose you now my king." She stated before she lay him back on the marble surface.

. . . . .

Empress Woe was distressed. The little girl was scurrying about making preparations for the 'Stone of Subjugation.' She was busy adding varied ingredients to a boiling cauldron. She put in a tar black diamond shaped stone the size of her fist. The stone was void right now and had no powers. It would soon have quite a few as soon as she finished with the concoction.

The body of her guardian angel stirred somewhere in the chamber. "Aiden," the almost lifeless body mumbled out.

Empress Woe was furious; here lay her mighty Keeper of the Dark, barely sustaining his life force because of the efforts she had gone through to pull him out of the material plane, for he had been all but annihilated by her arch enemy, and all he could think about now was that boy, the Alchemist. She had been healing him continuously for several hours, spending too much of her own energy on him. She angrily headed over to the semi conscious form of her dark seraph.

"You finally awaken Arangyunus." She stated icily.

Black strained as he gazed at his Empress through narrow slits of his eyes, he barely had the strength to open them. "Where is Aiden?"

The Empress gritted her teeth. This had gone far enough. She did not want a feeble lovesick nincompoop as her guardian. She would have to take matters into her hands directly now. She spat on Black's face before she haughtily strode off, back to her simmering cauldron.

The little girl picked up a stiletto and positioned her hand over the boiling concoction. Without flinching she pricked her hand as two drops of blood fell into the boiling mixture. Black fumes started fuming out as the cauldron's contents changed various shades of grey and silver. The little girl then put in her bare hand into the seemingly piping cauldron and pulled out the diamond stone she had immersed earlier. The stone was now dazzling an evil glint of Black and silver, similar to the shades of the cauldron's ingredients.

"I need to get to Aiden." Black stated feebly as he managed to sit upright after much effort. His whole body was reeling under excruciating pain. His skin felt like it had been left in an oven to bake. He could barely gather the strength to sit upright.

"No you need not." Empress Woe stated whirling around. She held an iridescent stone in her tiny palm. The 'Stone of Subjugation'.

The Ruler of the dark smiled evilly. Now all she had to do was let her guardian rest for some time till he healed and then the stone would do the remaining work for her. Till that time, she herself would have to descend onto the material plane and assume the Alchemist's lover's form.

Black strained his eyes to make out what his mistress held in her hand. He had no idea what the shiny gem was. He did not know that the shiny gem would soon be embedded inside him.

. . . . .

"I need to talk to you." Aiden stated flatly as he entered his room and shut the door behind him. Jason looked up from the automobile magazine he was reading as his face went pale.

"Uhhh?" was all Jason could muster with a deer caught in the headlights expression.

"We need to talk Jason." Aiden stated firmly.

"What aba.." Jason stammered. "What about?"

Aiden bit his lips nervously. All the determination he had gathered melted away. How would he proceed now?

"It's about Will." Aiden finally stuttered. He was losing his calm. "No, it's about me actually," he corrected himself.

"So?" Jason uttered after a few seconds of silence.

Aiden was having a hard time. This was way more difficult than his 'Electromagnetic Field Theory Examination'. What the hell would he say now?

"Listen Jase," Aiden finally started. "I'm a bit... different." Aiden cursed himself at the way this confrontation was going as he noticed Jason fidgeting nervously with his phone, rolling it around in one hand.

"Will is a close friend of mine." Aiden stated as he mentally banged his head against the wall. Hadn't he already thought of what he would say to Jason? Where had all of that disappeared to?

"In fact we're more than friends."

Jason was turning beet red as Aiden progressed. Unexpectedly he shot up from the chair he was sitting on. "I need to go." He stated in a mild voice as he made a beeline for the door. Aiden was taken aback at Jason's sudden movements.

"Wait Jason, I just need to..." the rest was left unheard as Jason swiftly exited and slammed the door behind him before Aiden could recover. Aiden stared at the closed door with an annoyed expression on his face. What had he been thinking? Why had it not gone off well? Should he chase after Jason? No, judging Jason, it was evident that the boy had bolted off as fast as his legs could carry him. What should he do now?

. . . . .

Aiden stepped out of the elevator onto Will's floor, still holding his phone to his ear. He had been trying both Scott and Will at regular intervals since a long time and pre-recorded messages relayed that both the phones were switched off. His anxiousness was driving him crazy. Had Will ditched him or something? No that was not possible; he had promised that he would always stay by his side. And where the hell was Scott?

He neared Will's door and rang the bell with his phone still attached to his ear. This time, Will's phone rung. And he could hear Will's muffled ringtone from the other side of the door.

Abruptly, the door swung open as Will stood in front of him with a ringing phone in his hand. Aiden disconnected his side as the phone ceased ringing. "Will, what happened?"

"What happened?" his lover asked with a grave expression on his face.

"What happened yesterday? Where did you disappear?"

"Oh, I got caught up in some official work." his lover stated nonchalantly. The Empress was impersonating her guardian for the moment. There was no problem with her entering the material plane during daytime. She would have to fill in temporarily till Arangyunus recovered. But what was actually proving difficult to handle were the feelings of icky love and possessiveness the Alchemist was

124

emanating; they were nauseating her. This would be more difficult than she had thought.

Aiden looked at his lover with an incredulous expression on his face. Something was amiss. "Will, are you ok?"

"Yeah I'm fine. Perfect." The Empress replied faking a smile, though she felt the least bit like it in the proximity of this boy.

"Listen Aiden," the Empress stated as the boy continued to stare at her. "I have some important work for the day. We'll meet at night." Empress Woe wanted nothing more than to get away form the boy. She continued unperturbed as his face fell.

"You can have this till then." She stated handing over a set of keys to Aiden. Aiden's eyes grew wide as he realized that Will had just tossed over to him his Lamborghini's keys.

"But I..."

"I need to hurry Aiden, I'm already late for work," the Empress of the Dark stated coldly.

"Ok." Aiden stated timidly before he stepped closer to gently kiss his lover. The Empress immediately stepped back. "Bye, have fun!" she stated before she slammed the door at an astonished Aiden.

Aiden wondered what the hell had just happened.

. . . . .

Aiden was in a sour mood when he entered his robotics class. Things were awry in his life and he had no proper explanation for them. He hoped spending some time with electronic circuits would take his mind off worrying matters. And he would probably meet Scott too, the man had been impossible to contact since the night before.

Dominic and Storm greeted him as he entered. Scott, their instructor was still to come. Aiden settled down next to the pair and took out the necessary equipment from his bag.

"Did you finish reading the microcontrollers book I gave you day before?" Dominic asked, turning sideways to face Aiden. Aiden slapped his forehead; he had completely forgotten that Dominic had given him that book to read up before they properly started the microcontroller bit of the project. Dominic had even stressed of the importance of him understanding the concepts properly before they started.

"Did you at least get the green LED's and 9V battery from the shop at Crawfy market?" Dominic had his eye brows raised. Aiden felt like shit. He had forgotten about that as well. And this was Dominic here grilling him. How the hell could he have forgotten something Dominic had asked him to do; and not only one thing, but two?

"Shit, sorry. I forgot," Aiden looked mournfully at his friend who gave him a highly disappointed look. Aiden felt like he would do anything to rid Dominic of that expression. Scott entered the room just then.

"So everyone's all ready to continue?" Scott asked, trying to sound cheerful but Aiden could sense that something was off. Scott looked drained and tired. And he was the kind of guy who always looked fresh. Even his golden blonde hair seemed somewhat matt. Aiden passed it off as his over active imagination and started working on the circuits before him.

White could sense the turmoil going on in the boy's head. He had awakened from Frigeria's soporific spell just a few minutes back and had argued with the raven haired angel to be allowed to go on to the material plane. Ultimately, he had come to meet Aiden against Frigeria's wishes. He still felt weak and there were still scars on his back and torso, but he would try to remain calm in front of Aiden. It seemed Aiden had not yet encountered Arangyunus, which meant the latter was still healing somewhere in the Kingdom Of Void. White continued to subtly assist the trio in their work as they assembled various wires and electronic components.

Aiden was having a hard time concentrating on his work. There were just too many other things racing through his mind. He was working for quite some time quietly next to Dominic when suddenly the latter spoke up. "Aiden, are you and Scott somehow involved together or something?"

Aiden turned 50 shades of red. What the hell was Dominic saying? Did Dominic know that Aiden was gay? Did that fact repulse him? And why the hell was he referring to Scott as well?

What the hell was happening to his world today?

Aiden was saved from further interrogation by Storm; his large frame ambled over to the pair and settled down with them to assist them in their circuit. Aiden could hardly work anymore. His hands were trembling and he could not make sense of what was going on. A few minutes later Scott called it a day and asked everyone to wrap up.

Aiden quietly collected his stuff as Dominic and Storm left the room. He wanted his friends to leave first and go ahead so he would not have to talk to them on the way out. At least the time being, until he readied himself mentally to answer any questions Dominic had.

White sauntered over and settled down on the stool next to Aiden. He could sense the disheveled mental state the boy was in. And it touched him to the core that the boy was so disturbed. Telling the boy about the devil Arangyunus was not an option currently. The boy would probably break down entirely. So what could he do to help?

"Where did you disappear yesterday?" Aiden asked in a slightly acerbic tone. White was surprised at the sudden question. But he knew he was partly at fault for the Alchemist's current state.

"I, err, got stuck in some important work," he fibbed. "A friend came over and I had to go pick him up at the airport."

"I wanted you to meet Will."

White exhaled long and hard. He definitely had met Will. It was just that the Alchemist had no clue of it. "It's ok; I'll meet him next time. I did message you stating that I had to leave though," he stated as if that justified everything. White was lying through his teeth. And he sucked at it. At that moment Aiden could clearly read it on Scott's face that the latter was lying and White himself was aware that Aiden could see right through him.

Aiden chewed his lips nervously. Life suddenly seemed shallow to him. Meanwhile White was having a hard time keeping his feelings in control. The Alchemist was radiating need for compassion like a raging fire. His sorrow was affecting the entire atmosphere around. He seemed so innocent and so vulnerable. The fragility of the boy suddenly overwhelmed him. He could not resist it any longer. He closed his eyes, moved towards Aiden and slowly lowered himself to kiss the boy.

Aiden did not move budge his sitting position. White had pressed his lips against him. But Aiden had not let himself be kissed. Two fingers separated the two pairs of lips; one index and one middle finger, both belonging to Aiden, that had been gently but firmly placed before their lips could meet. Those fingers of his acted as a barrier, preventing their lips from meeting.

White opened his eyes when he felt hard fingernails rather than soft lips. And then he saw the sorrow in the boy's eyes. The boy did not want this to happen.

Aiden silently raised himself from the stool and picked up his bag. White looked at him with deep rooted grief. What had he done? He did not know what to say anymore. He watched with a sorrowful expression as Aiden quietly left the room. He did not know what to say. Why had he suddenly lost control? Why had he done that?

White wished he had the power to turn back time.

. . . . .

Aiden slammed the door of Will's black Lamborghini as he got in. He turned the key and revved up the engine. The car purred to life as he ruthlessly pressed the accelerator and sped off.

He was confused earlier. Now his mind was in a state of utter chaos. His whole world had turned upside down. First there was Scott and Will who had left him in the lurch the previous night without any semblance of a proper explanation. Then there was Jason who he was slowly losing; trying to talk to Jason was like pouring water over a buffalo; it all just splashed down without affecting the buffalo in the slightest bit. Then there was Will who had jilted him a few hours back by neglecting his needs, and seemed to think that a sleek car could be used to bribe his lover. Dominic had shown disappointment in him on two fronts as well; first on responsibility and then had hinted that he knew Aiden was gay. And he had even accused him of being involved with Scott. And what the hell had Scott attempted right now? Why the fuck had he tried to kiss him?

Aiden pressed his foot on the accelerator even harder as he shifted the gear to a reckless level. He was pissed, angry and muddled. Who should he go to now? Will and Scott were out of the question. So were Dominic and Storm. He was avoiding even Tinka since the previous day's visit to Will's retirement home. Who would he turn to now?

Just then Aiden noticed Jason walking on the opposite side of the road. He had his I-Pod earphones plugged in and was strolling back to college campus. Jason's head turned as he followed the motion of the svelte black car as it sped by.

Aiden decided this was it. He braked abruptly as the tires screeched and took a maniacal u-turn. Jason watched open-mouthed, paralyzed on the spot as the car skidded to a halt next to him. The passenger door slid up as Aiden greeted him with a determined expression on his face.

"Get in Jase."

Jason frantically looked around before he shrugged his shoulders and got in. The door slid down.

'At least the car can be used to intoxicate Jason', Aiden thought to himself. He switched gears as the car zoomed ahead.

"Jason, I really needed to talk to you before, but you wouldn't let me."

Jason face grew flustered. Between the enthralling effect the car was having on him, and Aiden's inquisitions and confessions, he did not know how to respond.

Aiden steeled himself as he blurted out, "Jason, I'm gay."

Aiden turned to watch Jason's expression as the boy turned crimson. "Yeah… ok," Jason replied in a timid voice.

"This car is Will's," Aiden continued, "And he's my boyfriend." Aiden was not so sure anymore if he could use that term for Will. Was Will his boyfriend anymore? He sure was not acting like it since the previous night. Then he cursed himself for thinking negative thoughts about someone who had given him so much joy.

"Ok," was all Jason replied in an even feebler voice. Aiden did not know what to say anymore. Jason looked absolutely crestfallen; as if he himself had just been outed or something. The car screeched to a halt once more as Aiden slammed on the brakes.

"Jason, you can leave if you want to now." Jason let out a whoosh of air as he slid the door up and scrambled out.

"Jase," Aiden called out as the fumbling form bend over to listen before he dashed off. "I'm still your friend."

"Yes," was all Jason stated in a goofy manner before he literally fled from the spot. Aiden stared at his eyes in the rearview mirror. They looked bloodshot, as if he had not slept for days.

He wondered how things would turn out in the time to come.

·····

Black opened his eyes from a forced slumber. Immediately he made out the form of his Empress waiting for him to gain consciousness.

"You're awake Arangyunus," The little lass stated coldly. "Awake and unbridled."

Black tried to raise himself from the platform he lay on. He still felt weak though the agonizing pain he had felt when he had last gained consciousness was no longer there.

"And you shall be unbridled no more," the little girl stated as she held up a shiny stone for Black to see. Black was confused at his Mistress' behavior. What was she doing?

And with a sudden motion the Empress flung the stone at him. Black felt a stinging pain as the gem struck him on his torso directly over where his heart was and remained stuck there for a few moments. He looked helplessly at his Mistress, his eyes begging o know what she was doing to him.

The Stone suddenly burst out into black flames as it started to get absorbed into Black's body. Black looked in fear as the gem sunk slowly into his chest and his body absorbed it. He caught hold of the crystal with one hand and tugged at it fruitlessly. The stone showed no signs of stopping its sinking motion.

Black looked up with apprehension and terror on his face. What was Empress Woe doing to him?

And slowly the stone sunk in completely and incorporated itself into his heart. All signs of question and trepidation immediately vanished as the stone completed its preparation. Black stood rigid and straight as his eyes turned from intense green to icy white for a couple of seconds before they returned to their normal state; a sign that the parasite had worked. He then immediately fell to his knees to bow in front of his mistress.

"You had gotten too wild Aranyunus. It is time that I fully control you."

And that is exactly what the little girl intended to do with the 'Stone of Subjugation', the stone that lay buried deep inside the dark angel.

. . . . .

Episode Six

His own thoughts had caused him too much trauma and helplessness before, and Aiden was finally letting go and enjoying himself. A naked Will had him pressed against a wall as they fiercely kissed, while Will ground his crotch against a fully clothed Aiden. The younger boy elicited moans that were greedily captured by his lover's mouth, barely giving him any space to breathe.

There was some confusion in the back of Aiden's mind. Why had Will been acting weirdly and even cold-shouldering him earlier? But he let those thoughts melt away as he lost himself in the passionate lover that was Will; the great solid chiseled body, the perfect musculature, the soft lips and aquiline face; all topped off with a healthy dose of passion.

Will kissed Aiden almost punishingly. He was firmly geld against the wall as Will continued to ravage his mouth, then slipped his hand into the waist band of jeans and began tugging them down, forcing his lover to join his state of nakedness. Aiden was having a hard time breathing, sucking at the air in Will's mouth to sustain his own respiration. He was hot and heavy and could not sense anything other than the flood of sensations Will was making him experience.

Will suddenly jerked up Aiden's thighs, making them straddle his hips on either side. Still smothering Aiden's lips with his own, he stumbled as he walked for both of them towards the bedroom. Upon reaching there he unceremoniously dumped Aiden on the bed. Aiden writhed about and struggled to get out of his confining clothes moaning 'I want you so bad'.

While smiled evilly and pounced upon Aiden who had barely gotten rid of his underwear till then. Will was back to punishing Aiden's lips and greedily bit them as he forced his mouth upon them. Aiden was certain that his lips would be all swollen and puffy later, but he did not care about that. Will and he had had rough sex the first few days after they met, but it had become more of gentle love-making sessions ever since the day he was anxious when Tinka had first cast aspersions on Will. Now seemingly Will was back to wanting it rough and animalistic and Aiden was fine with that. He opened his eyes and noticed Will's hungry ones. Then he noticed something was a little off with Will's eyes. There was a white glint along the cornea which was slowly dissolving as he watched. Was he hallucinating?

As Will pressed himself further into the boy, he suddenly reached below and started guiding his rock hard erection into Aiden. Aiden was shocked. Will was not using a condom. He was pressing against his hole aggressively now. Aiden shut his eyes tightly and braced himself for the pain as Will continued to enter him while at the same time ravenously attacked his mouth. They had never had sex without a condom before. Why was Will wanting it now? Maybe he was so high that he had lost control; but should Aiden himself allow it?

Aiden groaned, more with pain than with pleasure, but his groans were lost in Will's mouth. Aiden knew that whatever was happening was not what he would have approved of in his normal state of mind, but then he thought of how Will had been snubbing him recently. If he denied Will right now, the chasm between them might grow further. Aiden had no intention of losing Will. He gasped with pain as Will entered him fully, his pubes coming in contact with Aiden's ass cheeks, Aiden on his back and his legs flung wildly into the air.

Will withdrew all the way outside and slammed back into the boy. Aiden yelped with pain and squirmed as he lightly pressed his knees against Will's chest, signaling him to take it slow. But it seemed Will had other things in mind. Will withdrew till the head once more and foisted his hard member inside Aiden's hole.

"Will…" Aiden cried out in the middle of mind-numbing pain; pain that was excruciating. That's when Will picked up pace.

Will wildly pulled in and out and stared to savagely fuck the Alchemist. Fucking him like a sore pig. Pistoning in and out, driving his member till the last millimeter, as Aiden's ass muscles lost all hope and screamed in pain. But Will had only just begun. The veins on his penis distended obscenely as he continued to brutalize the boy. He had pinned down Aiden's hands on either side of the boy and was ingesting all the boy's screams, capturing them with his own mouth.

Aiden was in hell. His anus ring was burning, making him experience pain he had never felt before in his life. The lack of lubrication, Will's pace and his huge dick were too much for him. He was struggling and writhing beneath the demonic form of Will which continued to assault him. His muscles were sore from the fruitless struggle he was using to get Will to stop, his strength insignificant in front of his powerful lover. Will had fingers of both hands tightly interlocked with Aiden as he held his hands against the bed sheet. Aiden was trying to bite onto Will's mouth but it was proving ineffective as Will even continued to batter his mouth. The boy was not even being able to ask for him to stop. Tears left his eyes owing to the unbearable pain

Suddenly Will let go of Aiden's mouth to gasp for breath. Aiden seized the moment as he let out a high pitched scream. "WIIILLLL STOP!"

Will stopped moving as Aiden looked up into the eyes of his lover. They were white in color, and he was sure of it this time. They were watering and turning lucid slowly, as if Will wanted to cry. And they were returning to their intense green shade. Suddenly Will balked as the forces of Subjugation overpowered him once more. He would continue his brutalization of the boy.

But Aiden had had enough. He instantly brought both his feet against Will's pectorals and kicked with all his strength.

Will went sailing through the air as he crashed into a wall behind, his head slamming the wall as he plummeted into it. And there he sat still upright, his eyes wide open. They were White in color.

Aiden mustered all his strength as he jumped off the bed. There were tears streaming down his face. Tears of pain. Aiden hated crying.

"What's wrong with you Will?" he bellowed almost pleadingly. Will did not answer. He just continued to stare at the boy in front of him. Aiden's ass was hurting bad. He was pretty sure he was bleeding, but could not muster the courage to reach a hand behind to check. He looked about frantically for his clothes and then quickly slipped on his jeans skipping his underwear. He was getting out of there as fast as possible; as fast as the current state of his body allowed him.

Aiden wiped the tears on his face with the back of his hand as he quickly collected his stuff and fled from the room.

Will stretched out a hand as if begging him to stop. "Aiden." He called out softly, but the boy was not listening. The door slammed as Aiden bolted from the flat.

. . . . .

Aiden's entire body hurt. His muscles were burning. His butt hurt like a thousand stinging needles. But none of that pain matched the pain in his heart. He hated the fact that tears had recently left his eyes; even though they had been tears of pain. He never cried.

Aiden ran out of Will's building entrance as fast as he could. He had no car this time. He would have to run towards college on foot. What would he do now?

'What was wrong with Will?' he questioned himself again and again. 'What happened to Will suddenly?' 'Why had Will tried to rape him?' Aiden felt contempt at himself as he thought about how he himself must somehow be at fault for all this.

His whole world had gone drastically awry in the last one day. From rejection to doubts and anxiety, from accusations to long formed friendships at the brink of destruction, from confused friends to misguided lovers, from lovers to savage abusers; what the fuck was happening to his world?

Aiden continued running towards his college as he contemplated what he should do. He wished that the earth would just open up and swallow him up. Maybe he should just jump over the bridge to his death. But isn't suicide for cowards who can't face the tribulations of life. Isn't that throwing away precious life?

A heavy fog was gradually descending as Aiden ran. It being late evening, the surroundings were dark and they were now being heavily shrouded. Aiden's footsteps resounded all along the pavements he ran. The boy was scared. Why had his lover treated him like that? Why had he been so brutal? What kind of beast had gotten into him? Is this how beautiful people toyed around with inferior looking ones? Play around with their feelings and then use them as trash cans? Was this what Will thought of him; treat him like a charity case for some time, coddle him all along and then trample all over him?

Aiden felt sick at himself for all the negative thoughts. There had to be an explanation for all of it. Will was not like this. After all, had he not said that he would always stay by his side? And what was that white glow in his eyes that he had noticed? There was one more thing Aiden did not want to admit to himself at the time, but he was certain that he had seen extreme sorrow and regret on Will's face when he had hastily departed from his apartment.

Aiden slowed down his running gasping for breath. The fog around him was getting thicker and thicker. It was hardly possible to see more than a few feet anymore. Their town barely experienced fog this thick.

Aiden halted to catch his breath. His body was still sore and his butt was absolutely raging with pain. Even the weather seemed to be working against him now. He balked as he heard footsteps coming towards him. Someone was approaching. He strained his eyes in the direction of the footsteps. A tall shape was slowly appearing amidst the thick smoke.

Aiden braced himself as he thought about how he would face his rapist of a lover.

The shape gradually emerged from the mist.

It was Scott; Scott White.

·····

Will sobbed uncontrollably as his entire body shook and shuddered. What was happening to him? Why could he not control himself? What had he just done? Why had he hurt his love?

Aiden had begged him to stop and he had ruthlessly continued. The eyes of his lover had cried out in pain and hurt and he himself wanted nothing more than to stop and comfort his lover. But he had not been able to do that. What had his Empress done to him?

The air before the shuddering fallen angel began to warp and deform as slowly a young girl with golden tresses and blue eyes appeared on the material plane. Empress Woe had appeared before her servant. But she did not have much time. Night would fall soon and she would be forced to return to the Kingdom of Void.

"You, Arangyunus, have become pathetic!" The little girl held out her right palm and stretched the fingers apart, hovering above Black's chest. A dark glow emanated from her digits as Black suddenly lurched forward and blood gushed out from his mouth.

"And I am forced to do this to you," the little girl continued as the eyes of her guardian were being forced to turn to a milky white shade.

The Empress had had enough. She had waited too long for the Alchemist to come willingly to her. And now even her own servant was serving her unwillingly. He had even managed to momentarily counter the dominance of the 'Stone of Subjugation', all saturated in those icky feelings of love and compassion he felt for the boy. Feelings that were even overwhelming his loyalty to her. She would not tolerate it. She would force Black to place her will at first priority, no matter what the cost.

She withdrew her hand as she finished maximizing the effects of the Stone embedded into Black's heart. Now he would obey her even as his heart bled.

All she had to do now was to make him find the Alchemist and quickly set matters right. Wooing the Alchemist would come to an abrupt halt now. She would resort to coercing the boy to do her will. And if the alchemist went out of control, she would kill him.

. . . . .

Aiden flinched as Scott neared him. He was in an unstable mood. Scott neared him with a look of sorrow, with empathy in his eyes, but Aiden was not sure how Scott would react now; and more importantly, how he should react. Shouldn't he just run away from there? Scott had tried to make a move on him earlier. What would Scott attempt to do now? Rape him?

"Aiden." Scott called out softly as he stepped towards him slowly.

Aiden had a pained expression on his face as he took a tiny step backwards. His body was burning all over. Should he shut out this friend too? He had been running away from everything.

"Aiden please." Scott called out. The mighty angel was having an arduous time with the boy. And all he wanted right now was to comfort and protect him.

"Please Aiden, I will not do anything that displeases you."

The pupils of Aiden's eyes were shaking unsteadily. Then suddenly he relaxed and let his body loose. Immediately Scott stepped forward and enveloped him in his alms. Aiden made no attempt to shrug him off. He just let himself loose in the warm embrace that was the mighty Keeper of the Light.

White hugged the alchemist protectively in his alms, the embrace firm enough to let the boy know of the security he intended to offer. Fog was thick around the conjoined pair, fog that the white angel had summoned. He put a hand over Aiden's head who sighed and rested his head upon the sturdy man's shoulder. The mighty angel had wanted to hug the boy since so long. Just hold him tight and kiss him. But he would have to curb all his longings.

White sensed the extreme discomfort and restlessness the boy was experiencing, even the physical pain burning through him. Slowly he crept into the boys mind and chanted a lulling spell into it. The boy would relax and fall asleep. White had promised never to enter the boy's mind unless a dire situation required him to do so. Now seemed the time.

Aiden felt his entire body relaxing, the physical pain was magically subsiding. His tense body was slowly falling slack against Scott's solid body. There was thick fog around them and visibility was reduced to zero. But he did not care for the time being. His eye lids were getting heavy as he felt something warm and fluffy enveloping his entire body, wrapping itself around him. He wondered what it was but his eyes would not open, he was too lost in the soporific effect Scott was having on him; soporific and calming. He trusted Scott, despite what he had attempted earlier. The last thing Aiden saw in his mind before he slipped into a peaceful slumber was Will's face; happy and smiling; telling him he would always stay by his side.

White had brought out his great wings. The spotless wings were wrapped around the boy, protecting him from the chilled air and from dangers unseen. He gently held the boy as he fell asleep and then easily lifted him into his alms, walking over to a bench on the pavement side and lying down on it along with Aiden on top off him, still cocooned in his pearly wings, wings that resembled soft white petals of roses, warm, safe and peaceful. He stretched out an arm from beneath wings as Aiden squirmed in his sleep.

"Guardian Ability 12; Sheltered Enclave." Spiritual energies dissipated from his hand and formed a spherical cordon around the lying pair. The cordon would prevent people from noticing them there throughout the night. It would also shield them from Empress Woe and Black's scouting techniques.

White slipped back his arm around Aiden who smiled in his sleep and held onto him tighter. The great white angel looked down at the peaceful sleeping face of the boy, feeling happy that he could at least momentarily rid the boy of the demons that had possessed him until a few minutes back. He knew not what lay ahead of them, but he knew on thing, he would give his all to protect the boy.

. . . . .

The Empress was furious. She had spent a restless eight hours - the night time on the material plane, fruitlessly searching for the alchemist. But the boy had simply vanished. All efforts to try and trace him had been in vain. And now she was back on the material plane; she had gotten there at the first crack of dawn and ordered Black to try and track down the Alchemist as well. Where was the boy? Had Witenhoem gotten him before? The consequences of that would be drastic.

The Empress had split from her guardian to speed up the search. She had been telepathically relaying messages to Black all along but the two of them were having no luck. She beckoned Black to meet up with her soon.

Using spells and tracing techniques seemed to be pointless. She and Black would have to physically travel to various places the boy would frequent and see if they could pick up any trace of him.

. . . . .

Aiden lolled about lazily as something vibrated against his leg. He felt the hard surface on which he lay and wondered where the warm feeling that had enveloped him till a few moments back had vanished. Suddenly he jerked up awake. His phone was buzzing in the pockets of his jeans, and that had been the juddering feeling against his leg.

He looked about frantically as he dug his hand into his pocket to retrieve the phone. It was early morning. He had been sleeping on a sidewalk bench all night? How did he end up here? He glanced at his phone display. 7:03 AM on a Monday morning; and it was Dominic calling.

"Hello." Aiden whispered into the phone holding in his breath as memories of the previous day crashed through his mind, overwhelming all his senses.

"Aiden, it's me. Where are you?"

"Uh, I'm…" Aiden looked about frantically and caught sight of Scott who was squatting atop a five foot fence with his alms hanging down loose. Scott grinned sheepishly as he realized Aiden had noticed him. Blue eyes and shining golden hair; he was every bit as stunning as Aiden remembered him to be.

"Aiden I am at your dorm room right now, and you're not here. I need to talk to you," Dominic stated impatiently from the other side of the line. "Where are you?"

Aiden was still staring at the picturesque vision of the beautiful man before him. Had this man watched over him all night? That was too weird!

"I'm just, just outside right now," Aiden finally stammered back into the phone. "Why do you need to talk?" he whispered fearing the worst.

"Can you meet me outside Café beans in 20 minutes?"

"Yeah, that'll be…"

"Fine then, see you there."

Aiden heard the phone click as Dominic disconnected the line. What was going on? He looked at his phone display to find three missed calls by Dominic. Was he sleeping so peacefully that he had not waken up earlier? He usually slept like a watchdog; awaking at the slightest sound or movement.

"Scott," Aiden took a deep breath before asking. "Did I spend the entire night here?"

"Yup." Scott replied cheekily as he jumped down form the fence.

"And you were there too?" Aiden asked incredulously.

"Yup; watching over you."

Aiden turned red. He was feeling all warm and tingly inside, but this was way too weird for him. "Err, I'm sorry about last night; was having a really rough time."

"No problem." Scott replied with a sad smile on his face. It was a pleasure to look after you."

Aiden was at a loss of words. A pair off joggers trotted by, frowning at a groggy boy who just awoke after a night's sleep on the sidewalk bench. He swung his legs and got off the bench in one swift motion. He had no idea what to say to Scott. But he had to meet Dominic in 20 minutes and he had to take care off his breath and hair before that.

"Ok, I gotta go now." He stated flatly as he collected himself and straightened his clothes.

"Ok," was all Scott stated.

Aiden stole one last glance at the scenic view of the hunk before he walked trotted towards the Café and slowly picked up pace till he attained a good jogging speed. He was meeting Dominic in the next few minutes. And he reckoned that they would probably have the conversation from hell.

. . . . .

Tinka hated 'Site Plan Study' days. But what she hated more were overeager teammates that dragged her onto the Site at 5:30 in the morning on a Monday. She had been awake and moving about for almost 2 hours now, and she was touchy as hell. She yawned without covering her mouth as Chad, one of her team members, and the highest GPA scorer in the class, ordered her to take a panoramic picture from the top of the railway bridge.

Tinka cursed under her breath as she climbed up the foot over bridge. There was no refusing Chad. He would make all four of them slog their butts till the entire project was completed to the last possible detail. Well maybe she would get a good grade this time and some of the hard work would pay off. She lumbered up the steps and walked to the middle of the over bridge. She took out her camera and focused on the scenery before her. Lots of green trees; that meant more coloring work in sheets, some structures; well that would mean lots of milieu consideration too and lots of people wandering about. Why the hell had her team chosen this place to present their project on? 'Oh yeah', Tinka reminded herself, 'Chad had found the site to be just right for their project.'

Suddenly Tinka noticed someone familiar. She zoomed in with her camera to make sure. Yup; it was him. What the hell was he doing here early Monday morning? And who was that little girl by his side?

The clunk of a metal piece was heard as the expensive camera left Tinka's hands and fell to the floor with a crash. Tinka gasped as restricted memories first unfettered themselves and then ran rampant in her mind. Memories of a dark horrific place. Memories of two terrible forms. Memories of a little girl with flowing yellow hair and crystal blue eyes. Memories of Aiden's lover Will thrashing about on the floor. Memories that had been sealed capsulated, locked away somewhere in her mind which she had just obtained the key for. And the stimulation for the key had been a glimpse of the little girl herself. The little girl that had been sitting on a throne in the dark chamber.

Tinka had just seen Will with that very little girl. Her head throbbed as forbidden memories unleashed themselves into her mind. It seemed bizarre that she had somehow forgotten all this. Or maybe she had been made to forget them! Things that were so unbelievable, that they could not possibly be true. Yet, she was certain that they were.

All her grogginess left her as the desperate girl dived into her bag for her phone and frantically dialed Aiden's number. What would she say to him?

.....

White was following the Alchemist everywhere. Concealing himself by invisible, he had followed the boy all the way to the coffee café and had even followed him inside the public washroom where the boy had washed his face and rinsed his mouth. Turning invisible caused White himself to lose his vision, following the inescapable laws of physics, but he could rely on other senses of his to tell him what was where.

He was still forming an enclave all around the boy, an enclave that prevented other beings from tracing the boy spiritually. But maintaining the enclave for such a long time was costing him much of his energy; he knew that the oncoming battle was unavoidable. The war would begin soon and he had to conserve energy for that.

He waited patiently in the background as Aiden stood outside the coffee café.

.....

Aiden shifted his weight from one foot to the other while waiting. He briefly thought about what had transpired between him and Will the previous night. All the negative vibes, the trauma and the pain. But surprisingly all that physical pain had disappeared; simply vanished. He was sure his butt would be sore as hell for at least a couple of days after what had transpired the previous day, but there seemed to be absolutely no pain whatsoever. Had it not been as violent and intense as he thought it had? Maybe he had been dreaming things.

The drone of a motorbike engine informed him that Dominic had arrived. Aiden stopped breathing for a few seconds, trying to read Dominic's expression as he got off his bike in the distance. Dominic gave a slight smile to him as he dismounted and made his way towards a queasy Aiden.

Suddenly Aiden's phone buzzed. He fished it out of his pocket to find Tinka calling. 'A lot of people seem to be awake and about today morning', he thought to himself as he pressed the red button and ended the phone call without answering it. Tinka would have to wait for now.

Dominic walked up to Aiden and stood unsteadily; Aiden himself was feeling discomfited and chewed on his lower lip; a sign that he was extremely nervous. The two glanced at each other in an awkward manner; till finally Dominic broke the silence.

"I had to talk about something, Aiden."

Aiden was trembling all over. Here was the guy he had been in love with for more than two years, and who was finally confronting him about his sexuality; though it was not at an opportune time, nor through his own choice, but here it was, all coming out finally. Here was the boy who he considered absolutely flawless; his chiseled face and aquiline looks that were obviously no where near Will's or Scott's, but whose character he knew from two years of experience was absolutely impeccable; the complete package and Aiden's ultimate idol.

Aiden was sure this ultimate idol was going to think of him as a much lesser person after this conversation. How many 'outings' were these few days going to witness?

"Aiden, I know that you're gay." Dominic let out in one breath as Aiden blanched. "I mean, I'm very sure of it; you are, aren't you?"

Aiden nodded his head slightly in agreement. Guilty as charged; there was no way out of this. He was momentarily distracted as his phone was buzzing in his hand again. It was Tinka. He disconnected the call once more.

"And I'm perfectly fine with that. I mean, you're still YOU right?"

"You are?" Aiden asked in a timid voice.

"I'm what?" Dominic asked confused.

"You're fine with it?" Aiden asked his voice trembling.

"Yeah. Yes, I am perfectly fine with it." Dominic stammered back. Nervousness interlaced with awkwardness was heavy in the air. Aiden felt like he would choke on the uneasy atmosphere alone and die.

"And Scott is your boyfriend?"

"No he's not!" Aiden bellowed his voice going out of control, then he reiterated in a softer voice, "No he's not."

"Err…then" Dominic was thrown off guard.

"Actually I have a boy friend and his name's Will," Aiden replied, though he was again not so sure anymore. "Scott's just a friend."

"Ha," Dominic stated softly. "Just a friend huh? Well Scott is always talking about you and always seems to be pre-occupied with you. I thought he was definitely your boyfriend or something."

"I mean he's pretty hot." Dominic stated after taking a deep breath.

Aiden swallowed a lump in his throat. Had Dominic just called another guy hot?

"He's not as hot as my boyfriend Will though." Aiden growled in a low voice.

That broke the uncomfortable awkwardness between the two as both of them suddenly burst out laughing. Aiden was all smiles as it looked like his friend was going to accept him.

"So who's this boyfriend of yours?"

"You won't know him, he's a social worker." Aiden stated triumphantly. "He lives just off the docks."

"So that's where you spend your nights!" Dominic raised his voice as he stated. "You're never available in the evenings and nights! You're sleeping with him everyday?"

Aiden blushed as he nodded and admitted the same to Dominic.

"Damn!" Dominic stated. "And to think I'm still a virgin."

Aiden was shocked. That was a bit too much information from Dominic for the present moment.

"I mean I've hardly kissed a girl before you know."

"Uh huh." Aiden stated as he nodded his head furiously. This conversation was taking an uncomfortable turn once more. He simply did not need to hear of all this from Dominic. Did Dominic want to be kissed? If so, Aiden sure was ready to do the honors!

"But I guess you don't need to know that." Dominic stated smiling, all his straight white teeth showing.

"Yeah, whatever." Aiden replied smiling. Somehow Dominic stating these facts were a sign from him that he totally accepted Aiden.

"But I need you to know that I am totally cool with it and you can talk to me about it and nothing changes between us," Dominic stated in one long sentence.

"Thanks. That means a lot to me."

"So you coming to class? We have an early lecture at 8 O' clock today."

"Yup, just a sec." Aiden stated as his phone buzzed once more. It was Tinka. Aiden knew she would be mad for him not taking her earlier calls, but this was way too important for interruptions.

"Yeah sorry!" Aiden stated as he picked up the call this time.

"Aiden!" Tinka's voice nearly screamed from the other side. "Why the fuck are you not picking up my calls?"

"Uhh, I was busy with Dominic here, we were…"

"Where the fuck are you right now?" Tinka screamed from the other side.

"Outside Café Beans. Why?"

Tinka calmed down a little before she spoke again. She needed to talk to Aiden but could not mention it was about Will. Aiden would shut down on her if she did.

"I need to tell you something. Just stay right where you are. I'll be there in 15 minutes!"

"Wait, wait, is it important? Can we talk during lunchtime? I have a lecture at 8."

"Balls to your lecture!" Tinka fumed from the other side. "Stay right where you are, I'll be there in a few."

Aiden was left muttering as Tinka disconnected the call. Dominic looked at him with a questioning look on his face.

"Sorry man." Aiden said to Dominic apologetically. "Can't come with you to class right now. Tinka's on my case right now. Have to stay here to meet her."

"No probs." Dominic sated cheerfully before he hesitated and asked next, "So I guess she isn't your girlfriend or anything? I always thought you two were a couple before."

"Thank heavens we're not a couple. We would NOT comprise a happy family."

Dominic chuckled before he said bye and left Aiden standing; all set for one more conversation. Aiden hoped this conversation would work out to be as pleasant as the previous one. Or would it? He wondered what it was that Tinka needed to so desperately discuss with him.

.....

Frigeria, the raven haired angel from the Kingdom of Light, stood watching patiently as the Alchemist said goodbye to one friend and waited for another. She could see that things were changing in the boy's life, taking all sorts of twists and turns. But the real tribulations were yet to come, and they were approaching fast.

She knew that White was following the boy, keeping a watch on him and was vigilant of enemy influences, constantly on the lookout for them. She knew he had turned invisible and had been following the boy all along. But she also knew that White had not detected her; while constantly being watchful for Empress Woe and Black, White had not sensed her presence, and it was for the better.

The Alchemist needed to know of certain things, things that the mighty white angel was scared of telling him or simply did not know about. It was time for Frigeria herself to intervene.

.....

Aiden once more waited impatiently as minutes ticked by, shifting his weight from one foot to the other yet again, wishing there was a bench nearby to sit on. The coffee shop was still not open so early in the morning.

He tried to stop thinking of what Tinka needed to talk to him about. He would know in a few minutes anyway. Instead his mind shifted to thoughts about Will. He was tired of trying to think of all possible explanations of last night's encounter with Will. And what was that white turbid color he had seen Will's eyes saturate into? That was eerie and... sad at the same time. 'Maybe I should call Will' Aiden muttered to himself after much rationalization.

Aiden lifted his handset and searched for Will's number. A high pitched voice screeched from behind as he was just about to press the call button.

"Thank God you're here!" It was Tinka.

"Hey Tinks," Aiden smiled at her. "What's going on?" Aiden had not met Tinka since Saturday and was not sure how he should talk to her presently. But she was still his best friend, wasn't she? He desperately wanted to tell her of the meeting with Dominic just before, but reasoned he would have to wait his turn.

"Ok, Aiden." Tinka stated grasping both of Aiden's elbows and half dragging a protesting Aiden towards the side alley of the coffee shop. "I have something to tell you and it's gonna sound really stupid and unbelievable, but it's the truth."

"Ok," Aiden was trying to remain patient.

"I know I have said this before but Will is not what he says he is and now I am sure of it."

Tinka paused to observe Aiden's expression. She hated going against Will again but she had to do it one more time.

"Will is not a normal human being." Tinka cleared her throat before she continued. "He's some sort of magician or sorcerer or something, and he's after you."

Aiden's eyes opened wide as he waited for Tinka to continue. Surely this was one of her jokes where she would burst out into laughter any moment and state that she'd 'got back at him'.

"Ok, this is gonna be weird but I am gonna tell you what I saw on Saturday when we went to the retirement home."

"Tinks, please stop."

"Aiden, I know you think I'm crazy or something but you have got to listen to me. Please. Just once, hear about what I saw."

Aiden swallowed as he nodded for Tinka to continue.

"The other day when I came out of the washroom I saw in another room, these slimy eerie squid like monsters and I screamed. Just then Will appeared behind me form nowhere and his hand glowed as he used some sort of weird… 'magic thing' on me. Everything turned black after that."

Aiden was biting his lips once again unable to understand what Tinka was trying to tell him.

"When I came to, I was in a dark eerie place, darkness with thousands of colorful stones glowing all around, and I saw Will writhing in pain before me. In that dark chamber was sitting this small blonde girl that stated that I had seen too much and then she did some psychic shit and my head started hurting."

Aiden opened his mouth to say something but Tinka interrupted him once again. Tinka was going on like a bullet train.

"And then I just remember being back with you in the recreation room. Somehow I had forgotten all about it till I saw Will and that same little girl today."

"Tinks, you've been dreaming." Aiden stated flatly.

"No, I'm not you bozo! Listen to me, it sounds far-fetched but I'm a hundred percent sure it's what I saw. You have to believe me."

"Believe what? All this crap?" Aiden asked incredulously.

"Believe her." A dulcet voice stated from behind, echoing as the tinkering of wind chimes.

Aiden whirled around to find a stunning dark haired woman in white robes slowly advancing towards him. Tinka suddenly saw silver butterflies before her eyes as she lost consciousness and fell to the floor with a thud.

Aiden whirled around once more to find Tinka on the floor and turned back to face this new arrival.

"Who the fuck are you?"

"Believe her; believe that your friend Will is actually the devil." The lady stepped forward and Aiden noticed how beautiful the lady looked, her black hair perfectly straight as it cascaded down her shining white dress.

"Hello Aiden, I'm Frigeria."

.....

White had been following Aiden at a distance, and had followed him as Tinka had pulled him into a side-alley. And he had been startled as he saw Tinka fall to the floor suddenly. Soporific spell? Frigeria was here? Suddenly he himself saw the same sleep inducing butterflies and fell to the floor against his strong will. The spiritual enclave he had been maintaining around Aiden collapsed as he did. Aiden's location was now susceptible to the Empress and to Black.

Not far away, the Empress suddenly received a positive signal from Aiden's search link, which disappeared as abruptly as it had appeared. She had traced Aiden and had lost the trace immediately. She telepathically confirmed with Black to learn that he had picked up the flickering trace too. That meant the Alchemist was on the material plane. And she was even sure that he was nowhere near his 'college' area. She had some idea of the area he was in now. She would have to physically find him.

Physically find him and immediately destroy him. The Alchemist falling into the hands of the enemy was too big a risk now.

.....

Aiden once again found himself in a situation where he had absolutely no idea what was going on. This mesmerizing lady did not seem threatening at all. In fact she had a really soothing aura. Was she going to try anything funny?

Aiden immediately remembered Tinka and fell on his knees, shaking Tinka's shoulders to try and wake her up.

"Tinks, wake up!" Aiden shook the girl back and forth.

"She will not wake up yet." Frigeria stated as suddenly she swished her hands and their surroundings started to deform and saturate into a light blue color.

Aiden stood up abruptly and looked about in a frenzied manner. All around his surroundings were disappearing, being enveloped in an azure color. The morphing of the surroundings reached completion as everything turned a soothing light blue, the ground, the walls, the alley; everything replaced with he same blue shade.

"What the...?" Aiden was still wondering what was happening. Only Frigeria, he and the unconscious form of Tinka remained in this azure universe now.

Frigeria felt White collapse in the vicinity as she send him into a sleepy subliminal state. It was imperative that he did not interfere now, for she had to make revelations to the boy that the mighty white angel would himself never dare to make. And definitely the ones he simply did not know of. She hoped she had set up her enclave perimeter in time to prevent the Empress from detecting Aiden. Nevertheless the enemy would be approaching soon.

"Who are you?" Aiden spat out at Frigeria.

The female angel paused and calmly stated. "I am Frigeria; chief angel healer of the Kingdom of Light."

"Huh?" Aiden had a stupefied expression on his face. The angel's voice resounded across the blue milieu, making it seem as if many melodious voices were speaking at once.

"An angel?"

"Yes, maybe this will convince you." And saying that Frigeria unfolded her great white wings, each more than 10 feet in length, which rose above the two forms and stretched up straight. Aiden could not believe what was happening.

"And I need to talk to you."

Aiden flinched at that line. He was probably hearing it for the umpteenth time in the last 2 days; especially today. First it was Dominic, then Tinka and now it seemed some heavenly angel also 'needed to talk to him'. He was dreaming, wasn't he?

"So err, where are we?"

"Safe, for now."

"And what do we need to talk about?"

"About Black and White."

Aiden's brow furrowed as he realized this 'angel' wanted to talk to him about Will and Scott. Well since this was a dream and Will and Scott seemed to be the most hot topic of discussion nowadays, he might as well play along. He waited for the dark haired angel to begin.

"Since time immemorial, the Kingdom of Light and the Kingdom of Void have been at war. Hazelhoem ruled the Kingdom of Light, a land whose guardian was Witenhoem, and the Kingdom of Void was governed by the seemingly four year old girl; Empress Woe and her Guardian was Arangyunus."

Aiden's brows furrowed further as he took in the big names being thrown at him.

"The Guardian Witenhoem was better known as White, the mighty white angel who was the protector of the Kingdom of Light while the guardian Arangyunus was better known as Black, the dark Seraph who was the protector of the Kingdom of Void. The two were sworn enemies since their time of conception and though counterparts of each other, were arch rivals, forever locked in a power struggle to eliminate the other."

Frigeria paused before continuing, "Then something unexpected happened 800 years ago. Black and White fell in love."

Aiden's eye brows shot up as his ears perked up as well. What was this angel talking about?

Frigeria held out a hand as a silver globe, the size of a football materialized, levitating above her palm. Aiden squinted his eyes and stepped closer, as he made out moving shapes in the sphere.

What he saw left him astounded. He saw Will in a tight embrace with Scott; the two were kissing passionately. But Scott looked almost celestial, with a golden sheen about him and what appeared to be white wings extending from his back. Will looked different with a silver glint across his entire body and massive silver grey wings with black streaks across the edges. Were these forms actually Scott and Will? Watching the scene, Aiden felt excited and repulsed at the same time.

He watched wide eyed as the two broke the kiss and Will gently ran the back of his hand across Scott's jaw.

"But outsiders it seemed, had more than just objections to this forbidden affair. It was love that was doomed from the very beginning."

The two figures in the silver globes vanished as an extremely cute girl with chubby cheeks, long curly golden hair and sparkling blue eyes sitting on an oversized throne appeared in it.

"Empress Woe, from whose elements Black was constituted, did more than just stop the affair. She obliterated Black."

"Obliterated?"

"Yes, she completely disintegrated him and wiped out his existence. She was capable of doing that since Black, her guardian was her own essence." The angel's voice still reverberated across but Aiden had gotten used to it by then

Aiden squirmed as he watched Will recoiling from pain, screaming his guts out as Scott held onto him. Then slowly Will's form burst into flames and exploded, leaving no trace other than soot and dust particles that clung onto Scott giving the beautiful form a funereal appearance. Scott sobbed uncontrollably, and screamed out his lover's name. Aiden was left astounded, was this really Will?

This was too realistic to be a dream.

"White went into a period of severe mourning after that. He mourned for more than a decade, screaming and crying in emotional pain. Even Hazelhoem could do nothing to comfort him."

"A decade?" Aiden asked bewildered as he watched Scott's figure crouched in the corner of a white marbled room, his body shuddering as he wept, his face hidden amidst his knees.

"Yes a decade. We are Perpetuals that live forever. The pain that White felt would not subside and as much as he desired, he could not end his own existence. It was a curse that he had to live with, forever."

Aiden watched the crying form as his heart wept out for Scott; the magnificent wings he had seen earlier had decayed into wispy tufts of molting feathers. Visions of Scott with blank expressions and those of extreme sadness flashed by in the globe.

"But even Perpetuals sometimes feel they have lived too long. The King of Light, Hazelhoem had aged himself against the Perpetuals intrinsic forces and wished to wipe out his own existence. His powers were waning and he could no longer fight Empress Woe of the Kingdom of Void."

"Hazelhoem wanted nobody other than White to succeed his throne; but he was painfully aware of the state the guardian was in and having waited far too many years for White to get over his emotional scars, he could wait no more."

Aiden watched as a wizened yet imposing old man with a long flowing white beard walked towards an emaciated Scott and gently lay a hand upon him.

"Hazelhoem, who could no longer bear to see the broken form of White, used the remainder of his fading powers and blood sealed White's memories. Encapsulating memories of him ever having fallen in love, of him ever having had a lover who he held dearer than his own existence, within his mind, locked away by the strongest powers of the ruler himself, before he gave up his own existence and safeguarded White from his own memories, leaving him to be the ruler; the Keeper of the Light."

"But then how is Will still alive?"

Frigeria paused to glance at the inquisitive boy, but continued anyway, "White then became the ruler of the Kingdom of Light, and the enemy of Empress Woe who was left without a Guardian herself. The two were enemies that fought many harsh battles as well as many cold wars between themselves. "

"About 5 centuries after this incident, Empress Woe started to reconstitute Black. Black with his former memories locked away in the chasms of his inner mind, a black that would serve as her Guardian and nothing else. It took her over 60 years to finish reconstituting him."

Aiden let out a low whistle listening to this being's tale. Could all this possibly be true?

"So where do I fit into all of this?" he asked impatiently.

"Legend has it hat someday the Alchemist would appear on the material plane; that he would seem human by all other standards, and legend says that this Alchemist would put an end to the war between the Kingdoms of Light and Dark. The Alchemist would possess power beyond the Perpetuals"

Aiden waited impatiently for Frigeria to continue though he feared he now knew the answer to his question. It seemed this angel had a knack for going all the way round whenever he asked her a direct question but the truth was that Frigeria herself was short on time and she had to explain everything to the boy as best and as swiftly as she could.

"That Alchemist is you."

The two of them fell silent as Aiden absorbed this piece of news.

"Me?"

"Yes you. Aiden Writer, I bow to thee, the Alchemist." Frigeria slowly got down on one knee as she bowed her head down, her wings ruffling as she did so. Aiden at once felt awkward. How the hell was he the Alchemist, and why was this angel bowing before him?

"But I don't have any... err... powers or anything. How can I be the Alchemist?"

"You are the Alchemist that had appeared on the material plane after eons of waiting and you are the one that will put an end to this endless battle."

"But what can I possibly..."

"It is you who will have to awaken." The angel bellowed rising sharply and suddenly, a striking change in behavior from a few seconds ago. Her clarion voice echoed as the many clang of bells everywhere. "It is you who must realize that you are the Alchemist and awaken his powers to end this massive battle."

"Err, Ok." Aiden was flustered. "But how?"

"That, my Lord, only you know."

Aiden was displeased at the enigmatic answer. What was he expected to do?

"It is you who must end this battle between the two most ardent lovers that are now enemies, for now they both love only you."

Aiden was taken aback at the last statement.

"And it is time for me to take my leave." Frigeria knew that Black and the Empress were fast approaching. She would have to somehow engage one of them on her own. And these moments would probably be the last few of her perpetual life. The azure surroundings started to dissolve as the ground and the walls of the valleys slowly came back into view. Tinka was also stirring from her slumber.

"Remember Aiden," the raven haired angel stated before she disappeared from view, "Be Strong!"

Aiden watched helplessly as the white clothed figure disappeared from the alley. He stooped down to awaken Tinka, shaking her slightly. The girl opened her eyes groggily.

"What happened?"

Suddenly Aiden heard the sound of running footsteps. He bend over backwards as he tilted half his body out of the alley to see who it was.

It was Will. Running towards him with an expressionless face.

"Will, it's…" but the rest of the words remained stuck in his throat, as out of the blue, Will pulled forth two jagged black blades in is hands and with a battle roar leaped up in the air, gaining altitude before he pounced onto the boy. Aiden stood rooted with fear on the spot, unable to move even an inch as Will brought down the double blades at a high velocity. One strike and Aiden would die. It was all over.

'CLANG.' The noise resounded as the dual blades of alacrity clashed with the Helos Sabre and sparks flew in all directions. Aiden stood shivering with fear as three swords trembled mere inches before his face. Scott had defended him.

Aiden looked questioningly towards Will. His face was expressionless; dead blank; but there were tears streaming down his cheeks.

Scott pushed with all his might and swung around his sword as Will jumped backwards and gradually up erect.

"You're not going to leave a single scar on him Black!" Scott growled.

Things were happening too fast for Aiden to even think about in his mind.

. . . . .

Empress Woe was heading towards the Alchemist. So Black had found the boy and had White engaged him? Very well, she would have to make an appearance now and finish off things. She stopped running as she paused running and slowly disappeared from the material plane. She would teleport directly to the location.

A few seconds later she reappeared on the same dimensions she had disappeared form. She looked around confused. She once again concentrated and tried to appear next to the two guardians and the alchemist. She had to finish the boy off.

Once again she was dumbfounded as she teleported back to the exact same spot. And then she understood. It was an illusionary technique, and she was stuck in someone else's world. She knew only one person who possessed illusory techniques as powerful as this one.

"Frigeria," she muttered with anger. Very well, it would take her some amount of time but she would soon get out of this technique and would kill Frigeria as well. Then she would proceed onwards towards the Alchemist.

. . . . .

Aiden was still trembling with fear as the two fighters assumed combat positions, their swords glistening in the morning sun. Suddenly Black straightened himself as a pair of colossal silver grey wings emerged from his back, tearing across the shirt and standing out in all their glory. The 15 foot wings were jagged with black streaks across the edges and appeared to be comprised of dark gossamer silk, yet seemed strong and erect.

White howled as he too let out the massive white wings Witenhoem was known for; the pearly whites that had dazzled thousands. The cloth on his torso tore across, leaving shreds as the wings unfurled fully and stood up in a v-formation.

Aiden stared wide-eyed, his mouth open. So these were their true forms?

"What's going on?" Tinka asked getting up unsteadily and then noticing the two angels; a dark Seraph and a Keeper of the Light.

"What the fuck?" was all Tinka elicited before she too acquired the expression Aiden had on his face.

"This ends today Arangyunus." White shrieked and leapt into the air flapping his wings as Black followed suit.

Two friends stood bewildered as the two massive shapes rose into the sky and their swords clashed. Aiden shook his head as he realized what the lady angel had been talking about earlier. And if Scott and Will were angels, then was he really this 'Alchemist'?

Aiden abruptly got up and ran towards the fighting figures. Thoughts of Will with tear strained eyes were dominating his mind. If he indeed did want to kill him, why did Will have tears in his eyes? He knew the answer this time; Will was in love with him and somehow was being forced to do things against his will.

Aiden tried to make his way towards the two angels as they clashed in the sky. It was not of much use; they were only going further apart and higher. He watched helplessly as they yelled and swung their swords at each other. How would he get the two to stop?

Aiden looked about as he noticed that 'people' had seen the sights too. And now they stood watching in awe as the spectacle unfolded ahead of them. Aiden did not even want to know what thoughts were going on inside their heads, as he strained his eyes to see the two warriors.

The final battle between Black and White had just begun.

. . . . .

Episode Seven

Jason chewed on his cheese sandwich quietly. He appeared calm on the outside but was actually fuming inside. He hated getting up early, especially on Mondays. In fact, early mornings had been an overbearing decision in the selection of his courses and lectures. He never took any classes that took place before nine. And today, his 'new' girlfriend had called him at 7 in the morning, ordering to meet up at 7:30 in the canteen, before her lecture. Aditi's call had rudely awakened him from his deep slumber, and she'd ordered him to be there. And now, it was 7:45 and there was no sign of the girl. 'So this is the kind of stuff you have to bear with when you go out with a beautiful chick', Jason pondered over his realization.

All the bitterness and resentment on Jason's face vanished as he caught side of a skimpily dressed Aditi in high heels walking hurriedly in towards him. His face immediately assumed a nauseatingly sweet expression, smiling with all his 32 out.

"Hey Jason." Aditi greeted him as she swung a bag around and swished into a chair. Aditi had green eyes now, Jason realized. She always wore lenses that changed her eye color. First it was blue, then brown and now green. Jason was not even sure of the actual color of her eyes.

"I have a lecture in ten, so I have to make this quick," Aditi continued.

Jason raised his eye-brows wondering what 'this' meant. His mind was hyperventilating with paranoia. Was Aditi going to dump him here? A fine start to the week it would be. The girl was fast and shrewd, and he was barely being able to keep up with her. She always got her way. But still, he was madly besotted with her. They called girls like her 'man-eaters' didn't they?

"You've been shunning Aiden and rebuffing him ever since I told you he's gay, haven't you?"

Jason was thrown off for an instant. Where did this topic emerge from?

"Err, huh?"

Aditi gritted her teeth; even though Jason was extremely cheerful and friendly, he was bigoted in some matters. And he was slow at understanding things; sometimes too slow. Aditi spoke clearly and slowly this time.

"Ever since I made you aware of the fact, that Aiden is not only gay but has a boyfriend, you've been totally snubbing him, not hanging out with him at all. Am I right?"

Jason kept his sandwich down on his plate. He had no clue as to how Aditi knew about such a thing, but over the last few days he had realized that the girl's gossip network and reach for new happenings was far more effective than CNN and BBC combined.

Jason made a face. "But he's… you know what."

"He's gay my dear. At least use the word."

Jason inhaled long and deep. This conversation was way too uncomfortable for him.

"Let me ask you this Jason; has Aiden ever made a move on you?"

"What?"

"Had Aiden ever tried to kiss you, grabbed your ass, cupped your crotch - done anything 'gay' with you?"

"What?! No!!"

"So then why are you so paranoid about him being gay? It's not like he wants to marry you or something."

Jason just stared at the girl with eyes that pleaded to change the topic. But since Aditi was on it now, he knew there was no way he was getting off the hook easily.

"Why are you snubbing your roommate, your good friend just on the account of his being gay? C'mon, which planet do you live on? Haven't you met gay people before?"

Jason just swallowed a lump in his throat. He hadn't actually, or had simply turned a blind eye towards them before. He didn't want to say anything, but he would have to hear Aditi till she felt she was through. There was no stopping her.

"I mean, he's probably been your friend for over two years and you can't even accept this part of him? Why are you being such a hypocrite?"

Jason finally opened his mouth. "Because he's a poof."

Aditi sighed. This was like trying to put toothpaste back into a tube.

"But that poof is still your friend you know. And you're letting him down. And he's probably hurt real bad that you can't accept him."

Jason had no answer to that. The girl was right. Through the past few meetings with him, he knew how that Aiden felt deep hurt because of him. He had felt disgust and discomfort. But Aiden had felt plain raw pain. Aiden's face and the expressions he wore when they made contact, had made it apparent to even him.

"He's your friend Jason, and a good one at that too. How can you lose him on something like this?"

Jason dropped his head low. He could barely hear Aditi anymore. All he could think of was Aiden's pained expression when he left him in the car that time. Aditi was making him confront things he had been averting since days. But now here it was, staring him right in the face.

"You can't go on like this you know. And I won't have a bigot for my boyfriend!"

Jason jerked up at the last statement. This was the first time Aditi had used the connotation boyfriend for him; even though it was in a negative aspect.

"Think it over Jason. But do all your thinking quick. You need to apologize to Aiden, and apologize fast. In fact, I want you done with your apology before I meet you in the lunch recess."

Jason opened his mouth to protest as Aditi shot up from the chair and collected her bags.

"And give him a call soon."

That was it. Her decision was made and Jason was to follow accordingly. He grunted as Aditi strode off, her hips swaying. She was one hot babe. Guys were turning around as she passed by. Someone even whistled and Jason turned a little blue with jealousy. He was mad after this girl. The olive honey baked complexion. The perfect figure and the great legs. There was no way he was going to lose her.

Jason eased back into the chair as he picked up his cheese sandwich and nibbled on it again. Aditi was right about him and Aiden, though he was having a tough time admitting it. He had been an asshole. He had no clue what the word bigot meant, but had not wanted to interrupt Aditi to ask that. But he was still being an asshole, and he knew that.

He squirmed once more as a thought of a naked Aiden doing things with Will crossed his mind. Yes, even thinking about that made his stomach turn. Even to the point where it made him feel absolutely disgusted at times. Was it possible for him to relegate those feelings and let friendship occupy higher priority? It was the right thing to do wasn't it? After all, this was his buddy Aiden who was in question.

Aiden, who always paid the most attention to him when he was sick and would assure his worried mother over the phone that he would take care of her son. Aiden who always went swimming with him in the evening when no one else would give him company even though Jason knew he was not so fond of it. Aiden who scolded him for not coming to him sooner when he skidded and took a nasty fall with his cycle and nearly broke his arm; he had felt drowsy after the incident and gone to sleep immediately and Aiden on finding out hours later had rushed along with him to the hospital and insisted that the doctor at least put the slightly swollen arm in a sling. Jason felt sick at himself as he though about how he was abandoning that same Aiden.

The confused roommate brought a hand to his head as he felt his head hurt slightly. This was more thinking and contemplation than he had ever done in his life. He fished out his phone as he dialed the number of his estranged roommate.

Aditi sashayed through the exit door of the canteen, feeling satisfied that she had brushed up Jason good. The sky rumbled and she glanced up at it. The weather was suddenly turning ominous. Thick black clouds were covering the sky fast. She wondered how she'd not noticed the dark sky a few minutes before, when she left to meet Jason. She reckoned she had just been inattentive; it's not like this kind of weather could just suddenly materialize. She mumbled about not getting an umbrella if it suddenly started raining. Her hair would probably get ruined.

She hurried to her lecture hall as streaks of lightning flashed across the sky.

. . . . .

The 'Hourglass of Retrogression' was a powerful artifact. It was a simple delicate glass flask, emblazoned with golden filigree that was owned neither by the Kingdom of Light nor by the Kingdom of Void - it was owned by both, conjointly. It was a super-dominant artifact that could be used to turn back time on the material plane, but one that required both the kingdoms to assent to its use. Its activation required a drop of blood from both the Kingdom's guardians; Black and White.

It seemed to White, that soon that omnipotent artifact would have to be put to use, for tens of thousands of people were witnessing the mega battle that was taking place, a battle between entities with titan wings, as they clashed across the sky, one burning golden, the other immersed in a silver glow. White had even noticed TV camera's aimed towards the dueling duo as people strained to comprehend what was taking place. But he hardly had time to think of it at the time, for the toughest conflict he had ever participated was in progress.

Black charged howling towards his opponent, gaining speed as he nosedived downwards, twisting his wings at an angle that streamlined his motion while White flapped upwards, gaining velocity each time his wings stroked. The two swung there swords out at each other as the dark sky was bathed blinding white by lightning and thunder fulminated.

When the lightning subsided, the two winged beings were on opposite sides - opposite to the ones they had been on before; their backs facing each other after the impact had taken place and their swords had clashed, their wings slowly allowing them to drift apart. Black smiled on one side as White gritted his teeth on the other. He had managed to counter only one of the swords. The other had slashed across his wings; wings that appeared to comprise only of feathers but had muscled veins and tissue underneath it all. The pain was mind numbing.

Black's unharmed wings stretched out as he whirled around and he stretched out both of his hands and chanted; "Internecine Ability 3; Whirling Blackness." A swirling sphere of black and grey shadows materialized in front of his palm.

White immediately held his hand straightforward as he mouthed, "Ability of the Light 21, Flaming Shot", and a red ball of fire materialized before his arm. Black swung out his sword wielding hand, as he flung the destructive ball at White who aimed his own flaming shot at the offensive projectile. The two spheres collided in the space between them, leaving behind burning red embers and black flames.

Immediately the two rushed towards each other again as the sword clashing continued as if in a pre choreographed method. Screeching sounds were heard and lightning flashed each time their swords met.

White was slowly realizing something was different about the Black he was fighting. Why was his enemy using such low spells in the middle of such a high level combat? And there was something wrong in his eyes too. Well, he would take advantage of that. He suddenly increased the pace of his sword movements, pushing back his adversary with quick rapid reckless strokes and swung around mightily till he got an opening. Immediately he raised one hand upright, still levitating in flight.

"Ability of the Light 74; Lightning bolt." Clearly visible waves of white colored energy dissipated from his hand as much higher up in the clouds static charge accumulated sparkling with the same color as on the white angel's hands, but on a much larger scale. White brought down his hand swiftly, guiding lightning from the skies to strike his opponent as a blinding flash obscured his view for a second.

Had he got him? Had he struck down his opponent? It had been a powerful spell. White felt movement behind as he swirled around to find Black inches behind him, with his sword striking out. He jerked backwards with all the momentum his wings could muster, barely missing the blow. So Black had used a teleport ability at the last moment? This 'different' Black was far more furtive and savage than the one he had fought before.

White understood he would have to be careful.

The adversaries sparred with a few more swings and separated once more. White breathed heavily. He was using up too much energy but his opponent hardly seemed enervated. He watched as Black brought both his sword wielding palms together and joined them in a finger lock.

"Internecine Ability 98; Million Scattering Brutal Shadows." White's eyes grew wide in surprise; this was a drastically high level spell.

He watched helplessly as the massive dark angel's form became hazy and slowly started disintegrating into tens of thousands of pieces. Pieces that would act as millions of blades and attack the enemy from every possible direction. Black had temporarily broken himself down to these Scattering blades that could cut up an enemy into zillions of tiny shreds in seconds.

White quickly held his hand perpendicular to his body for defense. "Guardian Ability 7, Golden Sphere."

Instantly a golden translucent bubble sphere surrounded White, encasing him in safety. But White knew even this force field would not be able to sustain continuous attacks from the brutal shadowed scattering blades. And playing extreme defense at a time like this was not a very smart thing.

White watched from inside the force field as hundreds of tiny black blades - the dissembled form of Black himself; hurled themselves with force and momentum onto the spherical enclave. He gritted his teeth as the particle blades began colliding, each attempting to slice the sphere or at least crack it; and there were a countless number of them. He would not be able to maintain his force field much longer.

He gripped the hilt of his sword tighter as he called upon his inner energies and burst into golden flames. The powers of the flames of the Helos Saber would hardly protect him from these ruthless shadowy blades, but would at least offer some resistance. His body was refulgent in golden flames and not a moment too soon. The golden sphere collapsed as the blades swarmed in and rushed onto him.

White let out a blood curdling scream as the blades tore across every possible millimeter of his body, shredding bits of meat, feather and cloth alike. The innumerable particulate blades formed a spate of destructive projectiles, totally encasing his form as it plummeted downwards from the sky. His body crashed into the rooftop of a building, cracking the roof floor where it landed.

White painfully opened his eyes. Black had reformed himself from the blades and was motionless in his co ordinates in the sky far far above. White understood that he was recuperating himself from the effects of the immensely powerful internecine spell he had just used. But he was still up in the sky? This was definitely not the ordinary Black; the dark angel should have been groveling on the ground with pain after using such a high level 'mutually destructive' ability.

White tried to budge but his body would not let him. Every modicum of his frame had been sliced, thousands of deep cuts and thousands of superficial ones. The pain was overbearing. His face, his torso, his legs, arms, shoulders, back; all were covered in blood. Blood that was blurring his vision. His wings were torn and ragged once again. Most of the cloth fabric on him had been reduced to shreds. Would he die here? Would this mark the end of a Perpetual? Would this bloody mess and pain be his death? And then he remembered Aiden. That's what he was fighting for here; the Alchemist who was a boy that he had sworn to protect. He did not know where the boy was right now, but it was good if he was away from the battle.

White felt strength surge within his body as thoughts of Aiden overwhelmed him. He would fight for the boy, and he would not die till he had eliminated all possible forces that worked against the boy. He heaved himself up, shuddering, trembling with throbbing pains and weakness, but he would do this for Aiden. It had started to rain heavily now, and water droplets that fell on his body trickled down after turning red in color, dissolving his blood. But White felt energies flowing back into his body as his resolve grew more and more determined. He shrieked Aiden's name out loud and then clasped his palms as he held them above his head. If Black was using his full power in this battle then so would he.

"Ability of the Light 99; Heaven's God; Flaming phoenix."

As those words left his mouth, yellow and orange flames of fire started whirling around his body. A swirling mass of flames that got larger and larger with each passing second; flames that formed a whirling tornado of hot energies that were slowly taking a gigantic form Flames that spread across for hundreds of feet making everything around for miles glow red in color. The flames were getting hotter as more and more energies imploded onto a critical point. The critical point would serve as the eye of the phoenix.

Fire swirled into the sky like the sun's solar prominences as steadily, they took on the form a giant bird; a bird of fire that constantly burned itself out; a bird whose entire body was composed of flames that burned at more than a thousand degrees; a bird with a dozen tales of fire that extended to hundreds of feet; a bird more than 500 meters in length and even greater wingspan; this bird was heaven's god - the flaming phoenix; summoned by White to fight his battle.

The phoenix screeched in a high pitched tone, its scream shattering window panes and glasses for miles across as it lurched towards Black. Thousands watched dumbstruck as the gigantic fiery bird sailed through the air towards the dark Seraph.

. . . . .

The Empress was incensed. Her cute chubby face was absolutely livid with anger. She had been wasting too much time in this virtual world of the darned angel Frigeria. She needed to get back to the real material plane fast; reach there, finish off the Alchemist and then help her guardian Black to eradicate White. She knew for sure that her guardian would not lose to White this time; not while the stone of Subjugation was embedded within him. The stone made him more resistant to damage; made him a killing machine.

But for now she had to get out of this damned virtual world. A world which was barely a hemispherical dome with a radius of about half a mile. Topographically, the whole area resembled the one where she had initially tried to teleport from when she tried to appear right next to Black and White and the Alchemist boy. But otherwise this world was swarming with humans that were nothing but illusions; young boys playing with dogs in a park as an old couple sat on a park bench watching them. Sharply dressed suited men and women scurrying about to get to work. A hot dog vendor shouting as he advertised his wares; very city picturesque. But the little girl was getting annoyed.

She knew that getting out of such a 'maze' involved solving clues and riddles and conundrums. But she had had enough. Her eyes turned as red as hot charcoal as two figures in front of her caught fire and screamed as they ran amuck. A few moments later everyone had either caught fire or had turned to ashes; the old couple, the hot dog vendor, the boys and suited men and women, even the dogs. And an angry little girl was turning everything into gutted ruins and cinders. She was getting out of this labyrinth one way or another.

·····

Aiden frantically raced up the steps of the town's clock tower. He had been trying to find a way to get closer to the two winged beasts that were his friends. He knew not what he would do if he got closer to them, but he was determined to get to them somehow. He had raced about for very long in the town trying to follow the two clashing angels as they fought in the town's skies. But their fight path had been highly erratic and they covered astounding distances in a few seconds.

Then he thought of getting to a high structure. He realized now it was a stupid thing to try, but he had to do something. So here he was, clambering the steps of the public clock tower, striding the steps two at a time. He had already climbed eight floors. There were still 6 more to go. And the flights of steps were huge. Each flight had adjacent open windows and he could see unbelievable sights of battle unfurling in front of his very eyes. A gigantic fiery bird? Were Will and Scott capable of using something like that? So all this time they could do things like that? Where the hell had he been all along? Dreaming in La-la land?

Aiden's phone buzzed in his pocket as he grumbled and fished it out. Tinka had been calling incessantly earlier and Aiden had finally answered her call to tell her he would talk later. She was still messaging him. But looking at the display Aiden froze. He wiped the sweat off his brow with the back of his hand as he paused ascending the steps a few seconds to catch his breath. Then he picked up Jason's call.

"Hello?" Aiden inquired, very aware of how his voice was sounding.

No answer from the other side. Aiden waited a few more seconds before he spoke again.

"Jase, are you there?"

Suddenly Jason's voice broke out from the other side. "Hey wazzup! How's the makeover dude?"

And for a few moments Aiden forgot everything else around him. This was Jason. This was how Jason was trying to make up to him. And this was his roommate straining to say he had accepted him. His hear felt warm and light.

"Yeah, fine. How are you?"

"Perfect." Jason replied.

The line went silent as both searched for something to say.

"So err, you have a lecture now right? At 8?" Jason inquired.

"Yeah, but I'm skipping that."

"Seriously? That's hardly like you. Where are you?"

Aiden paused as he once again noticed a colossal flaming red bird soaring through the sky. "Err Jason, you might want to take a look outside."

"Why what's..." there was silence on the other end for a few seconds before Jason's voice cracked loudly through Aiden's receiving end. "Holy Crap!"

"Yeah." Aiden muttered from the other side.

"What the fuck is that?"

"Will tell you later. Gotta go for now," Aiden quickly spoke into the phone.

"Uh huh." Jason managed to mumble form the other side.

"And Jason..."

"Yeah?"

"Thanks for calling. It means a lot to me."

"Yeeaah." Jason drawled softly from the other side. Apparently his eyes were still fixated on the fantastic sight he had just seen.

"Later then." Aiden stated quickly and promptly cut the phone. He had important matters to attend to now. Or was he just making a fool of himself?

Aiden continued his ascent up the long flights of steps. 3 minutes of strenuous efforts later, he finally made it to the terrace alongside the town clock. He stood dismayed as he saw the massive shoal of people who had gathered there and were watching the skies. Some dumbstruck, some in awe, some in shock and other with cameras and cellular phones aimed towards the skies.

Well, now that he had reached the top, what the hell was he going to do anyway? He noticed the time in the tower clock. It was 8:02 AM.

He waded through the sea of people straining their necks, looking up and aww-ing disbelievingly as they took in the fantastical sights unfurling before them.

. . . . .

White smiled satisfactorily even in his torn-down condition. Summoning the giant phoenix had been a good decision, even though it took unimaginable amounts of his strength to do it. But he could take a small respite as Black continued to engage the phoenix in combat. In fact Black could only dodge the giant bird as it screeched and lurched for him every time. It was as if a giant hawk was trying to capture a tiny gadfly. The rain that fell on the giant bird's form or anywhere near sizzled and evaporated.

Black was having a tough time. Heaven's god, the flaming phoenix was humongous, but was nowhere as fast and swift as he was. The fiery bird squawked and tried to follow his trajectory, but his maneuverability was too high; he was literally flying circles around the red flaming bird. But the flames were piping hot and were searing his skin. He would have to go on the offensive and start attacking the phoenix now. Then he could move onwards with his nemesis White.

The giant bird screeched an ear piercing scream as it plunged towards him but Black swiftly dodged it. "Ambulatory Ability 7; Shimmer Teleport" he chanted and slowly faded away from the present dimensions as he appeared directly behind the creature, being careful to avoid the trajectory of it's blazing wings and tail. He held out his arms once more to chant a powerful internecine spell.

"Internecine Ability 57; Ineluctable Disintegra…" Black withdrew with a plunge as the Helos Saber swung out at him, ghastly severing his left arm. The bloody form of the Keeper of the Light was soaring above him with a determined expression. He had not allowed him to complete his spell.

White swung his sword, his teeth gnashed as he dove inwards towards the dark Seraph, striking the Blades of Alacrity with powerful blows. Black countered them and dived towards White, only to be cut off by the flaming phoenix returning towards him once more. Black recoiled his trajectory, avoiding the gigantic creature, realizing that this had now become a two-to-one battle. He would have to balance it out.

The fallen angel clasped his palms in a seal formation and held them above the centre of his chest. He called forth the ancient energies that lay embedded within him.

"Ability of the Shadows 99; Hell's avatar, Angel of Death."

Static energy appeared around Black and a pillar of black light dropped down from the sky. The beam hit the ground hard as the Earth shuddered and cracked, before the entire ground split open in an earthquake with its epicenter where the black beam had hit the ground. Buildings crumpled and fell as the ground cracked further and further apart and dust and smoke shrouded the entire area. A low rumbling noise shook the surroundings and a giant form emerged as the dust settled – the angel of death - a giant black pterodactyl shaped winged creature with dimensions comparable to the flaming phoenix itself. It's beak was more than 50 meters long and had shining white criss-cross gartered markings on it Throughout the length of it's entire body were engravings that looked like they had been done in icy crystals. Even its eyes were as ice crystals, shining and cold. The giant bird let out a swirling breath of frost before it took to the air and soared towards its enemy, the flaming phoenix.

The two birds crashed high in the atmosphere as the black pterodactyl locked it's claws on the fiery phoenix. The blazing phoenix screeched and attacked the black angel of death with its own claws and fiery breath as the two massive creatures became a gigantic conglomeration of orange and black monsters that tumbled and somersaulted in the air before they crashed heavily onto the ground far below, the impact shaking the earth for miles, as tall buildings were instantly reduced to rubble and ruins.

The monstrous creatures disentangled themselves before hurling themselves at one another again, rolling along the earth, leaving a trail of blazing and freezing carnage in their wake. Clawing, shoving, biting, each avatar struggled to get the better of the other and win this battle for their respective masters. Parks, buildings, ponds, streets; everything was reduced to debris as the lumbering creatures tumbled over them. Finally the phoenix broke free of the grasp of the darker bird and took to the air while the later chased after it.

Aiden watched stupefied from atop the clock tower. The giant monsters had come as close to about 200 meters from the tourist tower he was on, before they leapt to the air. And even from that distance he had felt the forceful thrust of the hot and chilled air that blasted around him, leaving him stunned. All around him people screamed and ran as they panicked and tried to get off the roof.

A stampede ensued as people trampled on fallen others and rushed towards the only exit from the roof. A minute later, the massive tower terrace lay bare, completely devoid of human presence; all having been frightened out of their skins, having the desire to live and having fled from there. Devoid except for a lone boy standing silently as he watched the epic scale war unfold before him, Aiden stood there with sadness in his eyes; was all this happening because of him?

Aiden looked up to the sky, his mind filled with feelings as diverse as awe, sadness and confusion. Two enormous birds were combating each other in the skies as rain poured down, their forms left an eerie orange red glow for miles. Below on the ground was widespread destruction as buildings and structures toppled over like packs of cards. Hundreds of people were dying below and Scott and Will were fighting up there somewhere. And HE was the root cause for all this. Lightning flashed making his form a scary silhouette as the lone boy stood transfixed on the roof beside the clock tower.

White was battling his darker enemy with all his might. His muscles had ripped and were giving away as blood still oozed and trickled out of every pore of his body. The mighty swords were clashing against each other as White took note of the mayhem and destruction occurring below. He prayed silently that Aiden was safe.

White realized that sleight of swords would achieve him nothing. Black had been fighting tirelessly whereas he on the other hand was weakened form the beginning. He would have to resort to something else. He waited for a break in their fighting and upon finding one immediately raised the Helos Saber upwards as he voiced, "Ability of the Light 98; Holy Storm."

Chains of lightening accumulate higher above the fighting forms as the sky glowed with massive static charges lurking behind dark clouds. Static charges rife with lethal energies that now White could unleash. He brought down his hands as a massive bolt of white lightning struck down towards Black who barely managed to avoid it. White concentrated more of his powers and brought down one beam of lightning after another, Black flitting about trying to escape the bolts of massive energy.

"Got you!" White yelled as the dark Seraph took a direct hit and plummeted towards the ground, his body and wings in fumes. But White was not done yet. He mustered his remaining spell power and hit the crashing form of Black with all the remaining static charge behind the clouds. One, two, three... seven more direct shots later the great white angel was left out of breath as Black's form crashed onto the ground beneath.

White swooped down and landed next to his un-stirring enemy.

The smell of burning flesh was rife in the air as White observed Black's burning body lying face down on the ground. Had he finally defeated his foe? 'No!' he voiced in his mind as he heard Black mumbling something. "Ability of the Shadows 97; Shadow Morasses."

Instantly everywhere around White shadows deformed and rose of the ground as they burgeoned with engulfing profiles and leapt towards him. White swiftly took to the air as the shadows followed suit. But they only rose to a certain height.

White was shocked. His opponent had managed to use such a powerful spell in that condition? If the shadows struck him even once, it would most likely be over for him. Black was indeed a redoubtable opponent.

The soaring white angel watched as the shadows surging upwards followed him and then stopped as they reached their maximum stretching limit.

He waited to catch sight of his opponent as the dark forms receded. The darkness slowly vanished, but Black was nowhere to be seen.

White panicked. Where was Black? Had he stealthily taken leave from the battle to kill Aiden first? Immediately he concentrated to search for the boy's presence.

The humongous creatures of hell and heaven continued their aggressive tussle not far away as chaos and destruction ruled the skies.

·····

There are moments when great things happen. And there are those in which a lot of important things happen but only some remain etched in memory. As streaks of lightning flashed across the sky and thunder bellowed, rumbling low and deep, some of those moments were about to 'happen'. Important events that would change the course of history and even more important ones that hardly any would remember.

Aiden squinted his eyes as he looked towards the skies. He had caught sight of the two winged angels in the skies earlier – a fleeting glance of a few seconds till the rain and his limited vision deterred him from seeing them anymore. And now the boy stood, mouth agape, staring frantically into the skies before him, trying to catch sight of the people he loved, as large droplets of rain pattered down on his face making him blink several times. But all he could see were two gigantic creatures of ice and fire contesting in the skies above, and those were not the two angels.

Lightning flashed blindingly and Aiden felt a movement behind him. He whirled around to find a Dark silver angel, bleeding from several lacerations as his skin burned and smoke fumed from his body. His wings were chipped and cut at places but stood high above the timid boy.

"Will!" Aiden cried out but any thing else he had to say got caught in his throat as the dark Seraph lifted a sword in the air with an intent to kill. Black stepped forward, his sword raised high as fear instilled itself into the eyes of the young Alchemist.

Aiden stood paralyzed as the sword swung forward and shut his eyes. So this was how he would die? He waited for the inevitable.

Aiden stood there his body pulled tightly into himself. Was he dead? No. Certainly not. He had felt no pain of a sword slicing through his body. In fact he had not felt anything at all. Only the raindrops stinging his skin. He opened his eyes apprehensively. There in front of him was the dark angel, Will. His sword hung low in his hand as he stared at Aiden with confusion plastered all over his face. Confusion, question and fear.

"Why?" Will asked with pain on his face.

Aiden could not make sure because of the rain, but he knew there were tears streaming down the man's cheeks. And Aiden understood immediately. Aiden knew Will was bleeding his heart out. He wanted to know why he was trying to kill the person he loved. Will's eyes were steadily turning milky white.

"It's me Will." Aiden stated softly and Will bowed his head low in shame. But Aiden could see that his eyes were once again turning green. The 'Stone of Subjugation' that lay embedded within his heart had cracked but had not broken. It had not completely unharnessed itself before, and this time it released the powers of subjugation mixed with insanity full force. And it's depravity made it's way through Black's veins.

Will lifted his head and screamed. A scream of pain, of anguish and of hurt. And then he raised his sword to kill the boy once and for all.

This time Aiden had no fear in his eyes. He smiled sadly as the sword struck down.

SWISH!

It was White again to the rescue. Only this time he had stopped Black's sword with his body. The sword had sliced through his shoulder and collar bone and lay embedded in his chest, just above his heart.

"I told you that you're not leaving a single scar on him." The bloodied white angel gritted through clenched teeth before he heaved Black backwards and the jagged sword withdrew from his body, pulling out chunks of flesh as obscene amounts of blood splashed onto the wet floor below and turned all the accumulating water a deep crimson.

"Then you die first!" Black growled as he raised his dual blades and swung maniacally at White.

White barely countered and dodged the blows. He had reached his limit, having over drained himself and his energies several times over. His sword played lightly with the two savage blades of his opponent before it flew out his hand and he stumbled backwards landing with a splash on the ground, barely sitting upright in his pain.

"Yes Witenhoem, you were right", the pyrrhic victor bellowed. "This ends today!"

"NO WIIIIILLL!" Aiden screamed from behind.

And then it happened. Critical moments that would forever change everything. Moments that would shape things for centuries to come. Moments that would end the endless battle.

Black stopped short with his sword inches above White as the Stone of Subjugation shattered within his heart. The insurmountable stone had been defeated and that was the first moment that Black looked down at his enemy confused, totally free from the evil powers of subjugation that the Empress had impressed upon him.

That was the exact moment that Empress Woe appeared on the material plane, back from the virtual world of Frigeria after apparently having slain her foe. And she immediately realized that the stone had been destroyed and no longer was her guardian totally under her control.

And a couple of seconds later, while Black still looked with confused eyes towards his enemy, and tried to make sense of his position, White jerked up and pulled at one of his opponents blades and thrust the same into Black's chest, and through the darker angel's heart.

Aiden stood stunned. The little girl covered her mouth with a hand. White pushed himself back as he dark Seraph fell to the ground, his face with a confused expression as he tried to search for Aiden. White had finally finished his foe.

Everyone stood still for a period of time. A period that none present would be able to specify exactly. Aiden was the first to move. He walked quietly towards the slain body of his lover. The same lover that had tried to kill him. The man he loved. The boy walked over and fell on his knees looking mournfully into the dead face of his lover as a sword thrust out obscenely from the centre of his chest. Will was dead.

"Aiden?" White questioned softly as he looked to the face of the boy. And even though it was raining, White could see that the boy shed no tears. Aiden never cried.

And then one of those moments took place. Aiden's body suddenly started radiating with a yellow glow. A glow that was soft to start with and steadily turned blinding. Aiden's silhouette stood up as the ground beneath him started to sizzle and pop before it melted. His eyes had turned an aberrant shade of red. White and the Empress watched with their mouths agape.

The Alchemist had just realized his powers.

And within those seconds Aiden understood the nature of everything around him. His body gradually stopped glowing yellow and turned back to normal as he looked all around. He could see clearly now. The rain, the clouds, the structures, the life entities; and he understood everything about them. What they were composed of, how they functioned, how they were made and how they could be destroyed. He was an alchemist that understood the molecular structure of things, understanding them at the nucleus level. But Aiden could see far more than the sub atomic units. He could see the forces of life and light that flowed through everything – the 'lifetrons'. What we humans would call the forces of 'magic' for lack of a better word. And Aiden could compose and disassemble anything at his will.

Aiden lifted a hand upwards and the rain stopped. The dark thunder clouds receded slowly and the sun shone through.

He waved towards the two avatars of Hell and Heaven that were still engaged in battle and both the creatures writhed and shrieked before their molecular structures and animating forces broke down to nothingness.

He turned towards the Keeper of the Light and gently moved a hand over his chest and instantly all off White's wounds were healed as the skin hissed and even the feathers on his wings fledged from nowhere.

This was the power of the Alchemist – Infinite. Almost infinite.

"No, you will die here!" a little girl shrieked from behind as she fired a speeding black comet of fire and atomic power towards the young boy. The boy held a hand and dismantled the fiery black sphere in mid air, before it reached anywhere near him. Breaking it down to the most basic of atoms. He instantly changed the chemical composition of those elements and reformed a new sphere, shining bright blue in fumes and hurled it towards the Empress. All happened within the fraction of seconds and the little girl took the direct impact and fell to the floor stunned, unable to contemplate what had happened.

Aiden looked at the evil Empress. So she had been the cause of all of this. Instantly, he concentrated as he understood the structure that composed this Perpetual. Her chemical composition, her life forces, her animating veins and soul. He held out his hand and clenched his fist as the little girl got up unsteadily and winced and trembled with pain.

In the next instant her body exploded leaving behind dust and fumes.

The Alchemist had just obliterated one of the most powerful Perpetuals. And he'd done it effortlessly.

Aiden stepped back as White stared at him his mouth still agape and his eyes wide with wonder. What limitless kind of power did the Alchemist possess? The Alchemist had miraculously healed him, he could no longer feel pain and all his wounds had disappeared. There was no longer a single scratch on his body. It would require even Frigeria several days to heal wounds of the kind he had possessed.

Aiden turned around and stepped back, falling to his knees beside the corpse of the dark angel. The cadaver of the one he loved. He sighed deeply. This was not within his limitless power.

And within those moments, Aiden understood everything else there was to understand. He had already understood everything material and spiritual that ran things around everywhere. Now he understood everything that was not material.

White got up unsteadily and immediately embraced Aiden, holding the boy tightly in his arms. He had something to say to Aiden.

Aiden in those moments, remembered everything he had gone through in life.

He remembered Steve who had been such a good friend and had supported him through the roughest of times in his own caring manner. Steve who he played tennis with and who he had never been able to defeat.

He remembered Jason and how after going through severe trauma, his roommate had finally accepted him entirely. Jason, who always made a fool of himself around girls and loved any kind of sport.

He remembered Tinka and how she had been the most amazing friend he could possibly ever possess, sticking through his side through all the hard times. Tinka who always laughed and played pranks on him to get back.

He remembered Dominic, the person who he had loved for so long and had been terrified to face when it came to matters of his sexuality; even Dominic had readily accepted him as more than a friend. Dominic who worked hard and always tried to keep everyone happy.

He remembered Scott, who stepped down from the stars, literally, and offered him friendship and guidance that kept him afloat. Scott, who would protect Aiden with his own life.

And lastly he remembered Will. Will who had given him more love in a week than most people experience in several lifetimes. Will that had comforted him and told him that he would always stand by his side. The handsome man with deep green eyes who's smile could light up Aiden's entire day. And Aiden had had him in his life.

What more could he ask for?

"I Love you, Aiden." Scott spoke softly as Aiden felt his soft white wings gently caressing his skin. Aiden looked up to the taller angel's face and smiled sadly.

"No. It is not me you love." And with that Aiden dived into his mind as White recoiled. An unconditional dive that was unstoppable. Aiden searched amongst his memories till he found what he was looking for. An isolated corner locked away, far into the subconscious. A hidden treasure of memories that Aiden reached out and unlocked.

Immediately White gasped as a deluge of memories and emotions overwhelmed him and he reeled under their blow. Memories of a forbidden love. Memories of true love. Memories of years of love. Memories of Black and White and the passion of their love. Memories of the heartbreak.

Memories of his fiercely intense love for the person he had just killed.

Tears left White's eyes as he looked down in horror at the fallen angel. And in a confused state he hugged Aiden, weeping his heart out.

And within those moments Aiden's body started to glow once more. Glowing white, getting brighter and brighter with each passing second. White broke the embrace and looked at the boy questioningly.

"What are you doing Aiden?" He glanced down as slowly the fallen body of his long lost love started disappearing. White screamed as he realized what the Alchemist was doing.

"No! No! Stop! Don't do this!" White hugged the boy as if that would stop him from vanishing before his eyes. But even the mighty Keeper of the Light was powerless against the Alchemist.

"Aiden. Stop!" he pulled back his head and stared into Aiden's glowing face, begging him to stop. There were no tears in Aiden's eyes. Aiden never cried.

"Tell Will I loved him." Aiden stated calmly as his face got brighter and brighter. "And that he gave me more love than I had ever dreamed of."

White screamed as the boys form was effulgent in blinding light and he hugged the iridescent form fiercely. Not letting go, swaying softly with it.

And slowly Aiden's body disappeared as the light dissipated.

The glow subsided as White was left hugging Black in his arms. The Alchemist had wiped out his own existence. Wiped it out to resurrect Black, or Will, as he'd better known him. He had sacrificed his own life, for resurrecting a Perpetual was not within his normal scope of powers.

And all that was left in White's arms was Black himself, with the fondest memories of his mighty white angel lover.

White sobbed and broke down into the arms of his reunited love. Black held him tightly and stroked his back soothingly, stroking the petals that were his wings. Slowly White withdrew and looked into the greenest of eyes. This was the love he had lost centuries ago. One he had regained. One he had been reunited with. Black stroked White's face with his fingers, gently wiping away the tears and leaned his face ahead as he met White for a soft kiss.

Frigeria flapped her wings and landed on the terrace beside the two and watched what was happening before her with wonder. She had escaped from Empress Woe unharmed.

The two male angels stood kissing on the terrace, holding each other tightly. Their wings were draping down onto the floor below. And both knew not, how many hundreds of years it would be before an Alchemist would return to the material plane. Maybe 500 years, maybe 800, maybe a millennium. But both knew that while an Alchemist could possibly return to the material plane, a young boy called Aiden would not. A young boy who had stolen both their hearts. A boy with the will of fire and a heart bigger than the largest ocean.

And in those moments, two Perpetuals kissed softly on the terrace beside the giant clock, as a love lost for more than 800 years was found again.

. . . . .

Epilogue

"No my mighty ruler. You have to take care of them yourself!" Frigeria stated with an annoyed look on her face.

"Frigeria, you must attend to them. Please."

The raven haired female angel grumble under her breath. It had been over a week since the Empress of the Kingdom of Void had been annihilated and the mighty White angel was still not attending to matters of the Kingdom. He had been diligently preoccupied by a certain dark Seraph. And now, there were troglodyte merchants that were visiting the capital city of Immaculata, and important matters would be discussed but the mighty white angel would simply not attend to them, saying he had other matters to attend to.

"I will not attend troglodyte merchants while you booger your lover on the bed. For heaven's sake, you've spent almost all of last week conquering him and being conquered. To think that you bed the devil himself!"

"Frigeria. Please." The white angel pleaded softly with large beseeching eyes.

The black haired angel sighed. "All right." She was hugged tightly by the larger angel before she could put any more words in. "But you have to promise you will resume your duties tomorrow!"

But white was out of earshot. Warped and teleported to his bedroom chamber, where a certain dark Seraph waited for him.

Frigeria sighed deeply. "To think that the fiercest two warriors in the two Kingdoms would be reduced to this. A couple of mooney eyed lovers!"

The air deformed as White teleported stealthily into his own chamber, where Black stood with his back to him, staring out of the window as his gossamer silver wings draped down on the floor beneath.

White quietly stole behind his lover and enveloped him in his arms, wings, solid muscles and all as he kissed along the back of his shoulders, making his lover sigh.

"So it was true", The dark angel stated suddenly. "The Alchemist did put an end to the war between the kingdoms of Light and Void."

White smiled sadly at his lover. The boy had been discussed a hundred times before.

"And his powers were indeed beyond the Perpetuals." White stated. "It was a sight to witness. The way he waved one hand and the evil Empress just blew up and vanished."

"Indeed." Black stated sadly and silence descended as the two lovers once again got lost in thought about the courageous boy.

"So the matter with the 'Hourglass of Retrogression' has been dealt with?" Black inquired.

The 'Hourglass of Retrogression' was a powerful artifact. It was a simple delicate glass flask, emblazoned with golden filigree that was owned neither by the Kingdom of Light nor by the Kingdom of Void - it was owned by both, conjointly. It was a super-dominant artifact that could be used to turn back time on the material plane, but one that required both the kingdoms to assent to its use. Its activation required a drop of blood from both the Kingdom's guardians; Black and White.

"Yes it has." White stated whispering.

The time on the material plane for the day when the two angels had clashed had been turned back. Everything had been turned back and re-achieved - the collapsed buildings, the lost lives, the peace of mind and ignorance of people on the material plane. Everything, except a young boy called Aiden.

"And who keeps what memories?" Black asked once again.

White looked deep into the intense green eyes of his lover as he replied, "Tinka, the Alchemist's friend will remember and know everything. The rest of the world will bathe in ignorance while the Alchemist's friend will know that Aiden died in a car accident."

"So the memories have been modified so huh?" Black stated sadly.

"Yes." White whispered back and once again there was silence in the chamber as the two tightly embraced figures said nothing.

"Aiden was beyond philanthropic." Black stated out of the blue. "He was in fact, self-effacing."

"Yes. And he gave up the Alchemist's life and power to reunite us."

Black smiled at the beautiful angel that was his now. He turned around slowly and kissed his soft lips as he ran his hands along the firm muscles on his arms. White guided them to the marble bed where he laid down Black, draping the hard texture by his silky grey wings as he joined him.

"And you're mine now." White stated as thoughts of how he had pounded his lover all throughout the previous night came breezing back into his head. Black had stated that he would take his revenge on him. And White could hardly wait.

And he inhabitants of both the Kingdoms would stare with awe in the skies when both their rulers soared together, cutting across the clouds, the two great angels - Black and White.

. . . . .

About the Author

Sky is a student who is completing his Master's in Business Administration at the time of publication of this novel. He enjoys swimming, reading, tennis, painting, travelling and writing. At 24 years old, this is his first attempt at not only gay erotica, but also at writing a story of such length. This story had been swimming around in his head for a long time before he decided to pen it down. He hopes to reach out to as many people as possible with his stories.

www.ingramcontent.com/pod-product-compliance
Lightning Source LLC
Chambersburg PA
CBHW050657290626
47170CB00015B/1634